D0453229

THE JEWEL THAT WAS OURS

by the same author

LAST BUS TO WOODSTOCK
LAST SEEN WEARING
THE SILENT WORLD OF NICHOLAS QUINN
SERVICE OF ALL THE DEAD
THE DEAD OF JERICHO
THE RIDDLE OF THE THIRD MILE
THE SECRET OF ANNEXE 3
THE WENCH IS DEAD

THE JEWEL THAT WAS OURS

Colin Dexter

MACMILLAN
LONDON

Copyright © Colin Dexter 1991

All rights reserved. No reproduction, copy or transmission of this publication
may be made without written permission. No paragraph of this publication
may be reproduced, copied or transmitted save with written permission or in
accordance with the provisions of the Copyright Act 1956 (as amended). Any
person who does any unauthorised act in relation to this publication may
be liable to criminal prosecution and civil claims for damages.

The right of Colin Dexter to be identified as author of this work has
been asserted by him in accordance with the Copyright, Designs and Patents
Act 1988.

First published 1991 by
MACMILLAN LONDON LIMITED
a division of Pan Macmillan Publishers Limited
Cavaye Place London SW10 9PG
and Basingstoke

Macmillan paperback edition 1992

Associated companies in Auckland, Budapest, Dublin, Gaborone, Harare,
Hong Kong, Kampala, Kuala Lumpur, Lagos, Madras, Manzini, Melbourne,
Mexico City, Nairobi, New York, Singapore Sydney, Tokyo and Windhoek

ISBN 0-333-57659-4

A CIP catalogue record for this book is available from the British Library

Typeset by Macmillan Production Limited

Printed in England by Clays Ltd, St Ives plc

NOTE: Not all the characters in this novel are wholly fictitious.

For my wife, Dorothy

Espied the god with gloomy soul
The prize that in the casket lay,
Who came with silent tread and stole
The jewel that was ours away.

(*Lilian Cooper*, 1904–1981)

Acknowledgements

The author and publishers wish to thank the following who have kindly given permission for use of copyright materials:

Extract from *Oxford* by Jan Morris published by Oxford University Press 1987, reprinted by permission of Oxford University Press;

Extract from the introduction by Lord Jenkins of Hillhead to *The Oxford Story*, published by Heritage Projects (Management) Ltd, reprinted by permission of the Peters Fraser & Dunlop Group Ltd;

Extract from *Lanterns and Lances*, published by Harper & Row and by Hamish Hamilton in the United Kingdom and Commonwealth, copyright © 1961 James Thurber. Copyright © 1989 Rosemary A. Thurber;

Julian Symons for the extract from *Bloody Murder*;

Marilyn Yurdan for the extract from *Oxford: Town & Gown*;

Basil Swift for the extracts from *Collected Haiku*;

Martin Amis for the extract from *Other People*, published by Jonathan Cape;

Max Beerbohm for the extract from *Mainly on the Air*, published by William Heinemann Ltd;

A. P. Watt Ltd on behalf of Crystal Hale and Jocelyn Herbert for the extract from 'Derby Day', *Comic Opera*, by A. P. Herbert;

Extract from *Aspects of Wagner* by Bryan Magee, reprinted by permission of the Peters Fraser & Dunlop Group Ltd;

The Estate of Virginia Woolf for the extract from *Mrs Dalloway*, published by The Hogarth Press.

Every effort has been made to trace all the copyright holders but if any has been inadvertently overlooked, the author and publishers will be pleased to make the necessary arrangement at the first opportunity.

This novel is based in part on an original storyline written by Colin Dexter for Central Television's *Inspector Morse* series.

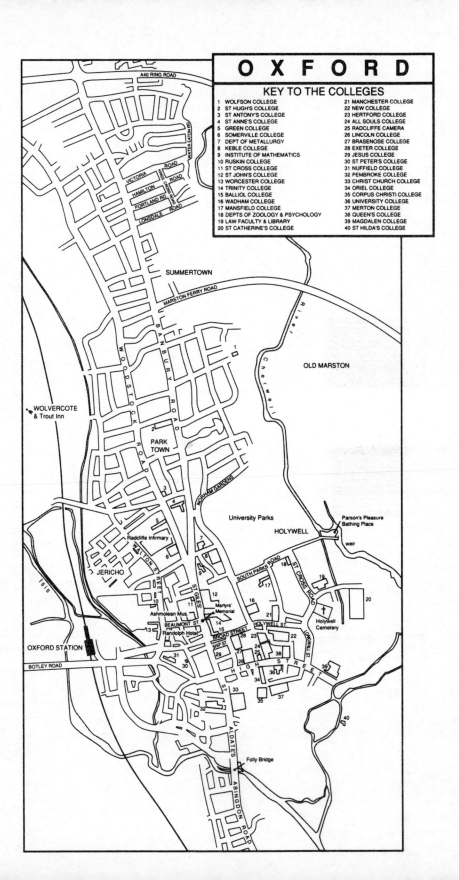

Part One

Chapter One

It is not impossible to become bored in the presence
of a mistress

(*Stendhal*)

The red-seal *Brut Imperial Moët & Chandon* stood empty
on the top of the bedside table to her left; empty like the
champagne glass next to it, and like the champagne glass
on the table at the other side of the bed. Everything seemed
empty. Beside her, supine and still, hands behind his head,
lay a lean, light-boned man in his early forties, a few years
older than herself. His eyes were closed, and remained closed
as she folded back her own side of the floral-patterned duvet,
rose quickly, put her feet into fur-lined slippers, drew a pink
silk dressing gown around a figure in which breasts, stomach,
thighs, were all a little over-ripe perhaps – and stepped over
to peer through the closed curtains.

Had she consulted her Oxford University Pocket Diary,
she would have noticed that the sun was due to set at 16.50
that early Wednesday evening in late October. The hour had
gone back the previous week-end, and the nights, as they said,
were pulling in fast. She had always found difficulty with the
goings back and forth of the clock – until she had heard that
simple little jingle on Radio Oxford: Spring Forward/Fall
Back. That had pleased her. But already darkness had fallen
outside, well before its time; and the rain still battered and
rattled against the window-panes. The tarmac below was a
glistening black, with a pool of orange light reflected from
the street lamp opposite.

When she was in her junior school, the class had been
asked one afternoon to paint a scene on the Thames, and
all the boys and girls had painted the river blue. Except

her. And that was when the teacher had stopped the lesson (in midstream, as it were) and asserted that young Sheila was the only one of them who had the natural eye of an artist. Why? Because the Thames might well be grey or white or brown or green or yellow – anything, in fact, except those little rectangles of Oxford blue and Cambridge blue and cobalt and ultramarine into which all the wetted brushes were dipping. So, would all of them please start again, and try to paint the colours they saw, and forget the postcards, forget the atlases? All of them, that is, except Sheila; for Sheila had painted the water black.

And below her now the street was glistening black . . .

Yes.

Everything seemed black.

Sheila hugged the thin dressing gown around her and knew that he was awake; watching her; thinking of his wife, probably – or of some other woman. Why didn't she just tell him to get out of her bed and out of her life? Was the truth that she needed him more than he needed her? It had not always been so.

It was so very hard to say, but she said it: 'We were happy together till recently, weren't we?'

'What?' The tongue tapped the teeth sharply at the final 't'.

She turned now to look at him lying there, the moustache linking with the neatly trimmed Vandyke beard in a darkling circle around his mouth – a mouth she sometimes saw as too small, and too prim, and, yes, too bloody *conceited*!

'I must go!' Abruptly he sat up, swung his legs to the floor, and reached for his shirt.

'We can see each other tomorrow?' she asked softly.

'Difficult not to, won't it?' He spoke with the clipped precision of an antique pedagogue, each of the five 't's articulated with pedantic completion. With an occasional lisp, too.

'I meant – afterwards.'

'Afterwards? Impossible! Impothible! Tomorrow evening we must give our full attention to our American clients, must we not? *Motht* important occasion, as you know. Lucky if we all get away before ten, wouldn't you say? And then—'

'And then you must go home, of course.'

'Of course! And you know perfectly well *why* I must go home. Whatever your faults, you're not a fool!'

Sheila nodded bleakly. 'You could come here before we start.'

'No!'

'Wouldn't do much harm to have a drink, would it? Fortify ourselves for—'

'No!'

'I see.'

'And it's healthy for the liver and kindred organs to leave the stuff alone for a while, uh? Couple of days a week? Could you manage that, Sheila?'

He had dressed quickly, his slim fingers now fixing the maroon bow-tie into its usual decadent droop. For her part, she had nothing further to say; nothing she could say. She turned once again towards the window, soon to feel his hand on the back of her shoulders as he planted a perfunctory kiss at the nape of her neck. Then the door downstairs slammed. Miserably she watched the top of the black umbrella as it moved along the road. Then she turned off the bedside lamp, picked up the champagne bottle, and made her way down the stairs.

She needed a drink.

Dr Theodore Kemp strode along swiftly through the heavy rain towards his own house, only a few minutes' walk away. He had already decided that there would be little, if any, furtherance of his affair with the readily devourable divorcée he had just left. She was becoming a liability. He realised it might well have been his fault that she now seemed to require a double gin before starting her daily duties; that she took him so very seriously; that she was demanding more and more of his time; that she was prepared to take ever greater risks about their meetings. Well, *he* wasn't. He would miss the voluptuous lady, naturally; but she *was* getting a little too well-padded in some of the wrong places.

Double chin . . . double gin . . .

He'd been looking for some semblance of love – with none of the problems of commitment; and with Sheila Williams he had thought for a few months that he had found it. But it was not to be: *he*, Theodore Kemp, had decided that! And there *were* other women – and one especially, her tail flicking sinuously in the goldfish bowl.

Passing through the communal door to the flats on Water Eaton Road, whither (following the accident) he and Marion had moved two years earlier, he shook the drenched umbrella out behind him, then wiped his sodden shoes meticulously on the doormat. Had he ruined them, he wondered?

Chapter Two

For the better cure of vice they think it necessary
to study it, and the only efficient study is through
practice

(Samuel Butler)

Much later that same evening, with the iron grids now being
slotted in from bar-top to ceiling, John Ashenden sat alone in
the University Arms Hotel at Cambridge and considered the
morrow. The weather forecast was decidedly brighter, with
no repetition of the deluge which earlier that day had set the
whole of southern and eastern England awash (including, as
we have seen, the city of Oxford).

'Anything else before we close, sir?'

Ashenden usually drank cask-conditioned beer. But he
knew that the quickest way to view the world in a rosier
light was to drink whisky; and he now ordered another
large Glenfiddich, asking that this further Touch of the
Malt be added to the account of the Historic Cities of
England Tour.

It would help all round if the weather were set fairer;
certainly help in mitigating the moans amongst his present
group of Americans:

- too little sunshine
- too much food
- too much litter
- too early reveilles
- too much walking around (especially that!)

Not that they were a particularly complaining lot (except for
that one woman, of course). In fact, by Ashenden's reckoning,

they rated a degree or two above average. Twenty-seven of them. Almost all from the West Coast, predominantly from California; mostly in the 65–75 age-bracket; rich, virtually without exception; and fairly typical of the *abcde* brigade – alcohol, bridge, cigarettes, detective-fiction, ecology. In the first days of the tour he had hoped that 'culture' might compete for the 'c' spot, since after joining the ranks of the non-smokers he was becoming sickened at seeing some of them lighting up between courses at mealtimes. But it was not to be.

The downpour over Cambridge that day had forced the cancellation of trips to Grantchester and the American War Cemetery at Madingley; and the change of programme had proved deeply unpopular – especially with the ladies. Yes, and with Ashenden himself, too. He had duly elected himself their temporary cicerone, pointing neck-achingly to the glories of the late-Gothic fan-vaulting in King's; and then, already weary-footed, shuffling round the Fitzwilliam Museum to seek out a few of the ever-popular Pre-Raphaelite paintings.

'They have a far better collection in the Ashmolean, Mr Ashenden. Or so I've *read*. William Holman Hunt, and – and Mill-*ais*.'

'You'll be able to judge for yourself tomorrow, won't you?' Ashenden had replied lightly, suspecting that the doom-laden lady had forgotten (never known, perhaps) the Christian names of a painter she'd pronounced to rhyme with 'delay'.

It had irked Ashenden that the Cambridge coach company would have to be paid in full for the non-outings that day. It had irked him even more that he had been obliged to forgo the whole of the afternoon in order to enlighten and entertain his ageing charges. He was (he knew it) a reasonably competent courier and guide. Yet in recent years he had found himself unable to cope properly without a few regular breaks from his round-the-clock responsibilities; and it had become his policy to keep his afternoons completely free whenever possible, though he had never fully explained the reasons for this to anyone . . .

In November 1974 he had gone to Cambridge to take the entrance examination in Modern Languages. His A-level results had engendered not unreasonable optimism in his comprehensive school, and he had stayed on for a seventh term to try his luck. His father, as young John knew, would have been the proudest man in the county had his son succeeded in persuading the examiners of his linguistic competence. But the son had not succeeded, and the letter had dropped on to the doormat on Christmas Eve:

From the Senior Tutor, Christ's College, Cambridge

Dear Mr Ashenden,   21.12.74

After giving full and sympathetic consideration to your application, we regret that we are unable to offer you a place at this college. We can understand the disappointment you will feel, but you are no doubt aware how fiercely competition for places

There had been a huge plus from that brief time in Cambridge, though. He had stayed for two nights, in the Second Court at Christ's, in the same set of rooms as a fellow examinee from Trowbridge: a lanky, extraordinarily widely-read lad, who apart from seeking a scholarship in Classics was anxious to convert the University (or was it the Universe?) to the self-evident truths of his own brand of neo-Marxism. John had understood very little of it all, really; but he had become aware, suddenly, of a world of scholarship, intelligence, imaginative enthusiasm, sensitivity – above all of sensitivity – that he had never known before in his comprehensive school at Leicester.

On their last afternoon together, Jimmy Bowden, the Trotskyite from Trowbridge, had taken him to see a double-bill from the golden age of the French cinema, and that afternoon he fell in love with a sultry, husky-voiced whore as she crossed her silk-clad legs and sipped her absinthe in some seedy bistro. It was all something to do with 'the synthesis of style and sexuality', as Jimmy had sought to explain, talking into the early hours . . . and then rising at six the following morning to stand outside Marks & Spencer to try to sell the *Socialist Worker*.

A few days after being notified of his own rejection, Ashenden had received a postcard from Jimmy – a black and white photograph of Marx's tomb in Highgate Cemetery:

> The idiots have given me a major schol – in spite
> of that Greek prose of mine! Trust you've had
> your own good news. I enjoyed meeting you and
> look forward to our first term together – Jimmy.

He had never replied to Jimmy. And it was only by chance, seven years later, that during one of his Oxford tours he'd met a man who had known Jimmy Bowden . . .

After gaining his pre-ordained First in both parts of the Classical Tripos, Jimmy had been awarded a Junior Research Fellowship at Oxford to study early Etruscan epigraphy; and then, three years later, he had died of Hodgkin's disease. He had been an orphan (as events revealed) and been buried in Oxford's Holywell Cemetery, amongst many dead, but once pre-eminent, dons – only some twenty feet or so, as Ashenden learned, from the grave of Walter Pater. Yet though Jimmy had died, some small part of his legacy lived on – for John Ashenden had for many years subscribed to several specialist film magazines, printed in the UK and on the Continent, for cinema buffs such as he himself had soon become. Exactly where and when the degeneration had set in (if, indeed, 'degeneration' it were) John Ashenden could not be all that sure.

Born in 1956, John had not grown up amidst the sexually repressive mores of his own father's generation. And once he started to work (immediately after school), started to travel, he had experienced little sense of guilt in satisfying his sexual curiosities by occasional visits to sauna clubs, sex cinemas, or explicit stage shows. But gradually such experiences began to nourish rather than to satisfy his needs; and he was becoming an inveterate voyeur. Quite often, at earlier times, he had been informed by his more experienced colleagues in the travel business (themselves totally immune, it appeared, from any corrupting influences) that the trouble with pornography was its being so *boring*. But *was* it?

From his first introduction, the squalid nature of his incipient vice had been borne upon him – groping his way like a blind man down a darkened aisle of a sleazy cinema, the Cockney voice still sounding in his ears: 'It's the real fing 'ere, sir, innit? No messin' about – nuffin like that – just straight inta fings!' And it disturbed him that he could find himself so excited by such crude scenes of fornication. But he fortified his self-esteem with the fact that almost all the cinemas he attended were fairly full, probably of people just as well adjusted as himself. Very soon, too, he began to understand something of that 'synthesis' that Jimmy had tried to explain to him – the synthesis of style and sexuality. For there *were* people who understood such things, with meetings held in private dwellings, the High Priest intoning the glorious Introit: 'Is everybody known?' That Ashenden had been forced to miss such a meeting of initiates that afternoon in Cambridge had been disappointing. Very disappointing, indeed.

But the next stop was Oxford . . .

Chapter Three

'O come along, Mole, do!' replied the Rat cheerfully,
still plodding along.

'*Please* stop, Ratty!' pleaded the poor Mole, in
anguish of heart. 'You don't understand! It's my
home, my old home! I've just come across the smell of
it, and it's close by here, really quite close. And I *must*
go to it'

(*Kenneth Grahame*, The Wind in the Willows)

'Arksford? This is *Arksford*?'

Seated on the nearside front seat of the luxury coach, John
Ashenden glanced across at the diminutive septuagenarian
from California: 'Yes, Mrs Roscoe, this is Oxford.' He spoke
rather wearily, yet wholly without resentment. Hitherto little
on the Historic Cities of England Tour (London–Cambridge–
Oxford–Stratford–Bath–Winchester) had appeared unequivocally satisfactory to the well-read, eager, humourless (insufferable!) Mrs Roscoe; and yet as he looked out of his own
side-window Ashenden could sympathise with that lady's disappointment. The eastern stretch of the A40 could hardly
afford the most pleasing approach to the old University City;
and as the coach slowly moved, one car-length at a time,
towards the Headington roundabout, a litter-strewn patch of
ill-kempt grass beside a gaudily striped petrol station lent
little enchantment to the scene.

The tour party – eighteen women, nine men (three
registered husband-and-wife combinations) – sat back in
their seats as the coach drove past the sign for 'City
Centre' and accelerated for a few miles along the featureless
northern section of the Ring Road, heading for the Banbury
Road roundabout.

For some reason Mrs Laura Stratton was ill-at-ease. She re-crossed her legs and now massaged her left foot with her right hand. As agreed, it would be Eddie who would sign the forms and the Visitors' Book, and then identify the luggage and tip the porter – while she would be lying in a hot herbal bath and resting her weary body, her weary *feet* . . .

'Gee, I feel so *awful*, Ed!'

'*Relax*, honey. Everything's gonna be OK.' But his voice was so quiet that even Laura had difficulty in picking up his words. At sixty-six, four years younger than his wife, Eddie Stratton laid his hand briefly on the nylon-clad left foot, the joints of the toes disfigured by years of cruel arthritis, the toe-nails still painted a brightly defiant crimson.

'I'll be fine, Ed – just once I get in that bairth.' Again Laura switched legs and massaged her other foot again – a foot which like its partner had until recently commanded the careful ministrations of the most expensive chiropodist in Pasadena.

'Yeah!' And perhaps someone else on the coach apart from his wife might have noticed Eddie Stratton's faint smile as he nodded his agreement.

The coach had now turned down into the Banbury Road, and Ashenden was soon into his well-rehearsed commentary: '. . . and note on each side of the road the cheerful orange-brick houses, built in the last two decades of the nineteenth century when the dons in the University – there, look! – see the date? – 1887 . . .'

Immediately behind Ashenden sat a man in his early seventies, a retired civil engineer from Los Angeles, who now looked out of his window at the string of shops and offices in Summertown: banks, building societies, fruiterers, hairdressers, housing agents, newsagents, wine shops – it could almost have been back home, really. But then it *was* back home, decided Howard Brown.

Beside him, Shirley Brown was the second wife who had seen a smile upon a husband's lips – a smile this time of wistful satisfaction; and suddenly she felt a sharp regret.

'Howard?' she whispered. 'Howard! I *am* glad – you know I am – glad we booked the tour. *Really* I am!' She laid her right arm along his long thigh and squeezed it gently. 'And I'm sorry I was such' (*pianissimo*) 'such an ungrateful bitch last night.'

'Forget it, Shirl – forget it!'

But Howard Brown found himself wishing that for a little while at least his wife would perpetuate her sullen ill-humour. In such a mood (not infrequent) she presented him with the leeway he needed for the (not infrequent) infidelities of thought and deed which he could never have entertained had she exhibited a quarter of the affection he had known when they'd agreed to marry. But that was in 1947 – forty-three years ago – before she'd ever dreamed of checking his automobile mileage, or scrutinising the postmarks on his private mail, or sniffing suspiciously at him after his coming home from the office . . .

'. . . and here' (Ashenden was in full and rather splendid spate) 'we see the Ruskin influence on domestic architecture during that period. You see – there! – on the left, look! – the neo-Gothic, mock-Venetian features . . . And here, on the left again, this is Norham Gardens, with the famous University Parks lying immediately behind. There! You see the iron gates? The Parks are one of the greatest open spaces in Oxford – still, even now, liable to be closed to the public at the whim of the University authorities – unless, of course, you get to know how to sneak in without being noticed by the keepers at the main entrance.'

'And to sneak *out* again, surely, Mr Ashenden?'

For once, one of Mrs Roscoe's inevitable interruptions was both pertinent and good-humoured, and her fellow passengers laughed their light-hearted approval.

Howard Brown, however, had been quite unaware of the exchange. He was craning his neck to look across at the Keeper's Lodge; and as he did so, like Mole, he sensed and smelled his old home territory, and inside him something long dormant woke into sudden life. He felt his eyes welling up with nostalgic tears, before fiercely blowing his nose and looking obliquely at his wife once more, gratified to observe that her lips had once again settled into their accustomed crab-crumpet discontent. She suspected nothing, he was virtually certain of that.

As the coach drew into St Giles', the sky was an open blue, and the sunlight gleamed on the cinnamon-coloured stone along the broad tree-lined avenue. 'Here we are, in St Giles'.' (Ashenden slipped into over-drive now.) 'You can see the plane trees on either side of us, ablaze with the beautifully golden tints of autumn – and, on the left here, St John's College – and Balliol just beyond. And here in front of us, the famous Martyrs' Memorial, modelled on the Eleanor Crosses of Edward the First, and designed by Gilbert Scott to honour the great Protestant martyrs – Cranmer and Latimer and, er . . .'

'Nicholas Ridley,' supplied Mrs Roscoe, as the coach turned right at the traffic lights and almost immediately pulled in on the left of Beaumont Street beneath the tall neo-Gothic façade of The Randolph Hotel.

'At last!' cried Laura Stratton, with what might have been the relief of a prisoner learning of a late reprieve.

In retrospect, it would have seemed an odd coincidence (though not an important one) that the middle-aged man housed in a nondescript block of flats at the top of the Banbury Road had been looking out from his second-floor double-glazed windows as the long luxury coach carrying Ashenden's group had passed by that late afternoon. Inside, a recently renewed needle glided through the well-worn grooves of the Furtwängler recording of *Götterdämmerung*; but the man's mind was more closely concentrated with an almost physical hurt on the greasy wrappings discarded by the previous night's fish-and-chip brigade as they'd walked homeward from the Chicken Barbecue in Summertown.

Chapter Four

'The cockroach *Blattella germanica*,' it was observed darkly in 1926, 'was at one time recorded as present in the Randolph Hotel kitchen'

(*Jan Morris*, Oxford)

Roy, concierge of the five-star Randolph Hotel, a cheerful, florid-faced man of sixty, had been on duty since midday, and had, as always, been fully apprised by the Reception Manager of the scheduled afternoon arrivals – especially, of course, of the biggish bus-load of American tourists at 4.30 p.m. Roy, who had started with the hotel as a page-boy in 1945 – forty-five years since – quite liked the Americans. Not that he'd ever wished to fly over there for a holiday or anything drastic like that; but they *were* a nice lot, usually, the Yanks; friendly, communicative, generous. And although an incorrigibly biased patriot himself, he had recently begun to query the automatic superiority of his own countrymen, particularly that night the previous month when he'd returned on a Euro-Ferry after an abortive 0–0 draw between England and Holland.

It was five minutes before schedule that from his cubby-hole immediately inside the main entrance he saw the patrician coach pull slowly in beside the white canopy, flanked by a pair of elegant lamp-posts, at the front of Oxford's premier hotel. And a few seconds later he was standing at the top of the steps outside, in his yellow-piped blue uniform, beaming semi-beatifically, and ready to greet the new arrivals with an appropriate degree of that 'warmth' attested to on several separate pages of the hotel's technicolour brochure. As he stood there, the flags – Union Jack, EEC, USA – fluttered lightly above him in the afternoon breeze. He enjoyed his work – always had; in fact seldom referred to it as 'work' at all. Seldom, too, did anything much go wrong in an establishment so happily and so predictably well-ordered as The Randolph. Seldom indeed.

But once in a while?

Yes, once in a while.

Phil Aldrich, a small, mournful-visaged dolichocephalic senior citizen (from California, too) moved from his habitual and lonely seat on the back row of the coach and came to sit next to Mrs Roscoe; his hearing was not quite what it had been and he wanted to know what was going on. The Deputy Manager had appeared on the coach itself to welcome them all and to announce that tea – or coffee, if preferred – was immediately available in the St John's Suite on the first floor; that all bedrooms were now ready for occupancy and that every hotel facility from telephone to trouser-press was at his guests' disposal forthwith; that even as he spoke their baggage was being unloaded, counted, checked, and portered to the appropriate rooms. It would save a good deal of time, the Deputy Manager concluded, if everyone would fill in now, on the coach, the Guest Registration Cards.

With appreciative nods observable on each side of the gangway, Ashenden duly distributed the Welcome Trusthouse Forte forms, already completed for the sections dealing with Company, Next Destination, Settlement of Account, Arrival, Departure, and Nationality. Only remaining for the tourists to fill in were the four sections headed Home Address, Telephone, Passport Number, and Signature.

Phil expressed an unqualified approval: 'Gee! That's what I'd say was pretty darned efficient, Janet.'

For once Mrs Roscoe was unable to identify any obvious flaw in the procedures, and, instead, appeared to concentrate her thoughts upon the perils of the unpredictable future.

'I do hope the people here realise the great difference between Vegetarian and Vegan—'

'*Janet!* This is one of the finest hotels in the UK—'

But Ashenden's voice now cut across their conversation:

'So! If we can all . . . St John's Suite, St *John*'s – that's on the first floor, just up the main staircase – tea or coffee – right away. I know some of you will just want to settle in and have a wash and . . . So if you take your forms to Reception – that's straight ahead of you as you go through the main doors here – and just sign the documentation forms there and get your keys . . . The lift, the guest-lift, is just to your right, in the corridor . . .'

'Get a *move* on!' hissed Laura under her breath.

'. . . I shall be calling round to your rooms later, just to make sure everything's . . .'

Ashenden knew what he was doing. Experience had taught him that the first hour or so in any new hotel was always the most vital, since some small problem, dealt with promptly, could make the difference between a contented life and an anxious existence. Blessedly, Ashenden was seldom, if ever, confronted with such positive complaints as cockroaches, mice, or the disgusting habits of a room's previous occupants. But a range of minor niggles was not unfamiliar, even in the best regulated of establishments: no soap in the bathroom; only two tubs of cream beside the self-service kettle; no instructions on how to operate the knobless TV; no sign – *still* no sign – of the luggage . . .

Eddie Stratton had managed to squeeze into second spot in the queue for keys, and Laura had grabbed their own key, 310, from his hand before he'd finished the documentation.

'I'm straight up, Ed, to draw me a bairth – I can't wait.'

'Yeah, but leave the door, honey – there's only the one key, OK? I'll have a cup of tea in the Saynt Jarn Suite.'

'Sure. I'll leave the door.'

She was gone.

As Laura hobbled away towards the guest-lift, Eddie

turned round and looked directly into the eyes of Mrs
Shirley Brown. For a few seconds there seemed to be
no communication between the two of them; but then,
after glancing briefly towards her husband, Shirley Brown
nodded, almost imperceptibly, and her eyes smiled.

Chapter Five

All saints can do miracles, but few can keep a hotel
(*Mark Twain*, Notebook)

'*At last!*' muttered Laura Stratton for the third (and final) time as she inserted her key and turned it clockwise (and correctly) in the lock.

The room itself did not open immediately off the main corridor on level three; but a small plaque fixed beside double swing-doors (a FIRE EXIT sign above them) had pointed the way to Room 310. Once through these doors Laura had found herself in a further corridor, only four or five feet wide, which ran parallel to the main corridor, along which (after she had turned left) she walked the five yards or so to the bedroom door – on her right. Just beyond this door, the corridor turned at right angles and came to an almost immediate stop in the shape of another double-doored FIRE EXIT – doubtless, as Laura guessed (again correctly), leading down some back stairs to the ground floor. It did not occur to her that a person could stand in this narrow square of space, pressed tightly back behind the wall, and remain completely unobserved from the narrow corridor leading to her room.

If anyone wished to remain thus unobserved . . .

Laura extracted the key and carefully let the door close, or almost close, behind her, with the tongue of the lock holding it slightly ajar. The two large black-leather cases were on the floor immediately inside, and she looked around to find herself in a most pleasantly appointed room. A double bed stood immediately to her right, covered by a pale-green quilt, with a free-standing wardrobe beyond it; facing her were the three lancet windows of the outside wall, with curtains down to the carpeted floor; and in front of these windows, from right to left, a tea-maker, a TV, a low, mirrored dressing table, and a red-plush chair. Her swift glance around missed little, except for the rather fine reproduction of Vermeer's *View of Delft* above the bed. Laura and her first husband had once seen the original of this in the Mauritshuis in The Hague, when the guide had mentioned that it was Marcel Proust's favourite painting; but strangely enough she had found it disappointing, and in the very few minutes of life remaining to her she was to have no opportunity of revising that rather harsh judgement.

She stepped to the window and looked across at the tetrastyle portico of Ionic columns, with the figure of Apollo, right arm raised and seated (a little precariously, as Laura judged) at the apex of the low-pitched pediment. Between the two central columns, a large Oxford-blue banner was suspended: *Musaeum Ashmoleanum apud Oxonienses*. Oh yes, Laura knew quite a lot about the Ashmolean Museum, and there appeared the flicker of a smile around her excessively lip-sticked mouth as she let the curtain fall back and turned to the door on her left, half-open, which led to the champagne-tiled bathroom. Without for the moment entering, she pushed the door a little further open: WC to the right; bath immediately facing her, the shower-curtains half drawn across; and to the left a hand-basin with a series of heated rails beside it, fully laden with fluffy white towels.

Laura had always slept on the left-hand side of any double bed, both as a young girl with her sister and then with both her husbands; and now she sat down, rather heavily, on the side of the bed immediately beside the main door, placed her white-leather handbag below the various switches for lights, radio, and TV, on the small table-top next to the bed – and removed her shoes.

Finally removed her shoes.

She fetched the kettle, filled it from the wash-basin in the bathroom, and switched on the current. Then, into the bathroom once more where she put the plug in the bath and turned on the hot tap. Returning to the main room again she picked up a DO NOT DISTURB sign, hung it over the outside door-knob, and returned to the bathroom to pour some pink Foaming Bubbly into the slowly filling bath.

Beryl Reeves had noted the single arrival in Room 310. At 4.40 p.m. she had put in a final burst of corridor hovering and hoovering, and knew even from her very limited experience that before she went off duty at 5.00 there would be several queries from these Americans about the whereabouts of the (non-existent) 'ice-machine' and the (readily available) replenishments of coffee sachets. Beryl was from Manchester; and her honest, if slightly naïve attitude to life – even more so, her *accent* – had already endeared her to many of her charges on Level Three. All in all, she was proving a very good employee: punctual, conscientious, friendly, and (as Morse was later to discover) a most reliable witness.

It had been exactly 4.45 that afternoon (and who could be more accurate than that?) when she had looked in at Room 310; noticed the sign hanging over the door-knob, wondering why the door itself was slightly ajar; peered momentarily into the room itself; but immediately retreated on seeing the steam emanating from the bathroom. Yes, she *thought* she would have probably noticed a white leather handbag if it had been somewhere just inside. No, she had *not* passed beyond the door and looked around the corner beside the Fire Exit. She had seen an American guest going into Room 308 shortly after this – a man; a friendly man, who'd said 'Hi!'. Yes, of course she would recognise him. In fact she could tell them who he was straightaway: a Mr Howard Brown from California.

Just before 6 p.m. the phone rang in the office of Chief Superintendent Strange at the Thames Valley Police HQ at Kidlington. The great man listened fairly patiently, if with less than obvious enthusiasm, to his colleague, Superintendent Bell from St Aldate's in Oxford.

'Well, it doesn't sound particularly like Morse's cup of tea, Bell, but if you're really short . . . No, he's trying to get a few days off, he tells me, says he never gets his full ration of furlough. Huh! If you take off the hours he spends in the pubs . . . what? Well, as I say, if you *are* short . . . Yes, all right. You know his home number? . . . Fine! Just tell him you've had a word with me. He's usually happier if Lewis is with him, though . . . What? Lewis is already *there*? Good. Good! And as I say, just tell him that you've had a word with me. There'll be no problems.'

Chapter Six

There are worse occupations in this world than feeling
a woman's pulse
> (*Laurence Sterne*, A Sentimental Journey)

'You here already, Lewis?'

'Half an hour ago, sir. The Super called me. They're
short-staffed at St Aldate's—'

'Must be!'

'I've already been upstairs.'

'No problems?'

'I'm – I'm not quite sure, sir.'

'Well – "Lead on, Macduff!" '

'That should be "Lay on Macduff!", sir. So our English
teacher—'

'Thank you, Lewis.'

'The lift's just along here—'

'Lift? We're not climbing the Empire State Building!'

'Quite a few stairs, sir,' said Lewis quietly, suspecting
(rightly) that his chief was going through one of his temporary
get-a-little-fitter phases.

'Look! Don't you worry too much about me, Lewis. If by
any chance things become a bit too strenuous in the ascent,
I shall stop periodically and pant, all right?'

Lewis nodded, happy as always (almost always) to be
working with the curmudgeonly Morse once more.

For a few seconds Morse stood outside Room 310,
breathing heavily and looking down at the door-knob.
He raised his eyebrows to Lewis.

'No, sir – waste of time worrying. Four or five people
been in.'

'Who's in there now?' asked Morse quietly.

'Only the quack – Doc Swain – he's been the house-doctor here for a few years.'

'Presumably the *corpse* as well, Lewis?'

'The corpse as well, sir.'

'Who else has been in?'

'The Manager, Mr Gascoigne, and Mr Stratton – that's the husband, sir. He was the one who found her – very shaken up, I'm afraid, he is. I asked Mr Gascoigne to take him to his office.' Lewis pointed vaguely to one of the lower floors.

'No one else?'

'Me, of course.'

Morse nodded, and almost smiled.

Mrs Laura Stratton lay neatly supine on the nearer side of the double bed. She wore a full-length peach-coloured dressing robe, and (so far as Morse could see) little else. And she was dead. Morse glanced briefly at the face, swallowed once, and turned away.

Dr Swain, a fresh-faced, youngish-looking man (early thirties?) was seated at the low dressing table, writing. He turned his head and almost immediately answered Morse's unspoken question.

'Heart attack. Massive coronary.'

'Thank you, Dr – *Swain*, I think?'

'And you are?'

'I am Morse. Chief Inspector Morse.'

Swain got to his feet and handed Morse a sheet of paper, headed 'Oxfordshire Health Authority', with an impressively qualified column of medical men printed top right, in which (second from bottom) Morse read 'M. C. Swain, MA, MB, BCh, MRCP, MRCGP'.

'Congratulations!' said Morse.

'Pardon?'

'Sixteen, isn't it? Sixteen letters after your name, and I haven't got a single one after mine.'

'Well, er – that's how things go, isn't it? I'll be off now, if you don't mind. You've got my report. BMA dinner we've got this evening.'

Seldom was it that Morse took such an irrationally instant dislike to one of his fellow men; but there are always exceptions, and one of these was Dr M. C. Swain, MA, MB, BCh, MRCP, MRCGP.

'I'm afraid no one leaves for the moment, Doctor. You know, I think, that we've got slightly more than a death here?'

'I'm told something valuable's been stolen. Yes, I know that. All I'm telling *you* is that the cause of death was a massive coronary. You can read it in *that!*' Swain flung his forefinger Morse's way, towards the sheet just handed over.

'Do you think that was before – or after – this valuable something went missing?'

'I – I don't know.'

'She died there – where she is now – on the bed?'

'On the floor, actually.'

Morse forced his features to the limits of credulity: 'You mean you *moved* her, Dr Swain?'

'Yes!'

'Have you ever heard of murder in the furtherance of theft?'

'Of course! But this *wasn't* murder. It was a massive—'

'Do you really think it necessary to tell me things three times, sir?'

'I knew nothing about the theft. In fact I only learned about it five minutes ago – from the Manager.'

'That's true, sir,' chipped in Lewis, greatly to Morse's annoyance.

'Yes, well, if the Doctor has a dinner to attend, Lewis – a BMA dinner! – who are we to detain him? It's a pity about the *evidence*, of course. But I suppose we shall just have to try our best to find the man – or the woman – responsible for this, er, this massive coronary, brought on doubtless by the shock of finding some thief nicking her valuables. Good evening, Doctor. Make sure you enjoy your dinner!' Morse turned to Lewis: 'Tell Max to get over here straightaway, will you? Tell him it's as urgent as they get.'

'Look, Inspector—' began Swain.

But Morse was doing a reasonably convincing impression of a deaf man who has just turned off his hearing-aid, and now silently held the door of Room 310 open as the disconcerted doctor was ushered out.

It was in the Manager's office, on the first floor of The Randolph, that for the first time Morse himself was acquainted with the broad outlines of the story. Laura Stratton had taken her key up to her room soon after 4.30 p.m.; she had earlier been complaining of feeling awfully weary; had taken a bath – presumably after hanging a DO NOT DISTURB notice outside her door; had been discovered at 5.20 p.m. when her husband, Mr Eddie Stratton, had returned from a stroll around Broad Street with a fellow tourist, Mrs Shirley Brown. He had found the door to 310 shut, and after being unable to get any response from within had hurried down to Reception in some incipient panic before returning upstairs to find . . . That was all really; the rest was elaboration and emotional overlay. Except of course for the handbag. But who is the man, with his wife lying dead on the carpet, who thinks of looking around to see if her handbag has disappeared?

Well, Mr Eddie Stratton, it seemed.

And that for a most important reason.

Chapter Seven

Almost all modern architecture is farce
(*Diogenes Small* (1797–1812), Reflections)

The Randolph boasted many fine rooms for dinners, dances, conferences, and exhibitions: rooms with such splendid names as Lancaster, Worcester, and the like – and the St John's Suite, a high-ceilinged room on the first floor where the reception had been arranged. In the daylight hours the view from the east window took in the Martyrs' Memorial, just across the street, with Balliol and St John's Colleges behind. And even now, at 6.45 p.m., with the floral, carpet-length curtains drawn across, the room still seemed so light and airy, the twin candelabra throwing a soft light over the maroon and pink and brilliant-white décor. Even Janet Roscoe could find little to criticise in such a grandly appointed room.

Sheila Williams, a large gin and tonic in her left hand, was trying to be pleasantly hospitable: 'Now are we all here? Not *quite* I think? Have we all got drinks?'

News of Laura Stratton's death had been withheld from the rest of the group, with only Sheila herself being officially notified of that sad event. It was a burden for her, certainly; but also a wonderful excuse for fortifying the inner woman, and Sheila seldom needed any such excuse.

'Mrs Roscoe! You haven't got a drink. What can I—?'

'I don't drink, Mrs Williams!' Janet turned her head to a sheepish-looking Phil Aldrich, standing stoically beside her: 'I've already told her *once*, Phil!'

'Janet here is a deacon in our church back home, Mrs Williams—'

But Sheila had already jerked into a tetchy rejoinder: 'Well I *do* drink, Mrs Roscoe! In fact I'm addicted to the stuff. And my reasons for such addiction may be just as valid as your own reasons for abstinence. All right?'

With which well-turned sentence she walked back to the table just beside the main door whereon a dozen or so bottles of gin (Booth's and Gordon's), Martini (French and Italian), sherry (dry, medium, sweet) stood in competition with two large jugs of orange juice. She handed over her half-empty glass to the young girl dispensing the various riches.

'Gin – large one, please! – no ice – and no more tonic.'

Thus, fully re-equipped for her duties, Sheila looked down once more at the yellow sheet of A4 which John Ashenden had earlier prepared, typed up, photocopied, and distributed. It was high time to get things moving. Of the tourists, only Howard and Shirley Brown (apart from Eddie Stratton) seemed now to be missing – no, that was wrong: apart from Eddie and *Laura* Stratton. Of the two distinguished speakers (*three*, if she herself were included), Theodore Kemp had not as yet put in an appearance. But the third of the trio, Cedric Downes, seemed to Sheila to be doing a splendid job as he stood behind a thinly fluted glass of dry sherry and asked, with (as she saw it) a cleverly concealed indifference, whence the tourists hailed and what their pre-retirement professions had been.

It was 7.25 p.m. before Dr Kemp finally entered, in the company of a subdued-looking Ashenden; and it was almost immediately apparent to Sheila that both of them had now been informed of the disturbing events that had been enacted in the late afternoon. As her eyes had met Kemp's there was, albeit for a moment, a flash of mutual understanding and (almost?) of comradeship.

'Ladies and Gentlemen . . .' Sheila knocked a table noisily and repeatedly with the bottom of an ash-tray, and the chatter subsided. 'Mr Ashenden has asked me to take you through our Oxford itinerary – briefly! – so if you will all just look at your yellow sheets for a minute . . .' She waved her own sheet; and then, without any significant addition (although with a significant omission) to the printed word, read vaguely through the dates and times of the itemised programme:

THE HISTORIC CITIES OF ENGLAND TOUR
27TH OCT–10TH NOV
(Oxford Stage)

Thursday 1st November

4.30 p.m. (approx.)	Arr. The Randolph
4.30–5.30 p.m.	English teas available
6.45 p.m.	Cocktail Reception (St John's Suite) introduced by Sheila Williams, MA, BLitt (Cantab), with Cedric Downes, MA (Oxon)
8.00 p.m.	Dinner (main dining room)
9.30–10.15 p.m.	Talk by Dr Theodore Kemp, MA, DPhil (Oxon) on 'Treasures of the Ashmolean'.

Friday 2nd November

7.30–9.15 a.m.	Breakfast (main dining room)
10.30–11.30 a.m.	Visit to The Oxford Story, Broad Street (100 yards only from the hotel)
12.45 p.m.	Lunch (St John's Suite) – followed by an informal get-together with our lecturers in the coffee-lounge
3.00 p.m.	We divide into groups (details to be announced later)
4.30–5.00 p.m.	English tea (Lancaster Room)
6.30 p.m.	The Tour Highlight! The presentation, by Mrs Laura Stratton, of the Wolvercote Tongue (Ashmolean Museum)
8.00 p.m.	Dinner (N.B. extra charge) in The Randolph. Otherwise group members are offered a last opportunity to dine out, wine out, and find out – wherever they wish – on our final night in this wonderful University City.

Saturday 3rd November

7.30–8.30 a.m.	Breakfast (Please be punctual!)
9.30 a.m.	Departure from The Randolph for Broughton Castle (Banbury), and thence to Stratford.

'The only thing that needs much expansion here' (Sheila was talking more confidently now) 'is the three p.m. spot tomorrow afternoon. So let me just fill in a bit there. Dr Kemp, Keeper of Anglo-Saxon and Mediaeval Antiquities at the Ashmolean – the museum just opposite us here! – will be taking his group around there tomorrow – as well as talking to us after dinner tonight, as you can see. Then, Mr Cedric Downes' (Sheila duly signified that distinguished gentleman) 'will be taking his own group around several colleges – including the most interesting of the dining halls – and addressing himself particularly to' (Sheila looked at her brief notes) ' "Architectural Design and Technique in the Sixteenth and Seventeenth Centuries". That, again, is at three p.m. . . . Well, you've heard almost enough from me now . . .' (Janet Roscoe was nodding) '. . . but I'd just like to mention that there is a *third* group tomorrow.' ('Hear, hear!' said Phil Aldrich happily.) 'You see, *I* shall be taking a group of you – perhaps only two or three of you, I don't mind – on an "Alice Tour". As most of you will know, the Reverend Charles Lutwidge Dodgson – "Lewis Carroll" – was in real life a "Student" – I shall explain that tomorrow – at Christ Church in the latter half of the nineteenth century; and we shall be looking at many mementoes of him, in the Deanery Garden, the Cathedral, and the Dining Hall; and also looking at a unique collection of old photographs, drawings and cartoons in the Bodleian Library. Well, that's what's on the menu. I'm sorry we're running just a bit late but . . . Anyway, it's my great pleasure now to introduce you to Cedric here – Mr Cedric Downes – who is going to set the scene for his talk tomorrow, in a rather light-hearted way, he tells me, by giving us a few thoughts on *modern* architecture. Ladies and Gentlemen – Cedric Downes.'

'Thank you, Sheila! I sometimes feel that some of our tourists must think that here in Oxford we're all mediaeval, Early English, Gothic, Tudor, Jacobean, Georgian, and so on. But we do have – though I'm no expert in this field – we do have a few fine examples of contemporary design. I don't want to get too serious about things – not tonight! But take St Catherine's, for example – the work of that most famous Danish architect, Arne er Johansen—'

'Jacobsen!' (*Sotto voce* from Kemp.)

'Pardon?'

'You said "Johansen",' murmured Kemp.

'Surely not! I said "Jacobsen", didn't I?'

A chorus of assorted tourists assured Downes that he had most certainly *not* said 'Jacobsen'; and for a second or two Downes turned upon his fellow lecturer a look of what might have been interpreted as naked detestation, were it not for the slightly weary resignation in his eyes. To his audience he essayed a charming smile, and resumed:

'I'm sorry! It's all these Danes, you know! You never actually meet one called "Hamlet", do you? And talking of *Hamlet*, I see you'll all be at Stratford-on-Avon—'

'I thought it was Stratford-uparn-Avon,' chirruped a shrill, thin voice.

But by now Downes was getting into his stride: 'How good it is for us all in Oxford, Mrs, er—'

'Mrs Roscoe, sir. Mrs Janet Roscoe.'

'How good it is for Dr Kemp and Mrs Williams and myself to meet a scholar like you, Mrs Roscoe! I was just going to mention – only in passing, of course – that the Swan Theatre there, in my view . . .'

But everyone had seen the door open, and now looked with some puzzlement at the newcomer, a man none of them had seen before.

'Mrs Williams? Is there a Mrs Williams here?'

The said lady, still standing beside the drinks-table, no more than a couple of yards from the door, raised the index-finger of her non-drinking hand to signify her identity.

'Could I have a quiet word with you, madam?' asked Sergeant Lewis.

Chapter Eight

Madame, appearing to imbibe gin and It in roughly
equal measures, yet manages to exude rather more of
the gin than of the 'it'

(*Hugh Sykes-Davies*, Obiter Dicta)

Inside the Manager's office, situated at the head of the first
flight of stairs, Morse found his attention almost immediately
drifting towards the large drinks-cabinet which stood to the
left of the high-ceilinged suite of rooms wherein Mr Douglas
Gascoigne, a bespectacled, intelligent-looking man in his early
forties, sought, and sought successfully, to sustain the high
standards of service expected from his multi-starred establishment. Early photographs, cartoons, diplomas, framed
letters, and a series of pleasing watercolours, lined the walls
of the main office, above the several tables on which VDU
screens, print-out machines, telephones, in- and out-trays, fax
machines, and file-cases abstracted from surrounding shelves,
vied with each other for a few square feet of executively
justifiable space. As in the St John's Suite, the curtains were
drawn, this time across the window behind Gascoigne as he sat
at his desk, concealing the view of the Ashmolean façade upon
which, though from a higher elevation, Mrs Laura Stratton
had gazed so very briefly some three hours earlier.

'It's just' (Gascoigne was talking) 'that we've never had
– well, not in my time – anyone actually *dying* in the hotel.'

'Some thefts, though, I suppose?'

'Yes, a few, Inspector. Cameras left around – that sort
of thing. But never anything so valuable . . .'

'Wonder why she didn't leave it in your safe, sir?'

Gascoigne shook his head: 'We always offer to lock away
anything like that but—'

'Insured, was it?'

'Mr Stratton' – the Manager lowered his voice and gestured to the closed door on his right – 'thinks probably yes, but he's still in a bit of a daze, I'm afraid. Dr Swain gave him some pills and he's still in there with one of his friends, a Mr Howard Brown.' And indeed Morse thought he could just about hear an occasional murmur of subdued conversation.

Lewis put his head round the door and signified his success in securing the appearance of Mrs Sheila Williams. Gascoigne got to his feet and prepared to leave the two detectives to it.

'As I say, just make use of any of our facilities here for the time being. We may have to keep coming in occasionally, of course, but—'

'Thank you, sir.'

So Gascoigne left his own office, and left the scene to Morse.

And to Sheila Williams.

She was – little question of it – a most attractive woman, certainly as Morse saw her: mid-thirties (perhaps older?), with glistening dark-brown eyes that somehow managed to give the simultaneous impression of vulnerability, sensuality, and mild inebriation.

A heady mixture!

'Sit down! Sit down! You look as if you could do with a drink, Mrs Williams.'

'Well, I – it *is* all a bit of a shock, isn't it?'

'Anything suitable in there, Lewis?' Morse pointed to the drinks-cabinet, not without a degree of self-interest.

'Looks like he's just about got the lot, sir.'

'Mrs Williams?'

'G and T – that would be fine.'

'Gin and tonic for the lady, Lewis . . . Ice?'

'Why dilute the stuff, Inspector?'

'There's no ice anyway,' muttered Lewis.

'Look,' began Sheila Williams, 'I'm not myself in charge of this group. I do liaise *with* the group and arrange speakers and so on – but it's John Ashenden who's the tour leader.'

Morse, however, appeared wholly uninterested in the activities of Mr Ashenden: 'Mrs Williams, I'm going to have to ask everyone in the group what they were doing between about four-thirty and five-fifteen this afternoon – that's between the time Mr Stratton last saw his wife and when he got back from his walk with, er, with Mrs Brown . . .'

As Sheila tossed back the last of her G and T, Lewis thought he saw the hint of a smile about her full lips; but Morse had turned to the wall on his left where he was minutely studying a late nineteenth-century Henry Taunt photograph of some brewery drays, and his last few words may well have been spoken without the slightest hint of implication or innuendo.

'I'm sure they'll all co-operate, Inspector, but they don't know yet about . . .'

'No. Perhaps we should wait a while? After dinner? No later than that. I wouldn't want Sergeant Lewis here to be too late in bed – Ah! Another, Mrs Williams?'

'I'm sorry . . . I seem to be—'

'Nothing to be sorry about, is there?'

'Same again then, please, Sergeant. Little less tonic, perhaps?'

Lewis's eyebrows rose a centimetre. 'Anything for you, sir?'

'No thank you, Lewis. Not on duty.'

Lewis's eyebrows rose a further centimetre as he collected Mrs Williams's glass.

The tour was, as Morse and Lewis learned, a pretty expensive, pretty exclusive business really. Most of them had been to England before (not all, though) and most of them were well enough off to be coming back again before *too* long, whatever the strength of the pound sterling. One of them wouldn't be, though . . . Yes, Sheila Williams knew quite a bit about the Wolvercote Tongue, although Dr Kemp was the real authority, of course. It seemed that Laura Stratton's first husband, a real-estate man operating in California and, in later life, quite a collector, had come to find himself in possession of a jewelled artefact which, after learning of its provenance, he had bequeathed – he had died two years since – to the Curators of the Ashmolean Museum in Oxford. Oh yes, she had seen it dozens of times, though only in a series of technicolour slides, from which she had been able to sketch out a diagram of the whole jewel, buckle *and* tongue; and in fact she herself had executed the final coloured illustration which was at that moment on show at the Ashmolean. Come to think of it, she was glad she *had* done the drawings; whatever happened now, people could know exactly how the Wolvercote Jewel in its entirety *would* have appeared. Doubtless the police would find the Tongue, but . . .

'We shall certainly do our best, madam,' Lewis had interposed, the tone of his voice suggesting something less than brimming optimism.

The Tongue itself? Well, again, *Kemp* was really the one to ask. But she could certainly tell them all about the look of it: of triangular shape, some 3 inches long, and 2 inches wide at the base; of a dull dirtyish brown colour (gold!), with (originally) three ruby-stones, one on each corner of the triangle – but now reduced to just the one, and that at the narrower end of things. The great, the unique, value of the tongue was the fact that it fitted (perfectly!) into the gold buckle which had been discovered during an archaeological dig at the village of Wolvercote in the early 1930s; and which, since 1947, had been proudly exhibited in the Ashmolean as evidence (hitherto unsuspected) of the exquisite craftsmanship of the goldsmith's art in the late eighth-century AD. Laura Stratton (so Sheila had learned from John Ashenden) had carried the jewel with her, in a black velvet-lined case, and kept it in her handbag – refusing to entrust the precious artefact either to transatlantic postal services, international tour operators, or burglar-and-fire-proof safe-deposit boxes. In the same handbag, it appeared, Laura had also carried a beautiful-looking string of wholly phoney pearls, which she had worn on most evenings with her dinner-dresses. Of any other valuables which might have been stolen with the handbag, Sheila had no idea whatsoever, although she volunteered the information that from her own recent experiences – and in spite of the equally recent strength of the pound sterling – some of the Americans seemed less than fully aware of the denominational value of the English currency they carried on their persons. With almost all of the party (she suspected) several £10, £20, even £50, notes would hardly be strangers in the purses and wallets of some of California's wealthier citizens. So a casual thief might have been pleasantly surprised by the sum of the monies often carried? But Mr Stratton – Eddie Stratton – *he'd* be the man to ask about such things, wouldn't he? Really?

She turned her large, melancholy eyes upon Morse; and for a few seconds Lewis found himself wondering if his chief wasn't temporarily mesmerised. So much so that he decided not to withhold his own contribution:

'You say, Mrs Williams, that the group won't perhaps mind me asking them all where they were between four-thirty and five-fifteen? Would you mind if you told us where *you* were?'

The effect of such an innocent question was quite unexpectedly melodramatic. Sheila Williams placed her empty glass on the table in front of her, and immediately burst into tears, during which time Morse glowered at his subordinate as if he had simultaneously broken all the rules of diplomacy, etiquette, and freemasonry.

But Morse himself, as he thought, was equal to the task: he nodded peremptorily to the empty glass, and immediately Lewis found himself pouring yet another generous measure of Gordon's gin, tempered again with but a little slim-line tonic.

Suddenly, and with a defiant glare at the two policemen, Sheila sat up in her chair, sought to regain a precarious state of equipoise, and drank down the proffered mixture in a single draught – much to Morse's secret admiration. She spoke just five words: 'Ask Dr Kemp – he'll explain!'

After she was gone, guided in gentlemanly fashion along

the corridor by Sergeant Lewis, Morse quickly opened the
drinks-cabinet, poured himself half a tumbler of Glenfiddich,
savoured a large and satisfying swallow, thereafter placing the
tumbler strategically on a convenient shelf, just below the line
of vision of anyone entering. Including Sergeant Lewis.

Strangely, neither Sergeant Lewis nor Inspector Morse
himself seemed particularly conscious of the fact that Mrs
Sheila Williams had signally failed to answer the only significant question that had been put to her.

Such is the wonderful effect of any woman's tears.

Chapter Nine

Often I have wished myself dead, but well under my
blanket, so that neither death nor man could hear me
(*George Lichtenberg*)

John Ashenden would later remember exactly what he
had done during the vital forty-five minutes that Morse
had specified . . .

It was a quarter to five when he had walked out of
The Randolph, and crossed over by the Martyrs' Memorial
into Broad Street. The sun no longer slanted across the
pale-yellow stone, the early evening was becoming much
cooler, and he was wearing a lightweight rain-coat. He
strode fairly quickly past the front of Balliol, the great
gates of Trinity, Blackwell's Book Shop; and was waiting by
the New Bodleian building to cross at the traffic lights into
Holywell Street when he saw them standing there outside the
Sheldonian, *sub imperatoribus*, her arm through his, neither of
them (as it seemed) taking too much notice of anything except
their mutual selves. Even more briskly now, Ashenden walked
past the King's Arms, the Holywell Music Room, the back
of New College – until he came to Longwall Street. Here he
turned left; and after two hundred yards or so went through
the wooden gate that led into Holywell Cemetery, where
under the stones and crosses – so many Celtic crosses! –
were laid to rest the last remains of eminent Oxford men,
in these slightly unkempt, but never neglected, acres of
the dead. A curving path through the grass led him to
a wooden seat above which, wired to a yew tree, was
a rectangular board showing the plot of the cemetery,
with the memorials of the particularly eminent marked by
numbers:

1 Kenneth Grahame (1859–1932)
2 Maurice Bowra (1898–1971)
3 Kenneth Tynan (1927–1980)
4 H.V.D. Dyson (1896–1975)
5 James Blish (1921–1975)
6 Theodore and Sibley, Drowned (1893)
7 Sir John Stainer (1840–1901)
8 Walter Pater . . .

That was him!

It took Ashenden some twenty minutes or so, treading through overgrown grasses, and parting ivy from many semi-decipherable inscriptions, to find the strong, squat cross:

In te, Domine, speravi
WALTER PATER
Died July 30 1894

Then, almost immediately, he saw that other stone, the one he was looking for – an even simpler memorial:

JAMES ALFRED BOWDEN
1956–1981
Requiescat

For several minutes Ashenden stood there silently under the darkening shadows: it seemed a wonderfully unforbidding piece of ground in which to find a final resting-place. Yet no one wanted to die – certainly not John Ashenden, as he remained standing by the grave, wondering whether Jimmy Bowden, during the pain of his terminal illness, had ever recanted the dogmatic and confident atheism he had once

propounded in the early hours of one most memorable day.
But Ashenden doubted it. He recalled, too, that final postcard
to which he had never replied . . .

There was no one else in the cemetery; no one there
to observe the strange little incident when Ashenden, after
looking round about him for a last reassurance, parted the
thickly twined rootage of ivy at the rear of Bowden's small
cross, took something from the right-hand pocket of his rain-
coat, and laid it carefully at the foot of the stone before
replacing the ivy and patting it, almost effeminately, back
into its pristine state.

He was in no hurry, and on his leisurely way back
to the cemetery gate he stopped and read several of the
gravestones, including 'Kenneth Grahame, who passed the
river on the 6th July 1932, leaving childhood and literature through him the more blest for all time'. Ashenden
loved the wording. He looked vaguely for 'Theodore and
Sibley, Drowned (1893)'; but it was too dark now, and he
could find no clue as to who they were and where they had
perished.

He regained the main street, and on his way back
to The Randolph called in the back bar of The King's
Arms to order a pint of cask-conditioned Flowers. For
which choice, Inspector Morse would have been quietly
proud of him.

Shirley Brown had disengaged her arm as she and Eddie
Stratton crossed into Beaumont Street at ten-past five.

'Whatever you say, Ed, I'd still like to know where
he was going.'

'Like I say, *forget* it, Shirl!'

'He was trying to get out of sight – quick. You *know*
he was.'

'You still reckon he saw us?'

'I still reckon he saw us,' said Shirley Brown, in her
Californian drawl.

They were the only two in the guest-lift; and Eddie

bade his temporary leave as they reached the third floor.

'See you in a little while, Shirl.'

'Yeah. And tell Laura I hope her feet are rested.'

Eddie Stratton had made no reply as he walked towards Room 310.

Chapter Ten

A foolish consistency is the hobgoblin of little minds
(*Ralph Waldo Emerson*, Essays)

Too long had Morse been in the police business for him
to believe that a death and a theft, or (as he was now
beginning to think) a theft and a death, were likely to be a
pair of fortuitously contingent events. Not that he was even
remotely hopeful about the *theft*. He would never mind pitting
his brains against a *murderer*; but he'd always discounted his
chances against a reasonably competent burglar – even, come
to think of it, against a reasonably *in*competent burglar. And
if, as seemed the consensus of opinion now, Laura Stratton
had left her door ajar for her husband to let himself in; if
she had carelessly left her handbag on the bedside table
immediately inside her partially opened door; if someone had
known of these things – even if someone had *not* known of
these things . . . well, certainly, the odds were pretty strong
on the prompt disappearance of the handbag. Give it fifteen
minutes? At the outside, thought Morse. We all might pray
(*some* of us might pray) 'Lead us not into temptation', yet most
people seemed perfectly happy to stick their cameras, binocu-
lars, radios, squash rackets, handbags . . . mm . . . yes, stick
any of 'em on the back seats of their cars, and then complain
to the police when they found their rear windows smashed
into splinters and—

Come off it!

The truth was, of course, that Morse had virtually lost
all interest in the case already, his only enduring memory
being the admiration he'd felt for the alcoholic capacity of
a lady named Mrs Sheila Williams.

He just managed to hide the tumbler when without even a

sociable knock Max put his head round the door and, seeing Morse in the Manager's chair, promptly entered and seated himself.

'They told me I'd find you here. Not that I needed much direction. Any pathologist worth his meagre remuneration tends to develop a fairly keen sense of smell.'

'Well?'

'Heart attack. Massive coronary.' (*Swain*'s words.)

Morse nodded slowly.

'God knows why you ask me along here to confirm the obvious. Where's the booze, by the way?'

Reluctantly, Morse pointed to the drinks-cabinet.

'You're not paying for it, are you?'

'What do you fancy?'

'Nothing for me, Morse. I'm on duty.'

'All right.'

'Is, er, is it drinkable – the Scotch?'

Morse got to his feet, poured a miniature into a plastic cup, and handed it over. For a few minutes the two old enemies sat sipping in friendly silence.

'You *quite* sure, Max . . . ?'

'Not so bad, is it, this stuff?'

'. . . about the time of death?'

'Between four-thirty and five-fifteen.'

'*Really?*' Never before had Morse heard anything remotely approaching such a definitive statement from the lips of the hump-backed police-surgeon. 'How on earth—?'

'Girl at Reception, Morse. Said the poor old dear had gone up to her room at four-thirty, on her own two tootsies, too. Then your people told me she was found by her ever-loving husband at five-fifteen.' Max took a large swallow of the Glenfiddich. 'We professionals in the Force, Morse, we have to interpret all the available clues, you know.' He drained his cup with deep appreciation.

'Another?'

'Certainly not! I'm on duty . . . And anyway I'm just off to a very nice little dinner.'

A distant temple-bell was tinkling in Morse's mind: 'Not the same nosh-up as whatshisname?'

'The very same, Morse.'

'He's the house-doctor here.'

'Try telling me something I *don't* know.'

'It's just that he looked at Mrs Stratton, that's all.'

'And you didn't have much faith in him.'

'Not much.'

'He's considered quite a competent quack, they tell me.'

'To be honest, I thought he was a bit of a . . .'

'Bit of a *membrum virile*? You're not *always* wrong, you know . . . Er, *small* top-up, perhaps, Morse?'

'You know him?'

'Oh yes. And you're *quite* wrong, in this case. He's not just a— No, let's put it the other way: he's the *biggest* one in Oxford.'

'She still died of a heart attack, though?'

'Oh yes! So don't go looking for any silly bloody nonsense here. And it's not Swain who's telling you, Morse – it's *me*.'

When, some ten minutes later, Max had departed for his BMA dinner, Morse had already performed what in political parlance would be termed a compromising U-turn. And when Lewis came in, with Dr Theodore Kemp immediately in tow, Morse knew that he had erred in his earlier thinking. The coincidence of a theft and a death (in whichever order) might often be shown to be causally connected.

But not in this case.

Lewis would have to interview them all, of course; or most of them. But that would be up to Lewis. For himself, Morse wished for nothing more fervently than to get back to his bachelor flat in North Oxford, and to listen once again to the Second Movement of the Bruckner No. 7.

But he'd better see one or two of them.

Chapter Eleven

History, n. An account mostly false, of events mostly unimportant, which are brought about by rulers mostly knaves, and soldiers mostly fools
                    (*Ambrose Bierce*, The Devil's Dictionary)

Almost immediately Kemp slotted into Morse's preconceptions of the we-are-an-Oxford-man, although he was aware that he could well be guilty of yet another instant inaccuracy. The bearded, clever-looking, ugly-attractive man (late thirties – Sheila's age?) who sat down only after lightly dusting the seat with a hyper-handkerchief, had clearly either been told (by Sheila?) or heard (gossip inevitable) something of what had occurred. Other persons might have been irritated only temporarily by the man's affected lisp. Not so Morse.

'Abtholutely pritheless, Inthpector!'

'Perhaps you could tell us a little more about the Wolvercote Tongue, sir.'

Kemp was well prepared. He opened his black brief-case, took out a pile of pale-blue leaflets, and handed one across the desk to Morse, one to Lewis.

The Wolvercote Jewel

During the last century or so archaeologists and historians have become increasingly conscious of the splendid workmanship of the late Saxon period, and the discovery in 1931 of a gold 'buckle' at Wolvercote had been extremely exciting. Particularly so since this buckle linked up with a corresponding 'tongue', fully documented and authenticated, known to be in the collection of one Cyrus C. Palmer Jnr, a citizen of Pasadena, California. The *cloisonné* enamel of the pear-shaped tongue, set in a solid gold frame, decorated in a distinctive type of delicate filigree, and set (originally) with three large ruby-stones, appeared to match the Ashmolean buckle with exact precision. And if further proof were sought, the tongue's lettering – [AE]LFRED[1] MEC HE[HT GEWYR] CAN – was identical in figuration and engravure to that of the gold buckle – into which (as all experts now concur) the tongue had once fitted.

That the tongue will shortly fit into its buckle once more is due to the philanthropy of Mr Palmer and to the gracious co-operation and interest of his wife, (now) Mrs Laura M. Stratton. The only major problem remaining to be resolved (according to Dr Theodore Kemp of the Ashmolean Museum) is the exact purpose of this most beautifully wrought artefact, henceforth to be known, in its entirety, as 'The Wolvercote Jewel'. Whether it was the clasp of some royal garment, or whether it served some symbolic or ceremonial purpose, is a matter of fascinating speculation. What is certain is that The Wolvercote Jewel – tongue and buckle at last most happily conjoined – will now be numbered amongst the finest treasures of the Ashmolean Museum.

1 Alfred the Great, AD 871–901. For a full discussion, see *Pre-Conquest Craftsmanship in Southern Britain*, Theodore S. Kemp, Babington Press, June 1991.

'You write this, sir?' asked Morse.

Kemp nodded bitterly: the whole bloody thing now cancelled (Morse learned) – the ceremony that was all fixed up – the presentation – the press – TV. God!

'We learnt the dates of the kings and queens of England at school,' said Morse. 'Trouble is we started at William the First.'

'You ought to have gone back earlier, Inspector – much earlier.'

'Oh, I'm always doing that, sir.' Morse fixed his eyes on the pallid face across the table. 'What were you doing earlier this evening between four-thirty and five-fifteen, Dr Kemp?'

'What? What wath I doing?' He shook his head like a man most grievously distraught. 'You don't – you can't understand, can you! I wath probably buggering around in . . .' he pointed vaguely over Morse's head in the direction of the Ashmolean. 'I don't know. And I don't care!' He

picked up the pile of leaflets and, with a viciousness of
which Morse would not have thought the effeminate fingers
capable, tore them across the middle, and threw them down
on the desk.

Morse let him go.

Kemp was the second witness that evening who had
been less than forthcoming in answering the only pertinent
question that had been put to him.

'You didn't like him much, did you, sir?'

'What's that got to do with anything?'

'Well, somebody must have stolen this Wolvercote thing.'

'*Nobody* pinched it, Lewis! They pinched the *handbag*.'

'I don't see it. The handbag's worth virtually nothing
– but the, you know, it's priceless, he says.'

'Abtholutely pritheless!' mimicked Morse.

Lewis grinned. 'You don't think *he* stole it?'

'I'd rather not *think* at all about that inflated bladder
of wind and piss. What I *know* is that he'd be the last
person in Oxford to steal it. He's got everything lined up
– he's got this literature all ready – he'll get his name in the
papers and his face on the telly – he'll write a monograph for
some learned journal – the University will give him a DLitt
or something . . . No, he didn't pinch it. You see you can't
sell something like that, Lewis. It's only "priceless" in the
sense of its being unique, irreplaceable, crucial for historical
and archaeological interpretation . . . You couldn't sell the
Mona Lisa, could you?'

'You knew all about it, did you, sir? This Wolvercote
thing?'

'Didn't *you*? People come from far and wide to view
the Wolvercote Tongue—'

' "Buckle", isn't it, sir? Isn't it just the *buckle* that's
there?'

'I've never heard of the bloody thing,' growled Morse.

'I've never even been *inside* the Ashmolean, sir.'

'Really?'

'The only thing we learned about King Alfred was about him burning the cakes.'

'That's something though, isn't it? It's a fact – *perhaps* it's a fact. But they don't go in for facts in History these days. They go in for empathy, Lewis. Whatever that is.'

'What's the drill then, sir?'

So Morse told him. Get the body moved quietly via the luggage-lift while the tourists were still at dinner; get a couple of DCs over from Kidlington to help with statements from the group, including the speakers, re their whereabouts from 4.30 to 5.15 p.m.; *and* from the occupants of bedrooms adjacent or reasonably proximate to Room 310. Maids? Yes, better see if any of them were turning down counterpanes or restocking tea-bags or just walking around or . . . Morse suddenly felt himself utterly bored with the whole business. 'Find out the *system*, Lewis! Use a bit of initiative! And call round in the morning. I'll be at home – *trying* to get a few days' furlough.'

'We're not going to search the rooms then, sir?'

'Search the rooms? Christ, man! Do you know how many rooms there *are* in The Randolph?'

Morse performed one final task in what, by any criterion, had hitherto been a most perfunctory police enquiry. Briefly he spoke with Mr Eddie Stratton, who earlier had been sympathetically escorted up to the Browns' quarters in Room 308. Here, Morse found himself immediately liking the tall, bronzed Californian, in whose lived-in sort of face it seemed the sun might soon break through from behind the cloud of present adversity. Never particularly competent at expressing his personal feelings, Morse could do little more than mumble a few clichés of condolence, dredged up from some half-remembered funerals. But perhaps it was enough. For Stratton's face revealed little sign of grief; certainly no sign of tears.

★ ★ ★

The Manager was standing by Reception on the ground floor; and Morse thanked him for his co-operation, explaining that (as invited) he had made some, er, little use of the, er, the facilities available in the Manager's office. And if Sergeant Lewis and his men could continue to have the use of the office until . . . ?

The Manager nodded his agreement: 'You know it's really most unfortunate. As I told you, Inspector, we always advise our guests that it's in their own best interests *never* to leave any unattended valuables in their rooms—'

'But she didn't leave them, did she?' suggested Morse mildly. 'She didn't even leave the room. As a matter of fact, sir, she still hasn't left it . . .'

In this last assertion Morse was somewhat behind the times, for Lewis now came down the main staircase to inform both of them that at that very moment the body of the late Laura M. Stratton was being transferred from Room 310, via the luggage-lift, en route for the Chapel of Rest in the Radcliffe Infirmary, just up the Woodstock Road.

'Fancy a drink, Lewis?'

'Not for me, sir. I'm on duty.'

The faithful sergeant allowed himself a wry grin, and even Morse was vaguely smiling. Anyway, it would save him, Lewis, a quid or two – that was for sure. Morse never seemed to think it was *his* round; and Lewis had occasionally calculated that on about three-fifths of his chief's salary he usually bought about three-quarters of the considerable quantities of alcohol consumed (though little by himself) on any given case.

Morse nodded a curt understanding, and walked towards the Chapters Bar.

Chapter Twelve

Water taken in moderation cannot hurt anybody
(Mark Twain)

Pouring a modicum of slim-line tonic into the large gin that her present drinking companion had just purchased for her, Sheila Williams asked the key question: 'Might you have to cancel the rest of the tour, John?'

'Oh, I don't think it need come to that. I mean, they've all *paid* for it, haven't they? Obviously we could refund if, well, if Mr Stratton or—'

'He's fine. I've spoken to him. *You* haven't.'

'I can't do everything, you know.'

'Please don't misunderstand me, John, but wasn't it perhaps a little unfortunate that you were nowhere within hailing distance when one of your charges busts her arteries and gets burgled into the bargain?'

Ashenden took a sip from his half-pint glass of bitter, appearing to acknowledge the truth of what Sheila had just said, though without volunteering any further comment. He'd once read (or heard) – Disraeli, was it? (or Jimmy Bowden?) – that a man ought never to apologise; never to explain.

He did neither now.

'We go ahead with everything, Sheila – except for the presentation bit, of course.'

'Unless they find it.'

'Which they won't.'

'Which they won't,' agreed Sheila.

'In spite of this fellow—'

'*That's him!*' whispered Sheila, laying a beautifully mani-cured hand across Ashenden's fore-arm. '*That's* Morse!'

Ashenden looked across at the greying man, of middle

height and middle age, who beamed briefly at the brunette behind the bar as he ordered a pint of best bitter.

'Drinks too much – *beer*,' volunteered Ashenden, sticking in the last word rapidly as he found Sheila's eyes switch to his with a glare of displeasure. 'Bit overweight – round the middle – that's all I meant.'

'Yes! I know.' Her eyes softened, and Ashenden was aware – had *often* been aware – that he found her attractive, especially (what a cussèd world it all was!) as she was now, when all that seemed required was a pair of strong arms to cart her up to the nearest bed.

But she suddenly ruined every bloody thing!

She had moved closer to him, and spoke close to his ear – softly and sensuously: 'I shouldn't really tell you this, John, but I find him awfully attractive. Sort of, you know, dishy, and . . . sexy . . .'

Ashenden removed the hand that had found his sleeve once more. 'For Christ's sake, Sheila!'

'Clever, too, John! *Very* clever – so they say.'

'And what's that supposed to mean?' Ashenden's voice sounded needlessly tense.

'I'll tell you,' replied Sheila, the clarity of her articulation beginning to disintegrate: 'He's going to wanna know wha' – wha' you were up to between – between – about – four-thirty and five-fifteen.'

'What's that got to do with *him*?'

'It's not *me* wants to know, darling. All I say is, that's . . . that's wha' he's goin' to ashk – ask you. That's wha' he's goin' to ask *everybody*.'

Ashenden looked down silently at his drink.

'Where *were* you, John?' (Was the lovely Sheila sober once again already?)

'There's no law against anyone having a look round the colleges, is there?'

'Quite a few people were wondering where you'd got to—'

'I've just told you, for heaven's sake!'

'But where *exactly* was it you went, John? Tell me! Come on! Tell mummy all about it!'

Ashenden decided to humour her: 'If you must know I went and had a look round Magdalen—'

But he got no further. A few yards away Morse was walking towards the Bar-Annexe as Sheila greeted him:

'Inspector! Inspector Morse! Come and join us!'

Morse's half-smile, grudging and potentially aloof, suggested he might have preferred his own company. But Sheila was patting the settee beside her, and Morse found himself looking down into the same dark-brown, pleading eyes that had earlier held such a curious fascination for him on the floor above.

'I, er—'

'Meet John Ashenden, Inspector – our leader!'

Morse nodded across, hesitated, then surrendered, now positioning himself and his pint with exaggerated care.

'John was just saying he'd been round Magdalen this afternoon. That's right, isn't it, John?'

'Yep. It's, er, not a college I've ever got to know really. Wonderful though, isn't it? I'd known about the deer-park, but I'd never realised what a beautiful walk it was along the Cherwell there – those hundreds of acres of fields and gardens. As well as the tower, of course. Surely one of the finest towers in Europe, wouldn't you agree, Inspector?'

Morse nodded, seeming that evening to have a particular predisposition to nodding. But his brain was suddenly engaged, as it had never been engaged at any other point since arriving on the scene . . .

He had always claimed that when he had to think he had to drink – a dictum indulgently interpreted by his colleagues as an excellent excuse for the disproportionate amount of time the chief inspector seemed to spend at various bars. Yet Morse himself was quite convinced of its providential truth; and what is more, he knew that the obverse of this statement was similarly true; that when he was drinking he was invariably thinking! And as Ashenden had just spoken,

Morse's blue eyes had narrowed slightly and he focused on the leader's face with a sudden hint of interest, and just the slightest tingle of excitement.

It was twenty minutes later, after a dinner during which they had spoken little, that Howard and Shirley Brown sat brooding over their iced tomato-juices at a table just inside the main bar.

'Well,' maintained Howard, '*you*'ve gotten yourself an alibi OK, Shirl. I mean, you and Eddie . . . No prarblem! What about me, though?' He grinned wryly, good-humouredly: 'I'm lying there next door to Laura, right? If I'd wanted to, well—'

'What you thinking of, honey? Murder? Theft? Rape?'

'You don't think I'm capable of rape, Shirl!'

'No, I don't!' she replied, cruelly.

'And you saw Ashenden, you say. That gives *him* an alibi, too.'

'Half an alibi.'

'He saw *you* – you're sure?'

'Sure. But I don't reckon he thought we saw *him*.'

'Down Holywell Street, you say?'

'Uh-huh! I noticed the sign.'

'What's down there?'

'Eddie looked it up on the street map. New College, then Magdalen College – that's without the "e".'

DCs Hodges and Watson were now going systematically through their lists; and, almost simultaneously, Hodges was requesting both Mrs Williams and Mr Ashenden to accompany him to the Manager's office, with Watson asking Howard and Shirley Brown if they would please mind answering a few questions in the deserted ballroom.

On the departure of his two drinking companions – the lady reluctantly, the gentleman with fairly obvious relief – Morse looked again at the Osbert Lancaster paintings on the walls around him and wondered if he really liked these illustrations for *Zuleika Dobson*. Perhaps, though, he ought at last to *read* Beerbohm's book; even discover whether she was called 'Zuleeka' or 'Zuleyeka' . . .

His glass was empty and he returned to the bar, where Michelle, the decidedly bouncy brunette, declined to accept his proffered payment.

'The lady, sir. The one that was with you. She paid.'

'Uh?'

'She just said to get a pint for you when you came up for a refill.'

'She said "when", did she?'

'She probably knows your habits, sir,' said Michelle, with an understanding smile.

Morse went to sit in the virtually deserted Annexe now, and thought for more than a few minutes of Sheila Williams. He'd had a girl-friend called Sheila when he'd been an undergraduate just across St Giles' at St John's – the very college from which A. E. Housman, the greatest Latinist of the twentieth century, had also been kicked out minus a degree. A hundred years ago in Housman's case, and a thousand years in his own. Sheila . . . the source, in Milton's words, of all our woe.

After his fourth pint of beer, Morse walked out to Reception and spoke to the senior concierge.

'I've got a car in the garage.'

'I'll see it's brought round, sir. What's the number?'

'Er . . .' For the moment Morse could not recall the number. 'No! I'll pick it up in the morning if that's all right.'

'You a resident here, sir?'

'No! It's just that I don't want the police to pick me up on the way home.'

'Very sensible, sir. I'll see what I can do. Name? Can I have your name?'

'Morse. Chief Inspector Morse.'

'They wouldn't pick *you* up, would they?'

'No? Funny lot the police, you know.'

'Shall I call a taxi?'

'Taxi? I'm walking. I only live at the top of the Banbury Road, and a taxi'd cost me three quid at this time of night. That's three pints of beer.'

'Only *two* here, sir!' corrected Roy Halford as he watched the chief inspector step carefully – a little *too* carefully? – down the shallow steps and out to Beaumont Street.

Chapter Thirteen

Solvitur ambulando
(The problem is solved by walking around)
(Latin proverb)

As he walked up the Banbury Road that Thursday night, Morse was aware that by this time Lewis would know considerably more than *he* did about the probable contents of Laura Stratton's handbag, the possible disposition of the loot, and the likely circle of suspects. Yet he was aware, too, that his mind seemed – was! – considerably more lucid than he deserved it to be, and there *were* a few facts to be considered – certainly more facts than Lewis had gleaned in his school-days about Alfred the Great.

Facts: carrying her handbag, a woman had gone up to Room 310 at about 4.35 p.m.; this woman had not been seen alive again – or at least no one so far would *admit* to seeing her alive again; inside 310 a bath had been run and almost certainly taken; a coffee-sachet and a miniature tub of cream had been used; a DO NOT DISTURB sign had been displayed on the outside door-knob at some point, with the door itself probably left open; the woman's husband had returned at about 5.15 p.m., and without reporting to Reception had gone up to the third floor, in the guest-lift, with a fellow tourist (female); thence a hurried scuttle down to Reception via the main staircase where a duplicate key was acquired. On finally gaining access to his room, the husband had discovered his wife's body on the floor, presumably already dead; the hotel's house-doctor had arrived some ten or fifteen minutes later, and the body duly transferred from floor to bed – all this by about 5.40 p.m. At some point before, during, or after these latter events, the husband himself had noticed the disappearance of his wife's handbag; and at about 6 p.m. a call had been received by St Aldate's CID with a request for help in what was now looking a matter of considerably more moment than any petty theft.

Yes, those were the facts.

So move on, Morse, to a few non-factual inferences in the problem of the Wolvercote Tongue. Move on, my son – and hypothesise! Come on, now! Who *could* have stolen it?

Well, in the first place, with the door to 310 *locked*, only those who had a key: the Manager, the housekeeper, the room-maids – namely, anyone with, or with access to, a duplicate key to the aforementioned room. *Not* the husband. In the second place, with the door to 310 *open*, a much more interesting thieves' gallery was open to view: most obviously, anyone at all who would happen to be passing and who had glimpsed, through the open door, a handbag that had proved too tempting an opportunity. Open to such temptation (if not necessarily susceptible to it) would have been the room-maids, the occupants of nearby rooms, any casual passer-by . . . But just a moment! Room 310 was *off* the main corridor, and anyone in its immediate vicinity would be there *for a reason*: a friend, perhaps, with a solicitous enquiry about the lady's feet; a fellow tourist wanting to borrow something; or learn something . . . Then there was Ashenden. He'd said he would be going around at some point to all the rooms to check up on the sachets, shampoos, soaps, switches. Opportunity? Yes! But hardly much of a motive, surely? What about the three guest speakers? Out of the question, wasn't it? They hadn't been called to the colours at that point – weren't even *in* The Randolph. Forget them! Well, no – not altogether, perhaps; not until Lewis had checked their statements.

So that was that, really. That set the 'parameters' (the buzz-word at HQ recently) for the crime. No other portraits in the gallery.

Not really.

No!

Or were there?

What about the husband? Morse had always entertained a healthy suspicion of anyone found first on the scene of a crime; and Eddie Stratton had been a *double*-first: the first to report both the death of his wife, *and* the theft of the jewel. But any man who finds his wife dead – dead! – surely he's not going to . . . Nobody could suspect that.

Except Morse.

And what about – what about the most unlikely, improbable, unthinkable . . . Unthinkable? Well, *think* about it, Morse! What about the wife herself: Mrs Laura Stratton? Could she have been responsible for the disappearance of the jewel? But why? Was it insured? Surely so! And doubtless for a hefty sum. All right, the thing was unsellable, unbuyable; the thing was useless – except, that is, as a link in a cultural continuum in a University Museum. Or else – yes! – or else as an insurance item which in terms of cash was worth far more lost than found; and if the Strattons were getting a bit hard up it might not have been so much *if* it were lost as *when*. And what – it was always going to hit Morse's brain sooner or later – what if the thing had never been there to get lost in the first place? Yes, the possibility had to be faced: what if the Wolvercote Tongue had never been inside the handbag at all? (Keep going, Morse!) Never even left America?

Morse already found himself in the Summertown shopping centre; and it was some five minutes later, as he came to his bachelor flat just south of the A40 Ring Road, that the oddest possibility finally struck him: what if the Wolvercote Tongue didn't *exist* at all? But surely there would have been all sorts of descriptive and photographic pieces of evidence, and so on? Surely such an authority as Dr Theodore Kemp could never have been so duped in such a matter? No! And he'd almost certainly flown over to see it, anyway. No! Forget it! So Morse almost forgot it, and let himself into his flat, where he played the first two movements of the Bruckner No. 7 before going to bed.

He woke up at 2.50 a.m., his mouth very dry. He got

out of bed and went to the bathroom, where he drank a glass of water; and another glass of water. In truth, water – a liquid which figured little during Morse's waking life – was his constant companion during the early hours of almost every morning.

Chapter Fourteen

It is only shallow people who do not judge by appearances. The true mystery of the world is the visible, not the invisible

(*Oscar Wilde*, The Picture of Dorian Gray)

The bachelor Morse had only the wraith-like, gin-ridden spectre of a lush divorcée to share his pillow that night, unlike the male speakers scheduled for the following day's Historic Cities of England programme, both of whom, when Morse had made his first visit to the bathroom, were dutifully asleep beside their respective spouses and in their own homes – homes in North Oxford, separated by only about a quarter of a mile.

The traveller who heads north from the centre of Oxford may take, at St Giles' Church, either the fork which leads up the Woodstock Road, or the right-hand fork, the Banbury Road, which leads after a mile or so to Summertown. Here, just past the shopping area, he will come to the new, yellow-bricked premises of Radio Oxford on his left; and then, almost immediately on his right, the first of the four roads – Lonsdale, Portland, Hamilton, Victoria – which stretch between the main Banbury Road and the River Cherwell (pronounced by most of the locals 'Charwell'). At all hours, each of these roads is suitable only for one-way traffic because of the continuous lines of parked cars on either side. The majority of houses here, built in the 1920s and 30s, are without integral garages; and many an amateurishly painted sign, alongside the edges of the pavement or on boards beside front gates, urges with courtesy, warns with threats of trespass, or simply begs with a pathetic

'Please', those motorists who commute to Summertown not to park their wretched vehicles *there*. In vain! For the life-blood along these roads ever flows, as it were, through arteries clogged with atherosclerosis.

But Dr Kemp no longer drives a car . . .

Any person meeting for the first time those two distinguished academics, Theodore Kemp and Cedric Downes, would be fairly sure to come to the following judgements. Kemp would perhaps appear to merit such epithets as artistic, flamboyant, high-brow, selfish, aloof, rakish – the list could go on and on, in much the same direction; and this impression would be formed largely from a certain arrogance in the pale features, an affected upper-class diction, the almost invariable silk shirt and bow-tie, the casual elegance of the light-beige light-weight suits which he favoured in both summer and winter to bedeck his slim and small-boned figure. And what of Downes? Certainly not by any means such a clear-cut impres-sion: rather languid in movement, somewhat overweight, a not-quite-top-echelon-public-school-man, a slightly bored ex-pression round the mouth, the promise of a humorous twinkle in the eyes, a semi-florid colouring, a heavyish suit with trousers sorely in need of a press, longish and lank brown hair, and a careless, unpretentious drawl in a voice which still bore the flat traces of his Midlands origins. Everything about him qualified; everything 'rather', 'quite', 'somewhat'. And finally – most importantly, maybe – the obvious impression that he was going a bit, more than a bit, deaf. For increasingly noticeable was his habit of shepherding any interlocutor to his right-hand side; his frequent cupping of the hand behind his right ear; and occasionally his use of an NHS hearing-aid, recently provided for his rapidly developing otosclerosis.

Which things being so, it might be assumed that Kemp was probably having all the fun that was going in life in general, and in Oxford in particular; whilst the seedier, world-weary Downes was slowly running out of steam, and like as not running out of luck, too. Yet such an assumption would not be wholly correct: in fact it would be some considerable way distant from the truth.

Kemp's life had not blossomed as once it had promised. After fathering (as was rumoured) almost as many illegitimate offspring as almighty Zeus himself, and after successfully disclaiming most of the responsibility for such excessive multiplication of the species, he had married a rather plain, though neatly figured woman, named Marion (with an 'o'), whose parents were rumoured to be fairly wealthy. Then, now two years since, he had managed to crash his BMW in such a way that his not-wholly fair but fully pregnant wife had lost both her child and the use of her lower limbs, whilst he himself had received only a broken collar-bone, with a few slivers of glass embedded in his back. But at least Marion had survived: the driver of the other car involved, a twenty-nine-year-old married woman, had been instantly killed. Definitive responsibility for the accident could not be fully determined, since the coroner found some of the evidence confusing, and far from competently reported. Yet Kemp *had* been drinking: and the charge he faced, a charge resulting in a fine and a three-year disqualification, had been one of driving whilst under the influence of alcohol, not that of reckless or of dangerous driving. Some of those who knew Kemp well, most of his University colleagues, and all of those who could never abide the man, considered him to have been extremely fortunate. Such disapprobation had probably accounted for the refusal of his college to elevate his status as a post-graduate researcher (or 'graduate researcher', as the pedantic Morse would have preferred) to that of the fellowship which had suddenly fallen vacant. Six weeks after this humiliation, he had been appointed to the post of Keeper of Anglo-Saxon and Mediaeval Antiquities at the Ashmolean. He now lived in a ground-floor flat in Cherwell Lodge, a brick-built block along Water Eaton Road – the latter stretching from the bottom of Victoria Road into the Cutteslowe Estate. The enforced move, made to accommodate his wheel-chaired wife, had taken place at exactly the wrong time in the housing market, and his property was presently worth little more than a quarter of the price likely to be fetched by that of his fellow-lecturer, the one who had temporarily forgotten the name of a Danish architect.

At the age of forty, five years previously, Cedric Downes had married Lucy, an engagingly attractive woman, eleven years his junior, fair-skinned and blonde, fully-figured and fully-sexed – though with a tendency towards a nervousness of manner on occasion – and with an IQ which was rated quite high by those meeting her for the first time, but which usually dipped a little upon more intimate acquaintance. Downes, a mediaeval historian, was a Fellow of Brasenose, and lived in a large detached house at the far end of Lonsdale Road, its beautifully tended back garden stretching down to the banks of the River Cherwell . . .

In the back bedroom of number 6 Cherwell Lodge, Marion Kemp lay supine. Marion Kemp *had* to lie supine. It would have been beneficial to the two of them, certainly would have guaranteed longer periods of sleep, if after the accident they had abandoned the double bed and settled for twin beds – perhaps even for separate rooms. Surprisingly, however, her husband would hear nothing of such a suggestion, and at first she had felt pleased and, yes!, flattered that he still wished to lie each night beside her fruitless body. And even on that Thursday night some of the hatred which for so long had been slowly coalescing in her soul had perhaps abated minimally . . .

As he had promised, he had been home at 10 p.m., had clearly not been drinking much at all, had brought her a cup of Ovaltine and a digestive biscuit, and quite definitely had *not* been with that bitchy, boozy, whoreson *Williams* woman!

Unlike Lucy Downes, Marion Kemp did not convey any immediate impression of a lively mind. Yet those who knew her well (a diminishing group) were always aware of a shrewd and observant intelligence. Earlier she had watched

Theo carefully as he had spoken to her about what had occurred that evening, and she had been wholly conscious of his own colossal frustration and disappointment. But in truth she could not find herself caring two milk-tokens about the loss of the Wolvercote Tongue; nor indeed find herself unduly distressed about the death of some bejewelled old biddy from the far side of America. Yet she could find no sleep in the small hours of that Friday morning, her mind considering many things: above all the growing suspicion that the man asleep beside her was looking now beyond that bloody Williams woman . . .

And Marion thought she knew exactly where.

Cedric Downes had come home rather later than usual that Thursday evening. He had been one of the last to give the police an account of his movements from 4.30 to 5.15 p.m. ('Is this *really* necessary, officer?') God! He'd had a tutorial at that time! And now, when finally he went through into the bedroom, all was very quiet, with Lucy lying motionless along her own side of the bed. He nestled gently against the contours of her body, hoping that she might sense his need for her, but realising almost immediately that she was distanced, and would not be conjoined. He turned on to his right-hand side, as now he usually did when seeking sleep. With his left ear becoming so deaf, he would consciously press his right ear deep into the pillow, thereafter hearing virtually nothing of the nightly groans of the central-heating pipes, or the inexplicable creaking of the wood, or the rushing of the wind in the towering pine trees. Briefly his mind dwelt on the evening's events; briefly dwelt on his loathing for Kemp; but within a few minutes he could feel the tug of the warm tide and soon he was floating down to the depths of slumber.

Not so his wife, still breathing quietly and rhythmically, and not so much as twitching a lumbrical muscle.

But very much asleep that night was Sheila Williams, the bedroom window wide open in her dingily stuccoed semi in the lower reaches of Hamilton Road, a house (as it happened) almost exactly equidistant from that of Kemp and that of Downes.

At 4.45 a.m. Morse made his third visit to the bathroom – *and suddenly he remembered*. He went into his living room, looked along his book-shelves, extracted a volume, consulted its index, turned to the pages given, and read through the entry he had sought. His head nodded a few degrees, and his dry mouth widened into a mildly contented smile.

He was asleep when Lewis rang the doorbell at 8.30 a.m.

Chapter Fifteen

The best-laid schemes o' mice and men
  Gang aft a-gley,
And lea'e us nought but grief and pain
  For promised joy
                    (*Robert Burns*, To a Mouse)

Few English families living in England have much direct contact with the English Breakfast. It is therefore fortunate that such an endangered institution is perpetuated by the efforts of the kitchen staff in guest houses, B & Bs, transport cafés, and other no-starred and variously starred hotels. This breakfast comprises (at its best): a milkily-opaque fried egg; two rashers of non-brittle, rindless bacon; a tomato grilled to a point where the core is no longer a hard white nodule to be operated upon by the knife; a sturdy sausage, deeply and evenly browned; and a slice of fried bread, golden-brown, and only just crisp, with sufficient fat not excessively to dismay any meddlesome dietitian. That is the definitive English Breakfast. And that is what the French, the Germans, the Italians, the Japanese, the Russians, the Turks . . . and the English, also, with their diurnal diet of Corn Flakes and a toasted slice of Mother's Pride – that is what they all enjoy as much as almost anything about a holiday.

The Americans, too, though there are always exceptions.

Janet Roscoe leaned across the table, lowered the volume switch on her abnormally loud voice, and spoke to Sam and Vera Kronquist, the third of the married couples originally registered on the tour.

'I just don't know how he' – her sharp eyes singled out Phil Aldrich, seated at the next table – 'how he can even think of eating – *that*.'

The vehement emphasis accorded to this last word might perhaps have suggested that Janet's co-worshipper in Sacramento's Temperance Hall of Christian Scientists was devouring a plateful of raw maggots or the roasted flesh of sacrificial infants, instead of his slim rasher of streaky bacon. But Sam Kronquist, though content with his croissant, was happily tolerant about the tastes of others:

'We're only on vaycation once a year, you know, Janet. So perhaps we can forgive him?'

Or perhaps not; for Janet made no reply, and in silence completed her own modest breakfast of naturally juiced grapefruit segments, and one slice of unbuttered toast smeared over with diabetic marmalade. She was just finishing her cup of black de-caffeinated coffee when John Ashenden, after his peripatetic trip around the other tables, came to tell the three of them that there would be a short meeting in the St John's Suite at 9.15 a.m. in order to fit the coming day's events into a schedule that would have to be slightly revised . . .

'If you refer,' began Ashenden, 'to your original sheets' (he held up a copy of the yellow sheets distributed the previous day) 'you will see that quite a few amendments, sadly, will have to be made to it. But the tour will quite definitely be going ahead as normal – or as normal as it can do in the circumstances. Eddie – Eddie Stratton – wants this, wants it to go ahead, and he believes that Laura would have wished that, too. So . . . First of all then: our visit to The Oxford Story, scheduled for ten-thirty. This has been put back to ten a.m. Make a note, please: ten a.m. instead of—'

'Don't you mean brought *forward*, Mr Ashenden?'

Yes, probably Ashenden *did* mean exactly what Mrs Roscoe said. And he beamed a smile towards her, in fact welcoming rather than resenting the interruption: '—has been brought forward to ten a.m. There's been a cancellation of a Spanish block-booking and it will help the people there if we take the earlier spot. Yes? No problems?'

Thereupon Ashenden duly distributed an extra sheet to each of his rather subdued audience:

The Oxford Story

It was here in Oxford that Lewis Carroll created the immortal 'Alice'; here that King Charles I held his Civil War Parliament; here where Archbishop Cranmer was burned at the stake; here where Penicillin was developed. So take a seat aboard a flying desk – Ride the Spiral! – and travel backwards through time to the earliest days of Oxford University when Friar Roger Bacon (1214–1294) sat in his rooms overlooking Folly Bridge and . . . But let *Oxford* tell its own story, as you sit comfortably in your car and witness whole centuries of fascinating men and glorious events. (Wheel-chair access and toilet facilities for the disabled.)

There being no murmurs of demurral, even from the customary quarter, Ashenden proceeded to extol the virtues of such a visit: to whisk oneself back to the origins of the University in the twelfth century, and thence be spiralled to the present day – seated, foot-happily – with the wonderful bonus, betweenwhiles, of listening to a commentary on the passing pageants by no less a personage than Sir Alec Guinness himself. The visit had in fact figured as an 'extra' in the published brochure, but in view of the, er, the sad, *sad* events . . . Well, the company had agreed that the £2 supplement should now be waived.

'That's a very kindly gesture, sir,' volunteered Phil Aldrich, and several of his fellow tourists audibly concurred.

Sam Kronquist, suffering from incipient prostate trouble, found himself wondering whether that final parenthesis signified a lack of toilet facilities for those persons as yet unwilling to label themselves 'disabled'; but he held his peace.

That meant, Ashenden continued, that there would be something of an uncomfortable gap between about 11.15 and 12.30; and he was very glad to be able to announce that Mrs Williams and Mr Downes and Dr Kemp had agreed to hold an impromptu question-and-answer session on Oxford: Town and Gown. This would be in the Ball Room, beginning at 11.30 a.m.

To the afternoon, then.

Ashenden exhorted his audience once again to consult the original sheet, confirming that, apart from the 6.30 p.m. presentation, the scheduled programme would go ahead as stated. Perhaps it would be sensible, though, to start the afternoon groups at 2.45 p.m., please, at which time Dr Kemp would meet *his* group immediately outside the main entrance to the Ashmolean; Mr Downes *his* group at the Martyrs' Memorial; Mrs Williams *her* group in the foyer of the hotel. Was that all clear? And would they all please try if possible to keep to the group they had first opted for? There was a nice little balance at the moment; not that he would want to *stop* anyone changing, of course . . .

Again the touring party appeared to find the arrangements wholly unexceptionable, and Ashenden came to his last point. Would everyone please change the time given on their sheets for dinner: this was now brought forward ('Right, Mrs Roscoe?') from 8 p.m. to 7.30 p.m. Three of the Trustees of the Ashmolean would be joining them, and he would assume unless he was informed to the contrary that everyone would be coming to this final dinner. It *had* been optional, he knew that; but in view of . . .

In the crowded hotel foyer, ten minutes later, Mrs Roscoe failed to decrease her decibel level as she called across to the Bacon Man from Sacramento: 'They tell me we sit in those cars two at a time, side by side, Phil . . .'

'Yeah! OK, Janet. Yeah, OK.'

Chapter Sixteen

As you go through, you see the great scientists, scholars, and statesmen; the thinkers, writers, actors, monarchs, and martyrs who are part of Oxford's history. By passing this doorway you have a glimpse of the people whom Oxford has moulded, and many of whom have, in their turn, gone on to help mould the world

(*Lord Jenkins of Hillhead*, The Oxford Story)

At 9.50 a.m. Cedric Downes led the way as the tourists trooped down the front steps of The Randolph, turned right, and moved across the road. Here, just by the Martyrs' Memorial, Downes stopped.

'Here we have . . .' He pointed to the heavy iron sign on which the letters MAGDALEN STREET were painted in white, and the group gathered around him. 'Everyone – nearly everyone – knows that this is pronounced "Maudlin" Street, as if it were a sentimental, tearful sort of street. That's what the bus drivers call it. Now out in East Oxford we've got a Magdalen Road, and the same bus drivers call that one "M-a-g-dalen" Road. I only mention this, my friends, to show you that life here in Oxford is never quite so simple as it may appear. Off we go!'

'I didn't know *that*, Phil,' said Janet Roscoe quietly. '*Very* interesting.'

The group progressed to Broad Street, where Downes brought them all to a stop again, this time immediately outside the Master's Lodge at Balliol. 'Here – on your left here – the plaque on the wall – this is where Latimer and Ridley, and later Cranmer, were burned at the stake in 1555 and 1556. Not difficult to remember the date, is it? You can see the actual spot, the cross there – see it? – right in the middle of the road.'

A little silence fell on the group: those with the faculty of a visual imagination watching as the long, grey beards began to sizzle, and then the ankle-length shirts suddenly leap up in a scorching mantle of fire, and others hearing perhaps those agonised shrieks as the faggot-fired flames consumed the living flesh . . . For a few moments it seemed that everyone was strangely affected by Cedric Downes's words. Perhaps it was the way he'd spoken them, with a sad and simple dignity . . .

'Here we are then! No more walking to do at all.' He pointed immediately across the way to the triple-arched entry of the three-storeyed building that housed The Oxford Story.

That same evening Miss Ginger Bonnetti (not 'Ginger', but christened Ginger) wrote a longish letter to her married sister living in Los Angeles, one Mrs Georgie (as christened!) Bonnetti, who had married a man named Angelo Bonnetti. (Morse would have had great joy in learning of this, for he gloried in coincidences; but since Miss Ginger Bonnetti was destined to play no further rôle in the theft of the Wolvercote Tongue, he never did.)

Hi, sis! We had a great morning in Oxford. There's a kind of tourist attraction here called The Oxford Story and we got into these sort of cars, but they're more like those old-fashioned desks from schooldays really – sitting side by side, remember? Made of some dark sort of wood with slightly sloping tops as if you'd just got to listen to the class teacher or write out the alphabet again if

you didn't. Then we went up a
sort of spiral gradiant at
.000001 mph – no kidding! I wish I
could remember all those great
names we saw, and I do mean
<u>great</u>! And you <u>sit</u>. You sit in these
double desks and listen to a
commentary from you guess who!
Sir Alec Guiness. I mean, the <u>voice</u>!
So the pen was working away as
we went around and I've kept a
brochure for you somewhere of all
these people, Roger Bacon, Thomas
Bodley, Charles First (what a
little guy <u>he</u> was), Hobbes and
Locke, Wilkins (? – I can't read my
own handwriting). Sir Christopher
Wren, Boyle (you remember <u>our</u>
Physics teacher?), John Wesley (or
is it Wessley?), Alice (yeah, the
same!), William Ewart Gladstone
and no end of those other PMs. And
of course Cranmer and the Protestant
Martyrs, and I'm starting to remember
I've forgotten so many of the others.
Does that last bit make sense,
Georgie? Anyway it was marvellous,
the only trouble was that the poor
fellow in front of me had to put

up with all this incessant chatter
from a really <u>dreadful</u> little woman
who's clearly trying to trap another
victim. But I've left the big news till
now. You remember I told you about
the jewel one of the group was going
to bring to the Oxford museum here?
Well yesterday this poor woman
had a coronary and died and
someone stole her handbag with
this jewel inside it! Where <u>is</u> safe
these days? You tell me that. She'd
been a little poorly and her husband
said she always knew it was
going to be sooner or later but it's
a bad time just now, for the tour
I mean. Eddie, he's the husband,
doesn't want us to be too upset and
the tour goes on as sheduled, and
well he was her second! He's a
pretty nice guy really. But I reckon
she was the one with the money and
I just hope she was pretty well
insured all round. So as you can see
we're having plenty happening here!
    Love to Angelo,
    Ginger

P.S. I forgot to tell you it was just a bit _spooky_ for a start in that Oxford Story.

P.P.S My room looks right out on the Ashmolean - see that X on the enclosed card?

In the Oxford Story Gift Shop, the group had stayed quite some time, examining aprons, busts, chess-sets, Cheshire cats, cufflinks, games, gargoyles, glassware, jewellery, jigsaws, jugs, maps, pictures, postcards, posters, stationery, table-mats, thimbles, videos – everything a tourist could wish for.

'Gee! With *her* feet, how Laura would have loved that ride!' remarked Vera Kronquist. But her husband made no answer. If he were honest he was not wholly displeased that Laura's feet were no longer going to be a major factor in the determination of the tour's itineraries. She was always talking about lying down; and now she *was* lying down. Permanently.

'Very good,' said Phil Aldrich as he and Mrs Roscoe and the Browns emerged through the exit into Ship Street.

'But the figures there – they weren't nearly as good as the ones in Madame Tussaud's, now were they?'

'No, you're quite right, Janet,' said Howard Brown, as he gently guided her towards Cornmarket and back towards The Randolph.

When, five days later, Mrs Georgie Bonnetti received her sister's interesting letter, she was a little disappointed (herself a zealous Nonconformist) that with neither cartridge from the double-barrelled rifle had her sister succeeded in hitting the saintly founder of Methodism. (The unbeliever Morse would have been rather more concerned about the other four mis-spellings.)

Chapter Seventeen

Clever people seem not to feel the natural pleasure
of bewilderment, and are always answering questions
when the chief relish of a life is to go on asking them
(Frank Moore Colby)

After his *in situ* briefing outside Balliol, Downes left the
scene of the barbarous burnings and strolled thoughtfully
along to Blackwell's. An hour and a quarter (Ashenden
had suggested) for The Oxford Story; then back to The
Randolph where he and Sheila Williams and Kemp (the
man would always remain a surname to Downes) had agreed
to hold the question-and-answer session with the Americans.
Downes sometimes felt a bit dubious about 'Americans'; yet
like almost all his colleagues in Oxford, he often found
himself enjoying actual Americans, without those quotation
marks. That morning he knew that as always some of their
questions would be disturbingly naïve, some penetrating, all
of them *honest*. And he approved of such questions, doubtless because he himself could usually score a pretty point or
two with answers that were honest: quite different from the
top-of-the-head comments of some of the spurious academics
he knew.

People like Kemp.

After spending fifty minutes browsing through the second-
hand books in Blackwell's, Downes returned to The
Randolph, and was stepping up the canopied entrance
when he heard the voice a few yards behind him.

'Cedric!'

He turned round.

'You must be deaf! I called along the road there three or
four times.'

'I *am* deaf – you know that.'

'Now don't start looking for any sympathy from me, Cedric! What the hell! There are far worse things than being deaf.'

Downes smiled agreement and looked (and not without interest) at the attractively dressed divorcée he'd known on and off for the past four years. Her voice (this morning, again) was sometimes a trifle shrill, her manner almost always rather tense; but there were far worse things than . . .

'Time for a drink?' asked Sheila – with hope. It was just after eleven.

They walked together into the foyer and both looked at the noticeboard in front of them:

HISTORIC CITIES TOUR ST JOHN'S SUITE 11.30 a.m.

'Did you hear me?' continued Sheila.

'Pardon?'

'I said we've got almost half an hour before—'

'Just a minute!' Downes was fixing an NHS hearing-aid to his right ear, switching it on, adjusting the volume – and suddenly, so clearly, so wonderfully, the whole of the hotel burst into happily chattering life. 'Back in the land of the living! Well? I know it's a bit early, Sheila, but what would you say about a quick snifter? Plenty of time.'

Sheila smiled radiantly, put her arm through his, and propelled him through to the Chapters Bar: 'I would say "yes", Cedric. In fact I think I would say "yes" to almost anything this morning; and especially to a Scotch.'

For a few delightful seconds Downes felt the softness of her breast against his arm, and perhaps for the first time in their acquaintanceship he realised that he could want this woman. And as he reached for his wallet, he was almost glad to read the notice to the left of the bar: 'All spirits will be served as double measures unless otherwise requested.'

They were sitting on a beige-coloured wall-settee, opposite the bar, dipping occasionally into a glass dish quartered with

green olives, black olives, cocktail onions, and gherkins
– when Ashenden looked in, looked around, and saw
them.

'Ah – thought I might find you here.'

'How is Mr Stratton?' asked Sheila.

'I saw him at breakfast – he seems to be taking things
remarkably well, really.'

'No news of . . . of what was stolen?'

Ashenden shook his head. 'Nobody seems to hold out
much hope.'

'Poor Theo!' pouted Sheila. 'I must remember to be
nice to him this morning.'

'I, er,' Ashenden was looking decidedly uncomfortable:
'Dr Kemp won't be joining us this morning, I'm afraid.'

'And why the hell *not*?' This from a suddenly bristling
Sheila.

'Mrs Kemp rang earlier. He's gone to London. Just
for the morning, though. His publisher had been trying
to see him, and with the presentation off and everything—'

'That was this *evening*!' protested Downes.

'Bloody nerve!' spluttered Sheila. 'You were here, John,
when he promised. Typical! Leave Cedric and me to do all
the bloody donkey-work!'

'He's getting back as soon as he can: should be here
by lunchtime. So if – well, I'm sorry. It's been a bit of
a disappointment for the group already and if you . . .'

'One condition, John!' Sheila, now smiling, seemed to
relax. And Ashenden understood, and walked to the bar
with her empty glass.

The tour leader was pleased with the way the session had
gone. Lots of good questions, with both Sheila Williams and
Cedric Downes acquitting themselves *magna cum laude*, especially Downes, who had found exactly the right combination
of scholarship and scepticism.

* * *

It was over lunch that Sheila, having availed herself freely of the pre-luncheon sherry (including the rations of a still-absent Kemp), became quite needlessly cruel.

'Were you an undergraduate here – at Arksford, Mr Downes?'

'I was here, yes. At Jesus – one of the less fashionable colleges, Mrs Roscoe. Welsh, you know. Founded in 1571.'

'I thought Jesus was at Cambridge.'

Sheila found the opening irresistible: 'No, no, Mrs Roscoe! Jesus went to Bethlehem Tech.'

It was a harmless enough joke, and certainly Phil Aldrich laughed openly. But not Janet Roscoe.

'Is that what they mean by the English sense of humour, Mrs Williams?'

'Where else would he go to do carpentry?' continued Sheila, finding her further pleasantry even funnier than her first, and laughing stridently.

Downes himself appeared amused no longer by the exchange, and his right hand went up to his ear to adjust an aid which for the past few minutes had been emitting an intermittent whistle. Perhaps he hadn't heard . . .

But Janet was not prepared to let things rest. She had (she knew) been made to look silly; and she now proceeded to make herself look even sillier. 'I don't myself see anything funny in blasphemy, and besides they didn't have colleges in Palestine in those days.'

Phil Aldrich laid a gently restraining hand on Janet's arm as Sheila's shrill amusement scaled new heights: 'Please don't make too much fun of us, Mrs Williams. I know we're not as clever, some of us, as many of you are. That's why we came, you know, to try to learn a little more about your country here and about your ways.'

It was a dignified little speech, and Sheila now felt desperately ashamed. For a few seconds, a look of mild regret gleamed in her slightly bloodshot eyes, and she had begun to apologise when immediately next to them, on a table below the window overlooking the Taylor Institution, the phone rang.

It was 12.35 p.m. when Mrs Celia Freeman, a pleasantly spoken and most competent woman, took the call on the telephone exchange at the rear of the main Reception area. Only approximately 12.35 p.m., though. When later questioned (and questioned most earnestly) on this matter, she had found on her note-pad that both the name of the caller ('Dr Kemp') and the name of the person called ('Mr Ashenden') had been jotted down soon after a timed call at 12.31 p.m. And it was at 12.48 p.m., exactly, that John Ashenden phoned back from the St John's Suite to Reception to order a taxi to meet the train from Paddington arriving 15.00, and to pick up a Dr Theodore Kemp at Oxford Station.

Chapter Eighteen

In the police-procedural, a fair degree of realism is possible, but it cannot be pushed too far for fear that the book might be as dull as the actual days of a policeman

(*Julian Symons*, Bloody Murder)

It was not until 10 a.m. that same morning that Morse had recovered the Jaguar; 10.15 a.m. when he finally put in an appearance at Kidlington HQ.

'Hope you had a profitable evening, Lewis?'

'Not particularly.'

'Not arrested the thief yet?'

Lewis shook his head. He'd already put in three hours' work, trying to sort out and collate various statements, and he was in no mood to appreciate the sarcasm of a man who had seemingly lost most of the little enthusiasm he'd started with.

'Well?' asked Morse.

'Nothing, really. These Americans – well, they seem a nice lot of people. Some of 'em not all that sure about *exactly* where they were – but you'd expect that, wouldn't you? Settling in, drinking tea, unpacking, having a wash, trying to get the telly going—'

'Studying the Fire Instructions, I hope.'

'Doubt it. But as far as I could see, they all seemed to be telling the truth.'

'Except one.'

'Pardon, sir?'

'Ashenden was lying.'

Lewis looked puzzled: 'How can you say that?'

'He said he had a look round Magdalen.'

'So?'

'He told me all about it – he was virtually reciting phrases from the guide-book.'

'He *is* a guide.'

'Pages 130-something of Jan Morris's *Oxford*. Word for word – nearly.'

'He'd probably swotted it up for when he was going round with the group.'

'Magdalen's not on the programme.'

'But you can't just say he's lying because—'

'Ashenden's a liar!'

Lewis shook his head: it was hardly worth arguing with Morse in such a mood, but he persisted a little longer. 'It doesn't *matter* though, does it? If Ashenden decided to go and look round Magdalen—'

'He didn't,' said Morse quietly.

'No?'

'I rang the Porters' Lodge there this morning. The College was closed to visitors all day: they're doing some restoration in the cloisters and the scaffolders were there from early morning. No one, Lewis – *no one* – was allowed in Magdalen yesterday except the Fellows, by order of the Bursar, an order the Head Porter assured me was complied with without a single exception – well only a fellow without a capital "f" who brought a stock of superfine toilet paper for the President.'

'Oh!' Lewis looked down and surveyed the sheets on his desk, neatly arranged, carefully considered – and probably wasted. They might just as well be toilet paper, too. Here was Morse making a mockery of all his efforts with just a single phone call. 'So he was telling us lies,' he said, without enthusiasm.

'Some of us spend most of our lives telling lies, Lewis.'

'Do you want me to bring him in?'

'You can't arrest a man for telling lies. Not *those* lies, anyway. He's probably got a fancy bit of skirt along Holywell Street somewhere. Just as well he *was* there, perhaps.'

'Sir?'

'Well, it means he wasn't in The Randolph pinching handbags, doesn't it?'

'He could have pinched it *before* he went out. Mrs Stratton was one of the first up to her room, and Ashenden was there for a good ten minutes or so—'

'What did he do with it?'

'We ought to have searched the rooms, sir.'

Morse nodded vaguely, then shrugged his shoulders.

'We wasting our time?' asked Lewis.

'What? About the handbag? Oh yes! We shall never find that – you can safely put your bank balance on that.'

'I wouldn't lose all that much if I did,' mumbled the dispirited Lewis.

'Has Max rung?'

'No. Promised to, though, didn't he?'

'Idle sod!' Morse picked up the phone and dialled the lab. 'If he still says it was just a heart attack, I think I'll just leave this little business in your capable hands, Lewis, and get back home.'

'I reckon you'd be as happy as a sandboy if he tells you she was murdered.'

But Morse was through: 'Max? Morse. Done your homework?'

'Massive coronary.'

'Positive?'

Morse heard the exasperated expiration of breath at the other end of the line; but received no answer.

'Could it have been brought on, Max – you know, by her finding a fellow fiddling with her powder-compact?'

'Couldn't say.'

'Someone she didn't expect – coming into her room?'

'Couldn't say.'

'No sign of any injury anywhere?'

'No.'

'You looked everywhere?'

'I always look everywhere.'

'Not much help, are you.'

'On the contrary, Morse. I've told you exactly what she died of. Just like the good Dr Swain.'

But Morse had already put down the phone; and five minutes later he was driving down to North Oxford.

Lewis himself remained in the office and spent the rest of the morning rounding off the dull routine of his paper work. At 12.50 p.m., deciding he couldn't emulate the peremptory tone that Morse usually adopted with commissionaires, he took a number 21 bus down to St Giles', where he alighted at the Martyrs' Memorial and began to walk across to The Randolph. Sheila Williams was stepping out briskly, without glancing behind her, up the left-hand side of St Giles', past the columns of the Taylorian and the front of Pusey House, before being lost to the mildly interested gaze of Sergeant Lewis. And as the latter turned into Beaumont Street, with the canopy of The Randolph immediately in front of him, he stopped again. A man walked down the steps of the hotel, looking quickly back over his shoulder before turning left and scurrying along the street towards Worcester College, where he turned left once more at the traffic lights, and passed beneath the traffic sign there announcing 'British Rail'. In normal circumstances, such an innocent-seeming occurrence would hardly have deserved a place in the memory. But these were not normal circumstances, and the man who had just left The Randolph in such haste was *Eddie Stratton*.

Diffidently, Lewis followed.

It was during this hour, between 1 p.m. and 2 p.m., as Morse and Lewis were later to learn, that the scene was irreversibly set for murder.

At 3.20 p.m., to an audience slightly smaller than anticipated, Cedric Downes was pointing to the merits of the stained-glass windows in University College chapel, and especially to the scene in the Garden of Eden, where the apples on the tree of knowledge glowed like giant golden Jaffas. At 3.30 p.m., in the Archive Room of the New Bodleian, Sheila Williams was doing her best to enthuse over a series of Henry Taunt photographs taken in the 1880s – also to an audience slightly smaller than anticipated. But the slides selected by Dr Theodore Kemp, to illustrate the development of jewelled artefacts in pre-Conquest Britain, were destined to remain in their box in the Elias Ashmole Memorial Room that sunny afternoon.

Chapter Nineteen

At Oxford nude bathing was, and sometimes still is, indulged in, which used to cause mutual embarrassment when ladies passed by in boats

(Marilyn Yurdan, Oxford: Town & Gown)

At 9.30 p.m. the University Parks had long been closed – since before sundown in fact. Yet such a circumstance has seldom deterred determined lovers, and others slightly crazed, from finding passage-ways through or over fences and hedges into this famous precinct – the setting for countless copulations since the Royalist artillery was quartered on its acres during the Civil War.

Two of these latter-day lovers, Michael Woods (aged seventeen) and Karen Jones (two years older), and both from the village of Old Marston to the east of the Parks, had sauntered over the high-arched Rainbow Bridge across the Cherwell, and come to 'Mesopotamia', a pathway between two branches of the river, when young Michael, encouraged by the fact that he was now resting the palm of his right hand upon the right buttock of the slightly forbidding Karen – and without any perceptible opposition on her part – steered the nymphet into the enclosure known as Parson's Pleasure. This famous and infamous bathing place is to be found at a point where the Cherwell adapts itself to a pleasingly circumscribed swimming area at a bend of the river, with a terrace of unsophisticated, though adequate, cubicles enabling would-be bathers to shed their clothing and to don, or not to don, their swimming costumes there. Green-painted, corrugated-iron fencing surrounds Parson's Pleasure, with the access gate fairly jealously guarded during the summer months, and firmly locked after the waters are deemed too cold for even the doughtiest of its homoerotic habitués. But whether from an unseasonable gale, or whether from recent vandalism, one section of the perimeter fencing lay forlornly on the ground that evening; and very soon the young pair found themselves seated side by side in one of the cubicles. In spite of her seniority in years, Karen was considerably the more cautious of the two in the progress of this current courtship. And justifiably so, for Michael, as vouched for by several of the village girls, was a paid-up member of the Wandering Hands Brigade. After several exploratory fingerings along the left femur, a sudden switch of tactics to the front of her blouse had heralded a whole new manual offensive – when at that point she decided to withdraw to previously prepared positions.

'Mike! Let's get out of here, please! I'm getting a bit chilly—'

'I'll soon see to that, love!'

'And it's a bit spooky. I don't like it here, Mike.'

He'd known, really, ever since they'd slipped through the hedge at half-past eight; known when he'd kissed her briefly on the Rainbow Bridge above the swollen and fast-flowing waters, testing the temperature and finding it not warm enough for any further penetration into the underclothing of a girl who seemed dressed that balmy evening as if for some Antarctic expedition. He stood up now, and (as she thought) with a surprisingly gallant, almost endearing gesture, refastened the only button on her blouse he'd thus far managed to disengage.

'Yeah! Gettin' a bi' chilly, innit?' he lied.

The moon as they walked from the cubicle was bright upon the waters, and Karen was wondering whether she might slightly have misjudged this lively, fun-loving youth when her eyes caught sight of something lying lengthways across the top of the weir in front of them.

'Yaaaaahhhhh!'

Part Two

Chapter Twenty

The moon jellyfish
like a parachute in air
sways under the waves
                    (*Basil Swift*, Collected Haiku)

It was halfway through the slow movement of Dvořák's American Quartet – with Morse mentally debating whether that wonderful work might just edge out the 'In Paradisum' from the Fauré *Requiem* for the number eight spot in his Desert Island cassettes – when the phone rang. For the second time that evening. Some while earlier, a weary-sounding Lewis had informed Morse that Mr Eddie Stratton had gone off somewhere just after lunchtime – from the railway station – and had still not returned to The Randolph. Naturally such a prolonged absence was a little worrying, especially in view of, well, the circumstances; and in fact an anxious Ashenden had rung Kidlington a few minutes previously, just in case the police knew anything. So Lewis thought he perhaps ought to mention it before going off duty . . . To that earlier call Morse had listened with a grudging, half-engaged attention; but he was listening far more carefully now.

Both Lewis and Max were already on the scene when Morse arrived, the surgeon (incongruously suited in evening-dress) immediately putting the chief inspector into the picture – in a somewhat flushed and florid manner:
    'The dead man lay there, Morse' – pointing to the moonlit water by the weir – ' "something pale and long and white", as the young lady said. Rather good, eh? Somebody'd poked him along here with a punt-pole; and when I arrived his body – his naked, semi-waterlogged body – was nudging against the

side of the bank – just here – just in front of the changing
cubicles, face down, his head washed clean of blood – much
blood, methinks, Morse! – his hair rising and falling—'

'Have you been rehearsing all this stuff, Max?'

'Just drinking, dear boy . . . hair rising and falling in
the water like some half-knackered jelly-fish.'

'Very fine!'

'I read that bit about the jelly-fish somewhere. Too
good to let it go, eh?'

'He needed a hair-cut, you mean?'

'You've no poetry in your soul.'

'What party was it *tonight?*'

'Oxfordshire Health Authority. Guest Speaker – no less!'
Max flicked his bow-tie with the index-finger of his right
hand, before pointing the same finger at the figure of a man
lying covered with a plastic sheet on the splashed grass beside
the water's edge.

'Who is it?' asked Morse quietly.

'Ah, I was hoping you could tell *me* that. You're the
detective, Morse. Have a guess!'

'A seventy-year-old Californian whose wife died yesterday
– died, according to the best informed medical opinion, of
purely natural causes.'

'And what did *he* die of?'

'Suicide – suicide by drowning – about three or four
hours ago, just as it was getting dark. Crashed his head
against a jagged branch as he was floating by. Anything else
you want to know?'

'Back to school, Morse! I'm not sure he's an American
or whether he was recently severed from his spouse. But
he's certainly not in his seventies! Forties more like – you
could put your pension on the forties.'

'I propose keeping my pension, thank you.'

'See for yourself!'

Max drew back the covering from the corpse, and even
Lewis gave his second involuntary shudder of the night. As
for Morse, he looked for a second or two only, breathed very

deeply, lurched a fraction forward for a moment as if he might vomit, then turned away. It was immediately clear, as Max had said, that there had earlier been much blood; soon clear, too, that the body was that of a comparatively young man; the body of the man whom Morse had interviewed (with such distaste) the previous evening; the man who had been cheated of the Wolvercote Jewel – and the man who now had been cheated of life.

Dr Theodore Kemp.

Max was putting his bag into the boot of his BMW as Morse walked slowly up to him.

'You got here early, Max?'

'Just round the corner, dear boy. William Dunn School of Pathology. Know it?'

'How did he die?'

'Blood probably coagulated *before* he entered the water.'

'Really? I've never heard you say anything so definite before!'

'I know, Morse. I'm sorry. It's the drink.'

'But you'll know for certain tomorrow?'

' "Tomorrow and tomorrow and tomorrow." '

'It wasn't suicide, then?'

'Oh no, Morse. That was *your* verdict.'

'No chance?'

'I'm only a pathologist.'

'How long in the water?'

'Couldn't possibly say.'

'Roughly?'

'Eight, seven, six, five, four hours . . . "Roughly", you said?'

'Thank you very much.'

Max walked round to the front of his car: 'By the way, I was talking to Dr Swain again this evening. He's reporting you to the Chief Constable.'

' 'Night, Max.'

' 'Night, Morse.'

★ ★ ★

When the surgeon had departed, Morse turned with un-warranted ferocity upon his ill-used sergeant: 'You told *me*, Lewis, that Mr Eddie bloody Stratton had been missing in quite extraordinarily suspicious circumstances since early afternoon, and that a frenetically distraught Ashenden had rung you up—'

'I didn't! I didn't say that!'

'What *did* you tell me, then?'

'Well, I did mention that Stratton had gone AWOL. And I *also* said that Dr Kemp hadn't turned up at the railway station when they'd arranged for a taxi to pick him up and take him—'

'What time was that?'

'Three o'clock, sir.'

'Mm. So if there's some evidence of a whacking great crack on his head . . . and if this had been deliberately inflicted rather than accidentally incurred . . . about seven hours ago, say . . . Three o'clock, you say, Lewis, when Kemp turned up again in Oxford?'

'When he *didn't* turn up in Oxford, sir.'

So many lights; the yellow lights of the arc-lamps that shone down on the river-bank; the white lights from the flashes of the police photographers; the blue lights of the police cars that lingered still around the scene. But little light in Morse's mind. He could hang around, of course, for the following hour or two, pretending to know what it was that he or anybody else should seek to discover. Or go back to HQ, and try to think up a few lines of enquiry for the staff there to pursue – men and women looking progressively more unwashed and unkempt and incompetent as the small hours of the morning gradually wore on.

But there *was* another option. He could drive down to The Randolph, and sort out that lying sod Ashenden! The bar would still be open, wouldn't it? At least for residents. Surely the bar *never* closed in a five-star hotel? Isn't that what you paid for? Yes! And occasionally, as now, it so happened that

duty and pleasure would fall together in a sweet coincidence;
and from Parson's Pleasure, after dutifully forbidding Lewis
to linger more than a couple of hours or so, Morse himself
departed.

It was twenty-five minutes after Morse had left the scene
that Lewis discovered the first, fat clue: a sheet of yellow A4
paper on which the details of the Historic Cities of England
Tour had been originally itemised; and on which the time of
the final item that day had been crossed through boldly in
blue Biro, with the entry now reading:

7.30 ~~8.00~~ p.m.   Dinner

Chapter Twenty-one

You did not come,
And marching Time drew on, and wore me numb
(*Thomas Hardy*, A Broken Appointment)

The parking plots on either side of St Giles' were now virtually empty and Morse drew the Jaguar in outside St John's. It was two minutes past midnight when he walked through into the Chapters Bar, where a dozen or so late-night (early-morning) drinkers were still happily signing bills. Including Ashenden.

'Inspector! Can I get you a drink?'

After 'a touch of the malt' had been reasonably accurately translated by Michelle, the white-bloused, blue-skirted barmaid, as a large Glenlivet, Morse joined Ashenden's table: 'Howard and Shirley Brown, Inspector – and Phil here, Phil Aldrich.' Morse shook hands with the three of them; and noted with approval the firm, cool handshake of Howard Brown, whose eyes seemed to Morse equally firm and cool as he smiled a cautious greeting. The reason for such a late session, Ashenden explained, was simple: Eddie Stratton. He had not been seen again since he was observed to leave the hotel just after lunch; observed by Mrs Roscoe (who else?) – and also, as Morse knew, by Lewis himself. No one knew where he'd gone; everyone was worried sick; and by the look of her, Shirley Brown was worried the sickest: what could a man be doing at *this* time of night, for heaven's sake? Well, perhaps supping Glenlivet, thought Morse, or lying with some lovely girl under newly laundered sheets; and indeed he would have suggested to them that it was surely just a little early to get *too* worried – when the night porter came through and asked Chief Inspector Morse if he was Chief Inspector Morse.

★ ★ ★

'How the hell did you know I was here, Lewis?'

   'You said you were off home.'

   'So why—?'

   'No answer when I rang.'

   'But how—?'

   'I'm a detective, sir.'

   'What do you want?'

A phone call made just before midnight to St Aldate's Police Station had been relayed to the murder scene at Parson's Pleasure: Mrs Marion Kemp, of 6 Cherwell Lodge, had reported that her husband, who had left for London early that morning, had still not arrived back home; that such an occurrence was quite unprecedented, and that she was beginning (had long begun!) to feel a little (a whole lot!) worried about him. She was herself a cripple, constantly in need of the sort of attention her husband had regularly given her in the evenings. She knew something, though not all, of his day's programme: she'd rung The Randolph at 10.45 p.m. and learned from the tour leader that her husband had not turned up at any point during the day to fulfil his commitments – and that in itself was quite out of character. After an evening of agonising and, now, almost unbearable waiting, she'd decided to ring the police.

   Such was the message Lewis passed on, himself saying nothing for the moment of his own extraordinarily exciting find, but agreeing to pick up Morse in about ten minutes' time, after briefly reporting in to St Aldate's.

'News? About Eddie?' asked an anxious Phil Aldrich, when the frowning Morse walked back into the bar.

   Morse shook his head. 'We get all sorts of news, sir, in the Force: good news, sometimes – but mostly bad, of course. No news of Mr Stratton, though. But I wouldn't worry too much, not about him, anyway . . .' (the last words mumbled to himself). He wondered whether to tell the four of them seated there about the death of Dr Kemp, for they'd have to know very soon anyway. But he decided they probably had enough on their minds for the moment; and swiftly tossing back the Glenlivet, he left them, making his way thoughtfully to the front entrance, and wondering something else: wondering whether any announcement of Kemp's death – Kemp's murder – would have come as too much of a surprise to *one* of the four people who still sat round their table in the Chapters Bar.

There was no time, however, for him to develop such a fascinating, and probably futile thought; for as he stood waiting on the pavement outside the hotel entrance, a taxi drew up, and with the help of the driver a very drunken man staggered stupidly into the foyer. Morse was usually reasonably tolerant about fellow-tipplers, and indeed occasionally rather enjoyed the company of slightly tipsy sirens; but the sight of this fellow pathetically fighting to extricate a wallet from an inner pocket, and then forking out and handing over three £10 notes – such a sight filled even Morse with mild disgust. Yet at least it was all a bit of a relief, wasn't it?

For the man was Eddie Stratton!

Clearly there could be little point in interviewing Stratton then and there; and already a solicitous (if censorious) Shirley Brown on one side, and a business-like (if unsmiling) Howard Brown on the other, were guiding the prodigal son to the guest-lift. No! Stratton could wait. With any luck he'd still be there the following morning.

Unlike the taxi driver.

Morse caught the man's arm, and held him back as he was walking down the steps.

'You must have brought him quite a way?'

'You wha'?'

'Thirty quid? Must have been – Banbury, was it?'

'Yeah – could a' bin. Nothin' to do with you, mate.'

'I'm not your mate,' said Morse, fishing for his warranty.

'So? Wha's the trouble?'

'Where did you pick him up?'

'North Oxford.'

'Expensive ride!'

'I didn't ask for—'

'You *took* it.'

'Not short of a quid or two though, these Yanks—'

'I quite like the Yanks.'

'Me too, officer.'

'There's a bottle there' (Morse pointed back to Reception). 'Leukaemia Fund. Doesn't look as if it's quite full yet.'

'How much?'

'Twenty?'

Shrugging, the taxi-man handed Morse two of the £10 notes.

'Where was it in North Oxford? What was the address?'

'I forget.'

'Shall we make it twenty-five?'

'Down the bottom of Hamilton Road, somewhere – ninety-seven, I think it was.'

'Name?'

'Same name as mine. Huh! Coincidence, eh?'

'I've always liked coincidences.'

'She rang up an' said, you know, take this fellah down to The Randolph.'

'Good! Thanks! Good night then, Mr, er . . .'

'Williams. Jack Williams.'

Lewis had pulled in behind the taxi, and was in time to find Morse slowly – reluctantly? – pushing two £10 notes into the slot of a Charity Bottle. He smiled happily. Morse had a *bit* of money – he knew that, but the chief's generosity, certainly in pubs, was seldom in evidence; and it was most reassuring to find that there was an unexpectedly munificent side to the chief inspector's soul. So Lewis watched, and said nothing.

Chapter Twenty-two

Duty is what one expects from others; it is not what
one does one's self
        (*Oscar Wilde*, A Woman of No Importance)

It was not difficult for Lewis to find his way to the Kemps'
home in Cherwell Lodge, the ground-floor flat on the extreme
right of the three-storey building, since it was the only
window in the whole street, let alone the block of flats,
wherein electric light still blazed at a quarter to one that
morning. By this time, Lewis had shown Morse the yellow
A4 sheet; and Morse had seemed so delighted with it that he'd
turned on the car's internal light in transit. He folded the
sheet along its original creases, and was putting it inside
his breast-pocket as Lewis quietly pulled the car alongside
the pavement outside number 6.

'We can ring from *there* – be easier really,' suggested Morse,
pointing to the Kemps' property. We'll need a WPC – there
should be one at HQ, don't you think?'

Lewis nodded.

'And a doc,' continued Morse. '*Her* doc, if he's not
too far sunk in slumber or wine.'

Again Lewis nodded. 'You're right, sir. The more the
merrier, isn't it, with this sort of thing? It's about the
only time I really hate the job, you know – with accidents and so on . . . having to tell the relatives, and all
that.'

It was Morse's turn to nod. 'Always hard, isn't it,
Lewis? I hate it too, you know that.'

'Well, at least there are the two of us tonight, sir.'

'Pardon?'

'I said, at least with the two of us—'

'No! Only *you*, Lewis. We can't waste precious resources at this unearthly hour.'

'You mean you're not—'

'Me? I'm just going to walk round to, er, talk to our other witness.'

'Who's that?'

'That, Lewis, is Mrs Sheila Williams. She could very well have something vital to tell us. It was Mrs Williams, remember, who ordered the taxi—'

'But she'll be in *bed*!'

By not the merest flicker of an eyebrow did Morse betray the slightest interest in the prospect of interviewing an attractively proportioned and (most probably) scantily clad woman at such an ungodly hour.

'Well, I shall have to wake her up then, Lewis. Our job, as you rightly say, is full of difficult and sometimes distasteful duties.'

Lewis smiled in spite of himself. Why he ever enjoyed working with this strange, often unsympathetic, superficially quite humourless man, well, he never quite knew. He didn't even know if he *did* enjoy it. But his wife did. For whenever her husband was working with Morse, Mrs Lewis could recognise a curious contentment in his eyes that was not only good for him, but good for her, too. Very good. And in a strange sort of way, she was almost as big an admirer of Morse as that faithful husband of hers – a husband whose happiness had always been her own.

'Perhaps, I'd better run you round there, sir.'

'No, no, Lewis! The walk may do me good.'

'As you say.'

'Er . . . just one more thing, Lewis. About the Jaguar. I left it just outside St John's, I think. If, er . . .' He held up his car-keys between the thumb and forefinger of his right hand, as if saving his nostrils the distress of some malodorous handkerchief. Then he got out of the car.

As Lewis watched him walk away up to Hamilton Road, he wondered, as he'd so often wondered, what exactly Morse was *thinking*; wondered about what was going on in Morse's mind at that very moment; the reading of the clues, those clues to which no one else could see the answers; those glimpses of motive that no one else could ever have suspected; those answers to the sort of questions that no one else had even begun to ask . . .

When Morse opened the ramshackle gate to number 97, his mind was anticipating a potentially most interesting encounter. If a diabetic patient was in need of so-called 'balance' – namely, the appropriate injection of human insulin for the control of blood-sugar levels – equally so did Morse require the occasional balance of some mildly erotic fancy in order to meet the demands of what until recently he had diagnosed as a reasonably healthy libido. Earlier that very week, in fact, as he'd filled up the Jaguar with Gulf-inflated gasoline, he'd found himself surveying the display of the semi-pornographic magazines arranged along the highest shelf above the dailies; and re-acquainted himself with such reasonably familiar titles as *Men Only*, *Escort*, *Knave*, *Video XXXX*, and so many others, each of them enticing the susceptible motorist with its cover of some provocatively posed woman, vast-breasted and voluptuous. And it was just after he'd flicked through one of them that Detective Constable Hodges (blast his eyes!) had come in, walked over to the newspaper stall, and picked up the top copy but one from the *Daily Mirror* pile. Morse had immediately picked up a copy of *The Times*, and proceeded to hold this newspaper like a crusader flaunting his emblazoned shield as he'd stood beside Hodges at the check-out.

'Nice day, sir?'

'Very nice.'

It had seemed to Morse, at that moment, that the dull eyes of Hodges had betrayed not the slightest suspicion of Morse's susceptibility. But even Morse – especially Morse! – was sometimes wholly wrong.

Chapter Twenty-three

Yet the first bringer of unwelcome news
Hath but a losing office
(*Shakespeare*, King Henry IV, Part 2)

Lewis watched the silhouette gradually form behind the opaque glass in the upper half of the front door.

'Hullo? Who is it?' The voice sounded sharp, and well educated.

'Police, Mrs Kemp. You rang—'

'All right! All right! You took your time. Let me take mine!'

With much clicking of locks and a final scrabbling of a chain, the door was opened, and Lewis looked down with ill-disguised surprise.

'For Heaven's sake! Didn't they *tell* you I was a cripple?' And before Lewis could reply: 'Where's the policewoman?'

'Er, *what* policewoman, Mrs Kemp?'

'Well, I'm not going to be put to bed by *you* – let's get that straight for a start!'

Lewis might almost have been amused by the exchanges thus far, were it not for the heavy burden of the news he was bearing.

'If I could just come in a minute—'

Marion Kemp turned her chair through one hundred and eighty degrees with a couple of flicks of her sinewy wrists, then wheeled herself swiftly and expertly into the front room. 'Close the door behind you, will you? Who *are* you by the way?'

Lewis identified himself, though Marion Kemp appeared but little interested in the proffered warranty.

'Have you found him yet?' The voice which Lewis had earlier thought well under control now wavered slightly, and

with her handkerchief she quickly wiped away the light film
of sweat that had formed on her upper lip.

'I'm afraid—' began Lewis.

But for the moment Marion simulated a degree of hospi-
tality. 'Do sit down, Sergeant! The settee is quite comfortable
– though I have little first-hand experience of it myself, of
course. Now, the only reason I rang – the chief reason – was
that I need a little help, as you can see.'

'Yes, I do see. I'm, er, sorry . . .'

'No need! My husband managed to crash into another
car on the Ring Road down near Botley.'

'Er, I'll just, er . . .' Lewis had seen the phone in
the entrance-hall and with Mrs Kemp's permission he now
quickly left the room and rang HQ for a WPC. He felt
profoundly uneasy, for he'd known the same sort of thing
on several previous occasions: surviving relatives rabbiting
on, as if so fearful of hearing the dreaded information.

'She'll be along soon, madam,' reported Lewis, seating
himself again. 'Very dangerous that stretch by the Botley
turn . . .'

'Not for the driver, Sergeant! Not on this occasion.
One broken collar-bone, and a cut on the back of his
shoulder – and even *that* refused to bleed for more than
a couple of minutes.' The bitterness in her voice had
become so intense that Lewis couldn't think of anything,
even anything inadequate, to say. 'It would have been
better if he'd killed me, and had done with the whole
thing! I'm sure *he* thinks that. You see, he can't get rid
of me – not the way he could get rid of any *normal* wife.
He has to keep coming back all the time to look after my
needs when . . . when he'd much rather be out having *his*
needs looked after. You *do* know what I'm talking about,
don't you, Sergeant?'

Lewis knew, yes; but he waited a little, nodding his
sympathy to a woman who, for the moment, had said her
immediate say.

'What time did your husband leave this morning?' he

asked quietly, noting a pair of nervous eyes suddenly flash across at him.

'Seven-twenty. A taxi called. My husband was banned for three years after he'd killed me.'

Lewis shook his head helplessly: 'He *didn't* kill you, madam—'

'Yes he did! He killed the woman in the other car – and he killed *me*, too!'

Lewis it was who broke the long silence between them, and took out his note-book: 'You knew *where* he was going?'

'His publishers. He's just finished a book and now he's doing some chapters for the new *Cambridge History of Early Britain*.'

'And he actually – *went*, did he?'

'Don't be silly! Of course he went. He rang me up from London. The post hadn't come when he left, and he wanted to know if some proofs had arrived.'

'What time did you expect him back?'

'I wasn't sure. There'd been some trouble at The Randolph. You know all about that?'

Lewis nodded – ever dreading that inexorable moment when she, too, would have to know all about something else.

'They'd changed the programme – I forget exactly what he said. But he'd have been home by half-past ten. He's never later than that . . .'

The slim, dark-haired, rather plain woman in the wheel-chair was beginning to betray the symptoms of panic. Talk on, Lewis! Write something in that little book of yours. Do anything!

'You've no idea where he might have gone to when he came back from London?'

'No, no, no, Sergeant! How could I? He'd hardly even have the time to see his precious Sheila bloody Williams, would he? That over-sexed, pathetic, alcoholic . . .'

Talk on, Lewis!

'He must have been pretty upset about the Wolvercote Jewel.'

'He'd been waiting long enough to see it.'

'Why didn't he go over to America to see it?'

'I wouldn't let him.'

Lewis looked down at the uncarpeted floor-boards and put his note-book away.

'Oh no! I wasn't going to be left here on my own. Not after what he did to me!'

'Mrs Kemp, I'm afraid I've got—'

But Marion was staring down into some bleak abyss. Her voice, so savagely vindictive just a moment since, was suddenly tremulous and fearful – almost as if she already knew. 'I wasn't very nice to him about it, was I?'

Blessedly the front-door bell rang, and Lewis rose to his feet. 'That'll be the policewoman, Mrs Kemp. I'll – if it's OK – I'll go and . . . Look, there's something we've got to tell you. I'll just go and let her in.'

'He's dead. He's dead, Sergeant, isn't he?'

'Yes, Mrs Kemp. He's dead.'

She made no sound but the tips of her taut and bloodless fingers dug into her temples as if seeking to sever the nerves that carried the message from ears to brain.

Chapter Twenty-four

There are several good protections against temptations, but the surest is cowardice

(*Mark Twain*, Following the Equator)

'Sit down, Inspector! Can I get you a drink?'

Sheila Williams, fairly sober and fully respectable, was drinking a cup of black coffee.

'What – coffee?'

Sheila shrugged: 'Whatever you like. I've got most things – if you know what I mean.'

'I drink too much as it is.'

'So do I.'

'Look, I know it's late—'

'I'm never in bed before about one – not on my own!' She laughed cruelly at herself.

'You've had a long day.'

'A long boozy day, yeah.' She took a few sips of the hot coffee. 'There's something in one of Kipling's stories about a fellow who says he knows his soul's gone rotten because he can't get drunk any more. You know it?'

Morse nodded. ' "Love o' Women".'

'Yeah! One of the greatest stories of the twentieth century.'

'Nineteenth, I think you'll find.'

'Oh, for Christ's sake! Not a literary copper!' She looked down miserably at the table-top; then looked up again as Morse elaborated:

'It was Mulvaney, wasn't it? "When the liquor does not take hold, the soul of a man is rotten in him." Been part of my mental baggage for many a year.'

'Jesus!' whispered Sheila.

The room in which they sat was pleasantly furnished, with

some good quality pieces, and several interesting and unusual reproductions of Dutch seventeenth-century paintings. A few touches of good taste all round, thought Morse; of femininity, too – with a beribboned teddy-bear seated upright on the settee beside his mistress. And it was in this room, quietly and simply, that Morse told her of the death of Theodore Kemp, considering, in his own strange fashion, that it was perhaps not an inappropriate time for her to know.

For a while Sheila Williams sat quite motionless, her large, brown eyes gradually moistening like pavements in a sudden shower.

'But how . . . why . . . ?'

'We don't know. We were hoping you might be able to help us. That's why I'm here.'

Sheila gaped at him. 'Me?'

'I'm told you had a – well, a bit of a row with him.'

'Who told you that?' (The voice sharp.)

'One of the group.'

'That Roscoe bitch!'

'Have another guess.'

'Ugh, forget it! We had a row, yes. God, if anyone was going to kill themselves after that, it was me – *me*, Inspector – not him.'

'Look! I'm sorry to have to ask you at a time like this—'

'But you want to know what went on between us – between Theo and me.'

'Yes. Yes, I do, Mrs Williams.'

'Sheila! My name's Sheila. What's yours?'

'Morse. They just call me Morse.'

'All bloody "give" on my part, this, isn't it?'

'What did pass between you and Dr Kemp, Mrs – er, Sheila?'

'Only my *life* – that's what! That's all!'

'Go on.'

'Oh, you wouldn't understand. You're married, I'm sure, with a *lovely* wife and a couple of *lovely* kids—'

'I'm a bachelor.'

'Oh, well. That's all right then, isn't it? All right for *men*.' She drained her coffee and looked, first wildly, then sadly around her.

'G and T?' suggested Morse.

'Why not?'

As Morse poured her drink (and his), he heard her speaking in a dreamy, muted sort of voice, as though dumbfounded by the news she'd heard.

'You know, I was married once, Morse. That's how I got most of this' (gesturing around the room).

'It's nice – the room,' said Morse, conscious that the shabby exterior of the property belied its rather graceful interior, and for a second or two he wondered whether a similar kind of comment might not perhaps be passed on Mrs Williams herself . . .

'Oh, yes. He had impeccable taste. That's why he left me for some other woman – one who didn't booze and do embarrassing things, or get moody, or stupid, or passionate.'

'And Dr Kemp – he'd found another woman, too?' asked Morse, cruelly insistent. Yet her answer surprised him.

'Oh, no! He'd already *found* her; found her long before he found me!'

'Who—'

'His wife – his bloody wife! He was always looking at his watch and saying he'd have to go and—'

She burst into tears and Morse walked diffidently over to the settee, where he temporarily displaced the teddy-bear, put his right arm along her shoulder, and held her to him as she sobbed away the storm.

'I don't know whether I'm in shock or just suffering from a hangover.'

'You don't get hangovers at this time of night.'

'Morning!'

'Morning.'

She nuzzled her wet cheek against his face: 'You're nice.'

'You've no idea why Dr Kemp—?'

'Might kill himself? No!'

'I didn't say "kill himself".'

'You mean—?' For a few seconds she recoiled from him, her eyes dilated with horror. 'You can't mean that he was murdered?'

'We can't be sure, not yet. But you must be honest with me, please. Did you know anyone who might have wanted to kill him?'

'Yes! *Me*, Inspector. Kill his wife as well while I was at it!'

Morse sedately disentangled himself from Mrs Williams. 'Look, if there's anything at all you think I ought to know . . .'

'You don't really think I had anything to do with – with whatever's happened?'

'You were seen walking up St Giles' towards North Oxford, just after lunch yesterday. And it wasn't Mrs Roscoe this time, either. It was Sergeant Lewis.'

'I was going – ' replied Sheila slowly, 'I *went* – to the Bird and Baby. Would *you* like a guess, this time? A guess about what I went for?'

'You were on your own there, in the pub?'

'Ye-es.' She had hesitated sufficiently, though.

'But you saw someone in there?'

'No. But – but I saw someone cycling past; cycling up towards Banbury Road. It was Cedric – Cedric Downes. And he saw me. I know he did.'

Morse was silent.

'You do *believe* me, don't you?'

'One of the secrets of solving murders is never to believe anybody – not completely – not at the start.'

'You don't *really* see me as a suspect, surely!'

Morse smiled at her: 'I promise to take you off the list as soon as possible.'

'You know, I've never been suspected of murder before. Thank you for being so civilised about it.'

'It'll be just as well if you don't say anything to the group about it. Not till we're a bit further forward.'

'And you're not very far forward at the minute?'

'Not far.'

'Couldn't *we* make a little more progress, Morse?' The fingers of her left hand were toying with the top button of her scarlet blouse, and Morse heard the siren voice beside his ear: 'What would you say to another little drink before you go?'

'I'd say "no", my lovely girl. Because if I'm not reasonably careful, if I do have another drink, in fact if I stay a further minute even *without* another drink – then I shall probably suggest to you that we proceed – don't forget that we don't "progress" in the police force, we always "proceed" – to, er . . .' Morse waved a hand vaguely aloft, drained his glass, rose from the settee, and walked to the door.

'You'd enjoy it!'

'That's what's worrying me.'

'Why not, then?'

Sheila had not moved from the settee, and Morse stood in the doorway looking back at her: 'Don't you know?'

A few minutes later, as he turned right into the Banbury Road, now beginning to think once more with some semblance of rationality, Morse considered whether his witness had been telling him the whole truth. Just as ten minutes earlier, as he had driven back to St Aldate's, Lewis had wondered the same about Mrs Kemp; in particular recalling the curious fact that, for a woman who had so manifestly hated her husband, she had reacted to the news of his death with such terrible distress.

Chapter Twenty-five

Going by railroad I do not consider as travelling at
all; it is merely being 'sent' to a place, and very little
different from becoming a parcel
(*John Ruskin*, Modern Painters)

At Kidlington HQ Morse and Lewis swapped notes at
7.45 a.m.: both felt very tired, but neither confessed to it;
and one of them had a headache, about which he likewise
made no comment. The Jaguar had been parked outside his
flat that morning, with the keys found on the door-mat; but
just as of his weariness and of his hangover, Morse made no
mention of his gratitude.

At least the morning plan was taking shape. Clearly the
biggest problem was what to do about the tour, scheduled to
leave Oxford at 9.30 a.m. bound for Stratford-upon-Avon. It
would certainly be necessary to make some further enquiries
among the tourists, particularly about their activities during
the key period between the time Kemp had arrived back in
Oxford, and the pre-dinner drinks when everyone except
Eddie Stratton, it appeared, was accounted for. *One* of the
tourists, quite definitely, would not be able to produce his
or her copy of the Oxford stage of the programme, for the
yellow sheet found in Parson's Pleasure was now safely with
forensics; might even produce some new evidence. And even
if no fingerprints could be found on it, even if several of the
tourists had already discarded or misplaced their own sheets,
there would not be too many Americans, surely, who regularly
wrote their sevens with a continental bar across the down-
stroke. Then there was Cedric Downes. He would have to be
seen a.s.a.p., and would have to come up with a satisfactory
explanation of exactly why and when he'd left The Randolph.

In addition it was to be hoped that Max could come up with some fairly definite *cause* of death; and it was even possible (if only just) that the surgeon might throw caution to the wind for once and volunteer a tentative approximation of the time it had actually happened.

An hour later, as he drove the pair of them down to Oxford, Lewis felt strangely content. He was never happier than when watching Morse come face to face with a mystery: it was like watching his chief tackle some fiendishly devised crossword (as Lewis had often done), with the virgin grid on the table in front of him, almost immediately coming up with some sort of answer to the majority of the clues – and then with Lewis himself, albeit only occasionally, supplying one blindingly obvious answer to the easiest clue in the puzzle, and the only one that Morse had failed to fathom. Whether or not he'd be of similar help in the present case, Lewis didn't know, of course. Yet he'd already solved a little 'quick' crossword, as it were, of his own, and he now communicated his findings to Morse. The first part of Kemp's day had probably been something like this:

Left home earlyish for his visit by rail to London to see his publishers; been picked up by taxi at about 7.20 a.m., almost certainly to catch the 07.59, arriving Paddington at 09.03; obviously with only some fairly quick business to transact, since he'd appeared confident of meeting his commitments with the tourists at lunchtime at The Randolph, and then again during the afternoon; likely as not, then, he would originally have intended to catch the 11.30 from Paddington, arriving Oxford at 12.30.

'Have you checked with BR?'

'No need.' Lewis reached inside his breast-pocket and handed Morse the Oxford–London London–Oxford Network South-East timetable; but apart from briefly checking the arrival time of the 13.30 from Paddington, Morse seemed less than enthusiastic.

'Did you know, Lewis, that before nine o'clock the third-class rail fare—'

'*Second*-class, sir!'

'—is about, what, seven times – eight times! – more expensive than getting a coach from Gloucester Green to Victoria?'

'*Five* times, actually. The coach fare's—'

'We ought to be subsidising public transport, Lewis!'

'You're the politician, sir – not me.'

'Remember Ken Livingstone? He subsidised the tube, and everybody used the tube.'

'Then they kicked him out.'

'You know what Ken Livingstone's an anagram of?'

'Tell me!'

' "Votes Lenin King." '

'They wouldn't be voting him king now, though.'

'I thought you might be interested in that little snippet of knowledge, that's all.'

'Sorry, sir.'

'Why are you driving so slowly?'

'I make it a rule never to drive at more than forty-five in a built-up area.'

Morse made no reply, and two minutes later Lewis drew up in front of The Randolph.

'You've not forgotten Ashenden, have you, sir? I mean, he was the one who took the call from Kemp – and he was the one who wasn't looking round Magdalen.'

'I'd not forgotten Mr Ashenden,' said Morse quietly, opening the passenger door. 'In fact I'll get him to organise a little something for me straightaway. I'm sure that all these tourists – *almost* all these tourists – are as innocent as your missus is—'

'But one of 'em writes these peculiar sevens, right?'

'They're not "peculiar"! If you live on the Continent its *ours* that look peculiar.'

'How do we find out which one it is?'

Morse permitted himself a gentle grin: 'What date did the tour start?'

Chapter Twenty-six

Wilt thou have this Woman to thy wedded wife, to
live together after God's ordinance in the holy estate of
Matrimony? Wilt thou love her, comfort her, honour,
and keep her in sickness and in health; and, forsaking
all other, keep thee only unto her, so long as ye both
shall live?

(Book of Common Prayer,
Solemnization of Matrimony)

At just after 9.30 a.m., Morse sat with Lewis, Ashenden,
Sheila Williams, and the (now fully apprised) Manager of
The Randolph in a first-floor suite which the latter had readily
put at police disposal. Without interruption, quietly, quickly,
Morse spoke.

'I've no wish to hold up the tour a minute longer than
necessary, Mr Ashenden, but I've got certain duties in this
case which will involve your co-operation. Likewise, sir' (to
the Manager) 'I shall be grateful if you can help in one or
two practical ways – I'll tell you how in a few minutes. Mrs
Williams, too – I shall . . . we, Sergeant Lewis and I, shall
be grateful for your help as well.'

Morse proceeded to expound his preliminary strategy.

The tour, originally scheduled to leave at 9.30 a.m., could
not now leave until well after a buffet lunch, if this latter
could be arranged by the kitchen staff (the Manager nodded).
A meeting of all the tourists would be summoned straightaway
(Ashenden felt a pair of unblinking blue eyes upon him) –
summoned to meet *somewhere* in the hotel (the Manager
nodded again – the St John's Suite was free), and Morse himself would then address the group and tell them as much or
as little as he wanted to tell them, believing, he admitted,

that Rumour had probably lost little of her sprinting speed since Virgil's time, and that most of the tourists already had a pretty good idea of what had happened. After that meeting had finished, it would help police enquiries if the tourists could be kept amused for the rest of the morning. And if Mrs Williams – and how very grateful Morse was that she'd agreed to his earlier telephone request to be present! – if Mrs Williams could possibly think of some diversion . . . some talk, some walk. Yes, that would be excellent.

So! There was much to be done fairly quickly, was there not?

Ashenden left immediately, with the manifold brief of herding his flock together, of informing the coach-driver of the postponed departure, of phoning Broughton Castle to cancel the special out-of-season arrangements; of explaining to the Stratford hotel the cancellation of the thirty lunches booked for 1 p.m.; and finally of reassuring the lunchtime guest-speaker from the Royal Shakespeare Company that her fee would still be paid.

The Manager was the next to leave, promising that his secretary could very quickly produce thirty photocopies of the brief questionnaire that Morse had roughed out:

(a) Name ....

(b) Home address ....
....

(c) Whereabouts 3–6.30 p.m., Friday 2nd Nov.
....
....
....

(d) Name of one fellow-tourist able to
corroborate details given in (c)
....

(e) Date of arrival in UK ....

(f) Signature .... Date ....

Sheila Williams, however, appeared less willing to co-operate than her colleagues: 'I willingly agreed to come here, Inspector – you know that. But my only specialism is mediaeval manuscripts, and quite honestly not many of this lot are going to be particularly ecstatic about *them*, are they? I could – well, I *will*, at a pinch – traipse around these inhabited ruins and try to remember whether Queens is apostrophe "s" or "s" apostrophe. But like Dr Johnson I must plead ignorance, Inspector – sheer ignorance.'

Here Lewis chipped in with his first contribution: 'What about shipping them all off on one of these circular tours – you know, on the buses?'

Morse nodded.

'Or,' pursued an encouraged Lewis, ' "The Oxford Story" – *brilliant*, that!'

'They went on it yesterday – most of them,' said Sheila.

'I suppose we could just ask them to stay in their rooms and watch the telly,' mused Morse; but immediately withdrew the suggestion. 'No! People will be arriving—'

'They could just walk around Oxford, couldn't they, sir? I mean there's an awful lot to see here.'

'Christ, Lewis! That's what I suggested, at the *start*. Don't you remember?'

'What about Cedric, Inspector?' (This from Sheila.) 'I'm pretty sure he's free this morning, and he's a wonderfully interesting man once he gets going.'

'Could he do the sort of talk Dr Kemp was going to give yesterday?'

'Well, perhaps not that. But he's a bit of a Renaissance Man, if you know what I mean. The only thing he's a bit dodgy on is modern architecture.'

'Good! That's fine, then. If you could ring this polymath pal of yours, Mrs Williams . . . ?'

'He'd take far more notice of *you* if you rang him, Inspector. And . . . he probably won't know yet about—'

'Not unless he was the one who murdered Kemp,' interposed Morse quietly.

★ ★ ★

Cedric Downes had himself been on the phone for about
five minutes, trying frustratedly to contact British Rail about
times of trains to London that day; yet he could have had little
notion of the irrational and frenetic impatience of the man who
was trying to contact *him*; a man who was betweenwhiles
cursing the incompetence of British Telecom and bemoaning
the cussedness of the Universe in general.

'Hullo! Is that British Rail?' (It was, by the sound of
it, Mrs Downes, surely.)

'What?' answered Morse.

'Oh, I'm sorry. It's just that my husband couldn't get
through to BR, and he rang the operator and I thought . . .'
Clearly Mrs Downes had little idea *what* she'd thought. Her
manner was rather endearingly confused, and Morse switched
on what he sometimes saw in himself as a certain charm.

'I do know what you mean. I've been trying to get
your number . . . er . . . Mrs Downes, isn't it?'

'Yes. I'm Mrs Downes. Can I help you?'

'If you will. Chief Inspector Morse here.'

'Oh!'

'Look, I'd much rather be talking to you than . . .'

'Ye-es?' The voice, as before, sounded a little helpless,
more than a little vulnerable. And Morse liked it.

'. . . but is your husband in?'

'Ah! You want Cedric. Just a minute.'

She must, thought Morse, have put her hand over the
mouthpiece, or perhaps Downes himself had been waiting
silently (for some reason?) beside the phone, for there was no
audible summons before a man's voice sounded in his ear.

'Inspector? Cedric Downes here. Can I be of help?'

'Certainly, if you will, sir. We have a bit of a crisis here
with the American Tour. I'm speaking from The Randolph,
by the way. The sad news is—'

'I know.' The voice was flat and unemotional. 'Theo's
dead – I already knew.'

'Do you mind telling me *how* you know?'

'John Ashenden phoned a couple of hours ago.'

'Oh, I see!' On the whole Morse was not unhappy that Ashenden had been ringing around. 'Why I'm calling, sir, is to ask if you're free to come to The Randolph this morning.'

'This *morning*? Well . . . er . . . er . . . Well, I've got commitments after lunch, but this morning's free, I think.'

'If you *could* get down here, sir, I'd be very grateful. We've got our hands a bit full with things.'

'Of course.'

'If you could—'

'Walk 'em round Oxford again?'

'A different route, perhaps?'

'Or I might be able to get the Oxford University Museum to open up a bit early – you know, Inspector, the dodo and Darwin and the dinosaurs.'

'Wonderful idea!'

'Glad to help, really. It's awful, *terrible* – isn't it? – about Theo.'

'You'll contact the Museum, sir?'

'Straightaway. I know someone there who's still trying to classify a few of the South American crabs that Darwin left to the Museum. Fascinating things, crabs, you know.'

'Oh yes!' said Morse. 'I'm most grateful to you, sir.'

'Anyway, I'll call in at The Randolph, so I'll see you soon.'

'Er, just before you ring off, sir?'

'Yes?'

'It's only fair to tell you that we shall be asking everyone here a few questions about what they were doing yesterday afternoon.'

'As is your duty, Inspector.'

'Including *you*, sir.'

'Me?'

'I shall be asking you why you were cycling up St Giles' towards North Oxford after lunch yesterday. So if you can have your answer ready? It's only a formality, of course.'

'Would that all questions were so easy to answer!'

'Where were you going, sir?'

'I was going home to get a new hearing-aid. I almost always carry a spare, but I didn't yesterday. At lunchtime the aid started going off and I suddenly realised that I wasn't going to get through the afternoon—'

'Your hearing's not all *that* bad, is it, sir? You don't seem to have much of a problem hearing me now.'

'Ah, but I'm very fortunate! My dear wife, Lucy, bought me a special phone-attachment – bought it for my last birthday, bless her heart.'

Something had stirred in the back of Morse's brain, and he sought to keep the conversation going.

'It sounds as if you're very fond of your wife, sir?'

'I love my wife more than anything else in the world. Can that be so surprising to you?'

'And you'd do anything to keep her?' It seemed a brusque and strange reply, but Downes seemed in no way disconcerted.

'Yes! Certainly.'

'Including murdering Kemp?'

From the other end of the line there was no manic laughter; no silly protestation; no threat of lawyers to be consulted. Just the simple, gentle confession: 'Oh yes! Including that, Inspector.'

For the moment, Morse was completely wrong-footed, and he would have discontinued the exchange without further ado. But Downes himself was not quite finished:

'It was Sheila, I know that, who saw me yesterday afternoon. And I don't blame her in the slightest for telling you. If you *have* got a murder on your hands, it's the duty of all of us to report anything, however insignificant or innocent it may appear. So I may as well tell you straightaway. As I biked up St Giles' yesterday afternoon I passed one of the group walking up to North Oxford. Would you like to know who *that* was, Inspector?'

Chapter Twenty-seven

It is a matter of regret that many low, mean suspicions
turn out to be well founded
   (*Edgar Watson Howe*, Ventures in Common Sense)

As Lewis saw things, Morse's talk to the tourists was not
one of his chief's more impressive performances. He had
informed his silent audience of the death – just 'death' – of
Dr Kemp; explained that in order to establish the, er, totality
of events, it would be necessary for everyone to complete a
little questionnaire (duly distributed), sign and date it, and
hand it in to Sergeant Lewis; that the departure of the coach
would have to be postponed until late afternoon, perhaps, with
lunch by courtesy of The Randolph; that Mr Cedric Downes
had volunteered to fix something up for that morning, from
about 10.45 to 12.15; that (in Morse's opinion) activity was
a splendid antidote to adversity, and that it was his hope
that *all* the group would avail themselves of Mr Downes's
kind offer; that if they could all think back to the previous
day's events and try to recall anything, however seemingly
insignificant, that might have appeared unusual, surprising,
out-of-character – well, that was often just the sort of thing
that got criminal cases solved. And here, sad to relate, was
more than one case – not only the theft of a jewel, but also
two deaths: of the person who was to present that jewel to
the Ashmolean, and of the person who was to take official
receipt of such benefaction.
   When he had finished Morse had the strong feeling
that what he had just implied was surely true: there *must*
be some connection between the disturbing events which
had developed so rapidly around the Wolvercote Tongue.
Surely, too, it must be from within the group of American

tourists, plus their tutors and their guide, that the guilty party was to be sought. And fifteen minutes later, with all the completed questionnaires returned, there was good reason to suppose that Morse could be right, since three of those concerned, Eddie Stratton, Howard Brown, and John Ashenden, appeared temporarily unable to provide corroboration of their individual whereabouts and activities during the key period of the previous afternoon – the afternoon when the original groups, three of them, had been re-formed slightly (following Kemp's telephone call), and when anyone wishing to absent himself for some purpose would have been presented with a wonderful opportunity so to do. And keeping check on who was doing what, and when, and where, could well have proved as complicated as calling the roll after Dunkirk.

For Morse, the information gleaned from the questionnaires was eminently pleasing; and when, at 10.50 a.m., Cedric Downes led the way out of The Randolph towards South Parks Road and the University Museum, with every single member of the group present (except Mr Eddie Stratton), he looked tolerably pleased with himself. Especially of interest was the fact that one of the two men clearly experiencing difficulty with section (c) on the examination paper, Howard Brown (Morse wondered why his wife hadn't been willing to cover for him), had filled in section (e) with the correct date of arrival, 27 October; or, to be more precise about the matter, '2̶7̶ October'.

Nor would Morse be forgetting the only man who had not been present at the meeting – the man who still lay with a wicked headache and a barely touched breakfast-tray beside him in Room 201, to which room Shirley Brown had shepherdessed him when, after his unexplained absence, he had reeled into The Randolph the previous night.

But it was with Ashenden that Morse's attention was immediately engaged. Ashenden! – the man whom Cedric Downes now claimed to have passed on his bicycle; the man who had lied about his visit to Magdalen; the man who, like Howard Brown (and possibly Eddie Stratton?), was as yet unable to produce a single witness to his whereabouts the previous afternoon.

Three of them. How easy it had been almost immediately to uncover three possible suspects for the murder of Theodore Kemp!

Too easy, perhaps?

Chapter Twenty-eight

Myself when young did eagerly frequent
Doctor and Saint, and heard great Argument
 About it and about: but evermore
Came out by the same Door as in I went
            (*Edward FitzGerald*, The Rubaiyat)

'How are you, Morse?'

'Optimistic.'

'Oh!' Max appeared disappointed by the reply as he peered down again at the grisly work on which he was engaged.

The contrast between the two men would have struck any observer that morning. The stout, hump-backed surgeon – circumspect, but perky and confident; Morse – looking distinctly weary, his jowls semi-shaven by an electric razor that had seemingly passed peak efficiency, and yet somehow, somewhere underneath, a man on the side of the angels.

'There's some deep bruising here,' began Max, pointing to Kemp's left temple, 'but the main blow' – he jerked the head towards him before caressing the crushed skull with a gentle reverence – 'was *here*.'

Characteristically Morse sought to swallow back the bitter-tasting fluid that had risen in his gorge; and the surgeon, with understanding, pulled the rubber sheet over the head again.

'Bit messy, isn't it? Bled a lot, too. Whoever killed him had a bucket of blood to wipe away.'

'He *was* murdered, then?'

'What? Ah! Slipped up a bit there, didn't I?'

'But he was, wasn't he?'

'Your job, that side of things.'

'Which blow killed him?'

'Paper-thin skull like that? Either! Little knock on the right place . . .'

'Probably the blow on the back of the head, Max.'

'Oh yes – certainly could have been that.'

'Or . . . ?'

'Yes – *could* have been the crack on the temple.'

'Someone could have hit him and then he fell over and hit himself on the fender or the door-jamb or the bedpost—'

'Or the kerb, if he was out in the street.'

'But you don't believe he was, do you?'

'Not my province, belief.'

'Could he have suffered either of the injuries in the water?'

' "Till that her garments, heavy with their drink, Pull'd the poor wretch from her melodious lay To muddy doom." '

' "Death", Max – not "doom". And he hadn't got any garments, had he?'

'Good point, Morse. And I've got something else to show you.' Max now exposed Kemp's torso and heaved the corpse a few inches off the table. Along the back of the right shoulder was a scratch, some five or six inches long: a light, fairly superficial scratch, it appeared, yet one made quite recently, perhaps.

'What caused that, Max?'

'Dunno, dear boy.'

'Try!'

'An instrument of some sort.'

'Not a blunt instrument, though.'

'I would suggest a sharp instrument, Morse.'

'Amazing!'

'*Fairly* sharp, I should have said.'

'Caused as he was floating along like Ophelia?'

'Oh, I couldn't possibly say.'

'Could it have been done before he was murdered – when he was wearing a shirt, say?'

'Ah! A not unintelligent question!'

Together the two men looked again at the light wound,

stretching down diagonally from the back of the neck towards the armpit.

'*Could* it have been, Max?'

'I think not.'

'Then he was possibly naked when he was murdered?'

'Oh, I wouldn't go *that* far. Anyway he might have hit a willow twig in the river.'

'What other possibilities are there?'

'The evidence extends only as far as the lower scapula, does it not? He could have been wearing an off-the-shoulder toga.'

Morse now closed his eyes and turned away from the body: 'A toga pinned together with the Wolvercote Tongue, no doubt.'

'Oh no! I can assure you of one thing: that was not upon his person.'

'You don't mean – you didn't . . . ?'

Max nodded. 'And he didn't swallow it, either.'

'And he didn't drown.'

'No. None of the usual muck one finds in the lungs when a man's fighting for his breath. Could he swim, by the way?'

'Don't know. I haven't seen his wife yet.'

The pathologist suddenly dropped his habitual banter, and looked Morse in the eye. 'I know you've got a lot on your plate, old boy. But I'd see her soon, if I were you.'

'You're right,' said Morse quietly. 'Just tell me, *please*, whether you think he was naked when he was murdered – that's all I ask.'

'I've told you. I don't know.'

'Not many reasons why people are naked, are there?'

'Oh, I dunno. Having a bath; standing on the weighing-scales; sun-bathing in Spain – so they tell me.'

'Having sex,' added Morse slowly. 'Not so much a willow's twig, perhaps, as a woman's talon.'

'Less likely, I'd say.'

'But you're sometimes wrong.'

'Not so often as you, Morse.'

'We'll see.'

Max grinned. 'Glad it was *you* who mentioned sex, though. I was beginning to suspect you'd misplaced your marbles.'

'No, no! No chance of that, Max. Not yet, anyway.'

And as Morse left the pathology block, a quiet little smile of confidence could be seen around the chief inspector's lips.

Chapter Twenty-nine

There are an awful lot of drunks about these days. It wouldn't really surprise me if you turned out to be one yourself

(*Martin Amis*, Other People)

Apart from his former wife, Mr Edward Stratton was the only one of the original group who had not listened to Morse that morning. Although his head was throbbing almost intolerably, he'd felt sober enough to ring for breakfast in his room, and had done his best to contemplate the 'Full English' he'd so foolishly ordered for 7 a.m. His brain drew a veil over the sickening consequences.

Edward Stratton had always been interested in machinery, or 'working parts' as he'd always liked to think of things. As a boy in high school he'd progressed from World-War-I aircraft-kits to model railways, his mind and his hands responding most happily to the assemblage of pistons, valves, wheels, with their appropriate adjustments and lubrications. Not marrying, he had set up a small business in specialised agricultural machinery – which had gone bust in 1975. After a long period of depression, and a short period of training, he had taken on a new career – one which also demanded dexterity with the hands: that of a mortician. Was there ever an odder switch of professions? But Stratton had soon grown proficient in the gruesome, sometimes disgusting, demands of his new job; and in the process of preparing an aged philanthropist for his silk-lined resting-place, he had met the man's disconsolate widow, Laura. And married her a year later. Or, perhaps, it may have been that *she* had married him. Convenience, that's what it had been for her – little more. Maybe for him, too? He'd assumed that she had money; everyone assumed that she had money. But he'd never known for certain and still didn't know now.

It was the Wolvercote Tongue which monopolised Stratton's thoughts as he sat on his unmade bed, head between his hands, that Saturday mid-morning. The thing was insured, he knew that – well insured. How otherwise? Yet insured in exactly what circumstances, under exactly what provisions, Stratton was wholly ignorant. *Why* had Shirley Brown had to mention the point on her brief visit to him earlier that morning, and sowed those slowly germinating seeds of doubt? Would it make a difference if it could be maintained that Laura had died *before* the Tongue was stolen? Would the money then go to the Ashmolean? But there could never be any proof on the matter, and if she had died *after* it was stolen, then surely the money would have to be credited to her estate, would it not? Stratton shook his aching head. He could get no real grip on the situation, and the more he pondered, the more confused his thinking became. But if he could get the police to believe it was *after* . . . because that would mean it was still in her possession when she died . . . wouldn't it . . . ?

Augh!

Stratton rose from the bed and walked to the bathroom. He was dipping his heavy aching head into a basin of cold water when he heard the sharp knock on the door, and was soon admitting Chief Inspector Morse and Sergeant Lewis into his bedroom.

The former had immediately recognised the symptoms of a Caesar-sized hangover and offered practical aid in the form of two tablets of Alka Seltzer which he appeared to carry regularly on his person.

And almost immediately Stratton had been talking freely . . .

They must have thought him a bit insensitive – running off like that, the day after . . . But he'd seen the advert in *The Oxford Mail*, and the prospect of an Open Day at Didcot had proved irresistible. He'd walked round the engine sheds, he said, where he'd looked long and lovingly at the old locomotives, and where he'd seen schoolboys and middle-aged men carefully recording numbers and wheel-arrangements in their note-books. ('All of them apparently sane, Inspector!') And then he'd had the thrill of actually *seeing* ('a life-time's ambition') the Flying Scotsman! He'd stayed there ('in Didcart') much longer than he'd intended; and when finally he tore himself away from the Cornish Riviera and the Torbay Express he'd walked back to Didcot Parkway Station at about five o'clock, and caught the next train back to Oxford, where he'd, er, where he'd had a quick drink in the Station Buffet. Then he'd been walking back to The Randolph when he suddenly felt he just couldn't face his excessively sympathetic countrymen, and he'd called in a pub and drunk a couple of pints of lager.

'The pubs were open, were they, Mr Stratton?' asked Lewis.

But it was Morse who answered: 'If you wish, Lewis, I will give you the names and addresses of the three of them there that open all day. Please continue, Mr Stratton.'

Well, at about half-seven he'd gone into a restaurant in St Giles', Browns; had a nice steak, with a bottle of red wine; left at about half-nine – and was strolling down to The Randolph when he'd met Mrs Sheila Williams, just outside the Taylorian, as she was making for the taxi-rank. They had stood talking for quite some time, each of them perhaps slightly the worse for wear, and then she had invited him up to her North Oxford home for a night-cap.

And that was it.

The strong-bodied American, with his rugged features, had spoken with a quiet simplicity; and as he'd watched him and heard him, Morse thought he could well have enjoyed a pint with the fellow. Yet in Morse's view it was always a good idea to ask a few inconsequential questions. So he did.

'You say you had a drink at Oxford Station?'

'Yep.'

'Which platform would that have been on?'

'Search me! But the same side the train came in, I'd swear to it.'

'And they have booze there, do they?'

'Sure do! I had a can – coupla cans. Expensive it was, too.'

Lewis's eyebrows lifted under a frown, and he looked across at his chief: 'I'm afraid that's not right, sir. Mr Stratton couldn't have got any beer or lager at Oxford Station – not yesterday. There was a great big notice outside: "No Refreshments" or something like that, due to modernisation.'

' "Owing to" modernisation, Lewis.'

'I've never known the difference.'

'No need. Just say "because of" and you'll always be right.'

'As I was saying, sir, the buffet was shut.'

'Interesting point!' remarked Morse, suddenly turning again to a now distinctly uncomfortable-looking Stratton. 'So if you didn't stay on the station between about five-thirty and six-thirty, where exactly *were* you, sir?'

Stratton sighed deeply, and seemed to be pondering his position awhile. Then he sighed again, before opening the palms of his hands in a gesture of resignation. 'Your Sergeant's right, Inspector. I asked if I could get a drink – anything. But, like he says, they were refurbishing all the places there. I *did* stay, though. I stayed about half an hour – longer, perhaps. I'd gotten myself a *Herald Tribune* and I sat reading it on one of the red seats there.'

'Bit chilly, wasn't it?'

Stratton remained silent.

'Was there someone outside you didn't want to meet?' suggested Morse.

'I didn't – I didn't want to go out of the station for a while. It, er, it might have been a little awkward for me – meeting someone who might . . . might be waiting for a bus, or a taxi.'

'You saw someone from the group on the train, is that what you're saying? Someone sitting in a compartment in front of you when you got on the train at Didcot?'

Stratton nodded. '*He'd* not got on at Didcot, though. He must have come from Reading, I suppose—'

'Or Paddington,' added Morse quietly.

'Yes, or Paddington.'

Morse looked across at Lewis. Paddington was beginning to loom slightly larger than a man's hand on the horizon; Paddington was where the murdered Kemp had stood and phoned The Randolph the previous day. So was it too much to believe that it was *Kemp* that Stratton had seen – about five o'clock, hadn't he said?

'You'll have to tell me, you know that,' said Morse gently.

'It was Phil Aldrich,' replied Stratton quietly, his eyes searching those of the two policemen with a look of puzzlement – and perhaps of betrayal, too.

Phew!

'Let me ask you one more question, please, sir. Do you stand to profit much from your wife's death?'

'I do hope so,' replied Stratton, almost fiercely. 'You see, I'm pretty hard-up these days, and to be honest with you I'm certainly not going to say "no" to any insurance money that might be pushed my way.'

'You're an honest man, Mr Stratton!'

'Not always, Inspector!'

Morse smiled to himself, and was walking over to the door when Stratton spoke again: 'Can I ask you a favour?'

'Go ahead!'

'Can you leave me another coupla those Alka Seltzer things?'

Chapter Thirty

Precision of communication is important, more important than ever, in our era of hair-trigger balances, when a false, or misunderstood word may create as much disaster as a sudden thoughtless act

(*James Thurber*, Lanterns and Lances)

Morse thought it must be the splendid grandfather clock he'd seen somewhere that he heard chiming the three-quarters (10.45 a.m.) as he and Lewis sat beside each other in a deep settee in the Lancaster Room. Drinking coffee.

'We're getting plenty of suspects, sir.'

'Mm. We're getting pretty high on content but very low on analysis, wouldn't you say? I'll be all right though once the bar opens.'

'It *is* open – opened half-past ten.'

'Why are we drinking *this* stuff, then?'

'Stimulates the brain, coffee.'

But Morse was consulting the Paddington–Oxford timetable which Lewis had picked up for him from Reception, and was nodding to himself as he noted that the 13.30 arrived at Oxford 14.57, just as Kemp had claimed. Now if Kemp had been held up, for some reason, for even longer than he'd expected . . . for considerably longer than he'd expected . . . Yes, interesting! The train Stratton must have caught – *said* he'd caught – must have been the 16.20 from Paddington, arriving at Didcot 17.10, and Oxford 17.29. For several seconds Morse stared across Beaumont Street at the great Ionic pillars of the Ashmolean . . . What time *had* Kemp left Paddington? For left Paddington he certainly had, at some point, after ringing through to The Randolph to explain his delayed departure.

But what if . . . ?

'You know, sir, I was just wondering about that telephone call. What if—?'

Morse grinned at his sergeant. 'Great minds, Lewis – yours and mine!'

'You really think there's a possibility it *wasn't* Kemp who rang?'

'Yes, I do. And it would give us a whole new time perspective, wouldn't it? You know, with the best will in the world, Max will never give us too much help if he thinks he *can't*. Quite right, too. He's a scientist. But if *we* can narrow the time down – or rather, widen it out, Lewis . . .'

For a while he appeared deep in thought. Then, pushing his half-finished coffee away from him, he stood up and gave Lewis his orders: 'Go and find Ashenden for me. I shall be in the bar.'

'There we are, then!' said John Ashenden.

It was twenty minutes later, and Morse had decided (insisted) that his temporary HQ in the Lancaster Room should be moved to more permanent quarters in the Chapters Bar Annexe. He had questioned Ashenden in detail for several minutes about the crucial phone call with Kemp, and asked him to write down in dialogue-form the exchanges as far as he could recall them. Ashenden himself now sat back in his armchair, crossed his lanky legs, and watched with slightly narrowed eyes as Morse took the sheet from him and proceeded to read the reconstructed conversation:

K. I've been held up at Paddington, John.

A. Oh no! What's you're trouble?

K. Just missed the train, but I'll catch the half-past one and be with you for quarter-past three, at the very latest. Sorry to let you down like this, and miss the drinks and the lunch and the first bit of p.m. Apologies apologies apologies, John!

A. Not the end of the world, though – not quite! (sotto voce.) I'll do my best to sort things out, of course, and let your group know. Trouble is I changed the time to quarter-to three.

K. I'm a bloody nuisance, I know.

A. It could be worse. Shall I arrange a taxi for you from the station?

K. Is it worth it?

A. Save ten minutes.

K. All right. I get in at just before three o'clock.

A. I'll ring Luxicars just in case there's not a taxi there.

K. Thanks.

A. Make sure you don't miss the next one!

K. No danger. Er, before I ring off can I have a quick word with Cedric please – if he's there?

A. He's here. I'll get him. Hold on!

'You write fairly well,' said Morse, after reading through the sheet for a second time, and still refraining from pointing out the single grammatical monstrosity. 'You ought to try your hand at some fiction one of these days.'

'*Fact*, Inspector – it's not fiction. Just ask that nosy Roscoe woman if you don't believe me! She was sitting near the phone and she misses *nothing*.'

Morse smiled, if a little wanly, and conceded the trick to his opponent. Yet he sensed that those next few minutes, after

Ashenden had finished speaking with Kemp, might well have been the crucial ones in that concatenation of events which had finally led to murder; and he questioned Ashenden further.

'So you called over to Mr Downes?'

'I *went* over to Mr Downes.'

'But he didn't want to talk to Dr Kemp?'

'I don't know about that. He was having trouble with his hearing-aid. It kept whistling every now and then.'

'Couldn't he have heard without it?'

'I don't know. Perhaps not. The line *was* a bit faint, I remember.'

Morse looked across at Lewis, whose eyebrows had risen a self-congratulatory millimetre.

'Perhaps you only *thought* it was Dr Kemp, sir?' continued Morse.

But Ashenden shook his head firmly. 'No! I'm ninety-nine per cent certain it was him.'

'And Sheila – Mrs Williams – she spoke to him then?'

'Yes. But you put it most accurately, Inspector. She spoke to *him*. And when she did, he put the phone down. So he didn't actually speak to *her* – that's what she told me anyway.'

Oh!

'We've still only got *his* word for it,' said Lewis, after Ashenden had gone. 'Like we said, sir, if it *wasn't* Kemp, we'd have a different time-scale altogether, wouldn't we? A whole lot of alibis that wouldn't wash at all.'

Morse nodded thoughtfully. 'Yes, I agree. If Kemp was already dead at twelve-thirty . . .'

'There was somebody else who heard him, sir.'

'Was there?'

'The woman on the switchboard who put the call through.'

'She wouldn't have known the voice, Lewis! She gets thousands of calls every day—'

'She'd be a very busy girl if she got a *hundred*, sir.'

Morse conceded another trick. 'Fetch her in!'

★ ★ ★

Celia Freeman was of far greater help than either Morse or Lewis could have wished. Especially Morse. For just as he had begun to survey the picture from a wholly different angle, just as he thought he espied a gap in the clouds that hitherto had masked the shafts of sunlight – the switchboard-operator dashed any hope of such a breakthrough with the simple statement that she'd known Theodore Kemp very well indeed. For five years she had worked at the Ashmolean before moving across the street to The Randolph; and for the latter part of that time she had actually *worked* for Dr Kemp, amongst others. In fact, it had been Dr Kemp who had written a reference for her when she'd changed jobs.

'Oh yes, Inspector! It was Dr Kemp who rang – please believe that! He said, "Celia? That you?", or some such thing.'

'Mr Ashenden said that the line was a bit faint and crackly.'

'Did he? You *do* surprise me. It may be a little faint on one or two of the extensions, but I've never heard anyone say it was crackly. Not since we've had the new system.'

'He never said it *was* "crackly",' said Lewis after she had gone.

'Do you think I don't know that?' snapped Morse.

'I really think we ought to be following up one or two of those other leads, sir. I mean, for a start there's . . .'

But Morse was no longer listening. One of the most extraordinary things about the man's mind was that any check, any set-back, to some sweet hypothesis, far from dismaying him, seemed immediately to prompt some second hypothesis that soon appeared even sweeter than the first.

'. . . this man Brown, isn't there?'

'Brown?'

'The continental-seven man.'

'Oh yes, we shall have to see Brown, and hear whatever cock-and-bull story he's cooked up for us.'

'Shall I go and get him, sir?'

'Not for the minute. He's on the walkabout with Mr Downes.'

'Perhaps he's not,' said Lewis quietly.

Morse shrugged his shoulders, as if Brown's present whereabouts were a matter of indifference. 'At least *Mr Downes* is on the walkabout, though? So maybe we should take the opportunity . . . What's Downes's address again, Lewis?'

Chapter Thirty-one

There is much virtue in a window. It is to a human
being as a frame is to a painting, as a proscenium to
a play

(*Max Beerbohm*, Mainly on the Air)

It was just before mid-day when Lewis braked sedately
outside the Downes's residence at the furthest end of
Lonsdale Road.

'Worth a few pennies, sir?' suggested Lewis as they
crunched their way to the front door.

'Thou shalt not covet thy neighbour's house, Lewis.
Just ring the bell!'

Lucy Downes was in, and soon stood at the door: an
attractive, slim, fair-haired woman in her early thirties,
dressed in a summerish cotton suit of pale green, with
a light-beige mackintosh over her left arm. Her eyes held
Morse's for a few seconds – eyes that seemed rather timid,
yet potentially mischievous, too – until her mouth managed
a nervous little 'Hullo'.

'Good morning, madam!' Lewis showed his ID card.
'Is Mr Downes in, please? Mr Cedric Downes?'

Lucy looked momentarily startled: 'Oh! Good Lord!
He's not here, I'm afraid, no! He's been showing some
Americans round Oxford this morning – and he's got a
lecture this afternoon, so . . . Er, *sorry*! Can I help? I'm
his wife.'

'Perhaps you can, Mrs Downes,' interposed Morse. 'We
spoke earlier on the phone, if you remember? May we, er,
come in for a little while?'

Lucy glanced at her watch. 'Yes! Yes, of course! It's just'
– she held the door open for them – 'I'm just off to – whoops!'

Morse had knocked his shin against a large suitcase standing just inside the door, and for a moment he squeezed his eyes tight, the whiles giving quiet voice to a blasphemous imprecation.

'Sorry! I should have – that wretched case! It's bitten *me* twice this morning already. Sorry!'

She had a pleasing voice, and Morse guessed that her gushy manner was merely a cover for her nervousness.

Yet nervousness of what?

'I'm just on my way,' continued Lucy. 'London. Got to change some curtains. A friend recommended a reasonably priced shop near King's Cross. But you really can't trust any of the stores these days, can you? I quite specifically ordered French pleats, and then – oh, sorry! Please sit down!'

Morse looked around him in the front living room, slightly puzzled to find the carpet, the decoration, the furniture, all that little bit on the shabby side, with only the curtains looking bright and new, and (in Morse's opinion) classy and tasteful. Clearly, in any projected refurbishment of the Downes's household, Lucy was starting with the curtains.

'I'd offer you both coffee but the taxi'll be here any time now. Cedric usually takes me to the station – ' she giggled slightly, 'I've never learned to drive, I'm afraid.'

'It's purely routine, madam,' began Morse, sitting down and sinking far too far into an antiquated, unsprung settee. 'We just have to check up everything about yesterday.'

'Of course! It's awful, isn't it, about Theo? I just couldn't believe it was true for a start—'

'When exactly *was* that?' Morse asked his question in a level tone, his eyes, unblinking, never leaving hers.

She breathed in deeply, stared intently at the intricate pattern on the carpet, then looked up again. 'Cedric rang up from The Randolph just before he came home. He said – he said he shouldn't know himself really, but one of the people there, the tour leader, told him and told him not to say anything, and Cedric' – she breathed deeply again – 'told me, and told *me* not to say anything.'

'Bloody Ashenden!' muttered Morse silently.

'His poor wife! How on earth—?'

'How many other people did you tell?'

'Me? I didn't tell anyone. I haven't been out of the house.'

Morse glanced at the phone on the table beside the settee, but let the matter rest. 'Dr Kemp tried to talk to your husband yesterday lunchtime.'

'I know. Cedric told me. He came back here.'

'What time was that?'

'One-ish? Quarter-past one – half-past?'

'He came back for his spare hearing-aid?'

Lucy was nodding. 'Not only that, though. He picked up some notes as well. I forget what they were for. Well, I don't really *forget*. I never knew in the first place!' She smiled nervously, and (for Lewis) bewitchingly, and (for Morse) heart-eatingly. 'Anyway he just grabbed some papers – and he was off again.'

'With his spare hearing-aid, too?'

She looked up at Morse with her elfin grin. 'Presumably.'

'I thought the NHS only issued one aid at a time.'

'That's right. But Cedric's got a spare – two spares in fact. Private ones. But he always votes Labour. Well, he *says* he does.'

'He's not all that deaf, is he, Mrs Downes?'

'He pretends he's not. But no, you're right, he's not *that* bad. It's just that when he talks to people he gets a bit frightened. Not frightened about not knowing the answers but frightened about not hearing the questions in the first place.'

'That's very nicely put, Mrs Downes.'

'Thank you! But that's what *he* says. I'm only copying him.'

'What time did he get home last night?'

'Elevenish? Just after? But he'll be able to tell you better than me.'

The door bell rang; and in any case the three of them had already heard the steps on the gravel.

'Shall I tell him to wait a few minutes, Inspector? He's a bit early.'

Morse rose to his feet. 'No. I think that's all. I – unless Sergeant Lewis here has any questions?'

'What are French pleats?'

She laughed, her teeth showing white and regular. 'Like that!' She pointed up to the curtains on the front window. 'It's the way they're gathered in at the top, Sergeant.'

'Oh! Only the missus keeps on to me about getting some new curtains—'

'I'm sure, Lewis, that Mrs Downes will be able to arrange a private consultation with Mrs Lewis at some convenient point. But some other time, perhaps? She does have a train to catch – her taxi driver is waiting impatiently on the threshold . . .'

'Sorry, sir!'

Lucy smiled again, especially at Sergeant Lewis, as he carried her heavy suitcase out to the taxi.

'You know when you're coming back, Mrs Downes?' Lewis asked.

'Seven o'clock. Just before – or is it just after?'

'Would you like me to ask your husband to meet you? We shall be seeing him.'

'Thank you. But he *is* coming to meet me.'

She climbed aboard, and the two policemen stood and watched as the taxi drove off into Lonsdale Road.

'Lovely woman, that!'

For the moment Morse made no reply, staring back at the house with a slightly puzzled air. 'Thou shalt not covet thy neighbour's wife, Lewis! Exodus, chapter something.'

'I didn't mean anything like that. You've got a one-track mind, sir!'

'You are perfectly correct, Lewis: one track only. My mind wants to know what the theft of the Wolvercote Tongue has got to do with the murder of Theodore Kemp. And I would be very surprised if that "lovely woman" of yours doesn't know a little more than she's prepared to admit – even to you!'

Chapter Thirty-two

Man has such a predilection for systems and abstract deductions that he is ready to distort the truth intentionally, he is ready to deny the evidence of his senses in order to justify his logic

(*Dostoevsky*, Notes from Underground)

Of a sudden, on the way back down the Banbury Road, Morse decided to view Parson's Pleasure by daylight. So Lewis drove down to the bottom of South Parks Road, where he was ushered through into the University Parks by a policeman on duty at the entrance to the single-track road which led down to the bathing area. Here the whole of the site was lightly cordoned off, and one of the Park Attendants was talking to (the newly promoted) Sergeant Dixon as Morse and Lewis moved alongside. The Park had closed at 4.30 p.m. the previous day, the detectives learned, yet it was not unknown for nimble adolescents and desperate adults to gain access to the Parks from half-a-dozen possible places. And the number of expended condoms discovered in and around the bathing-area suggested that not only ingress and egress, but congress too, were not unusual there, with the cover of the night, and the cover of the cubicles, combining to promote this latter activity – even when frost was forecast. But the cubicle in which the yellow sheet had been found could reveal no further secrets, and all hope had early been abandoned of learning anything from the scores of footprints which had criss-crossed the grassy area since the murder. Two divers had gone down into the river during the morning, but had found no item of relevance; and perhaps would not have recognised its relevance had they found it. Certainly no clothes, Sergeant Dixon asserted.

Morse walked over to the water's edge, the river-level high against the banks, and there he dipped his fingers in: not quite so cold as he would have thought. Dixon's mention of clothes had pulled his mind back to the discovery of Kemp's body, and he asked Lewis much the same question he had asked Max, receiving much the same answers.

'But I don't think he'd have been swimming here, sir.'

'Not unknown, Lewis, for people to bathe naked in this stretch.'

'Too chilly for me.'

'What about sex?'

'You don't have to take all your clothes off to do that.'

'No? Well, I'll take your word for it. I'm not an expert in that area myself.' He stood pondering the waters once more. 'Do you ever have any rows with your wife?'

' "Not unknown", as *you* would say, sir.'

'Then you patch things up?'

'Usually.'

'When you've patched things up, do you feel even closer together than before?'

Lewis was feeling puzzled now, and a little embarrassed at the course of the conversation: 'Probably a good thing now and then – clears the air, sort of.'

Morse nodded. 'We know of two people who had a row recently, don't we?'

'Dr Kemp and Mrs Williams? Yes! But she's got a whacking great alibi, sir.'

'A much better alibi than Stratton, certainly.'

'I could try to check on Stratton: Didcot – the pub he mentioned – Browns Restaurant.'

Morse looked dubious: 'If only we knew *when* Kemp was murdered! *Nobody*'s got an alibi until we know that.'

'You think Mrs Williams might have killed him?'

'She might have *killed* him all right. But I don't think she could have dumped him. I'd guess it was a man who did that.'

'He wasn't very heavy, Kemp, though. Not much fat on him.'

'Too heavy for a woman.'

'Even a jealous woman, sir?'

'Yes, I know what you mean. I keep wondering if Kemp had found some other floozie – and Sheila Williams found out about it.'

' "Hell hath no fury . . . " '

'If you must quote, quote accurately, Lewis! "Heaven has no rage, like love to hatred turned Nor Hell a fury like a woman scorned." '

'Sorry! I never did know much about Shakespeare.'

'Congreve, Lewis.'

'He seems to have been a bit of a ladies' man—'

'And if he couldn't make love to his wife because she was paralysed from the waist down . . .'

'I got the feeling she wasn't too worried about that, perhaps. It was Mrs Williams she had it in for.'

'She might have forgiven him if it had been anyone else, you mean?'

'I think – I think you ought to go to see her, sir.'

'All *right*,' snapped Morse. 'Give me a chance! We've got these Americans to see, remember? Aldrich and Brown – find out where *they* were yesterday afternoon. Where they *say* they were.'

Morse turned to look at the waters once more before he left, then sat silently in the passenger-seat of the police car as Lewis had a final word with Sergeant Dixon. In the side panel of the door he found a street map of Oxford, together with a copy of *Railway Magazine*; and opening out the map he traced the line of the River Cherwell, moving his right index-finger slowly northwards from the site marked Bathing Pool, up along the edge of the University Parks, then past Norham Gardens and Park Town, out under the Marston Ferry Road; and then, veering north-westerly, up past the bottom of Lonsdale Road . . . Portland Road . . . Hamilton Road . . . Yes. A lot of flood water had come down from the upper reaches of the Cherwell, and a body placed in the river, say, at Lonsdale Road . . .

And suddenly Morse knew where the body had been launched into the river and into eternity; knew, too, that if Lucy Downes could so quickly arouse the rather sluggish libido of a Lewis, then it was hardly difficult to guess her effect upon the lively carnality of a Kemp.

Lewis had climbed into the driving seat, and seen Morse's finger seemingly stuck on the map, at the bottom of Lonsdale Road.

'He couldn't have done it, sir – not Downes. He was with the Americans all the time – certainly till after we found the body. If anybody's got an alibi, he has.'

'Perhaps it was your friend Lucy Downes.'

'You can't think that, surely?'

'I'm not thinking at all – not for the minute,' replied Morse loftily. 'I am deducing – deducing the possibilities. When I've done that, I shall begin to *think*.'

'Oh!'

'And get a move on. We can't keep the Americans here all day. We're going to have to let 'em get on their way. Most of 'em!'

So Lewis drove back from Parson's Pleasure, back on to the Banbury Road, down St Giles', and then right at the lights into Beaumont Street. And all the time Chief Inspector Morse sat, less tetchy now, staring at the street map of Oxford.

No doubt, as Lewis saw things, 'deducing'.

Chapter Thirty-three

If you are afraid of loneliness, don't marry
(*Chekhov*)

Sheila Williams was feeling miserable. When Morse, himself looking far from serene, had come into The Randolph and demanded to see Messrs Aldrich and Brown immediately, he had resolutely avoided her eyes, appearing to have no wish to rekindle the brief moments of intimacy which had occurred in the morning's early hours. And the tourists, most of them, were getting restless – understandably so. Only Phil Aldrich had seemed as placid as ever, even after being interrupted in the middle of his lunch, and thereafter being seated in the Lancaster Room, writing busily on the hotel notepaper; and being interrupted just the once, and then only briefly, by Janet Roscoe – the latter intent, it appeared, on fomenting further dissatisfaction whenever possible.

Like now, for instance.

'I really do *think*, Sheila—'

'I do *envy* you so, Mrs Roscoe. I haven't had a genuine thought in *years*! Oh, Cedric! Cedric?'

He had been trying to steal silently away from the post-lunch chatter, but was stopped in his tracks at the foot of the great staircase as Sheila, glass in her left hand, laid the crimson-nailed fingers of her right hand along his lapel.

'Cedric! How that bloody woman has lived this long without getting murdered . . .'

Cedric grinned his sad, lopsided grin, removed the somewhat disturbing hand, and looked at her – her upper and lower lips of almost equal thickness, moist and parted, and temptingly squashable. She was a woman he had known for several years now; one with whom he had never slept; one who half repelled, and ever half attracted him.

'Look! I've got to be off. I've got a tutorial shortly, and I ought to sober up a bit betweentimes.'

'Why do that, darling?'

'Sheila! You're a lovely girl, but you – you let yourself down when you drink too much.'

'Oh, for Christ's sake! Not you as well.'

'Yes! *Me as well!* And I've got to go. I'm meeting Lucy off the train later on anyway, and if you want to know the truth' – he looked about him with rolling eyes – 'I'm completely pissed off with the whole of this bloody set-up. I've done my best, though. First I stood in for—' Suddenly he stopped. 'Sorry, Sheila! I shouldn't have said that. Forgive me!' He kissed her lightly on the cheek, then turned and walked out of the hotel.

As Sheila watched him go, she knew that in spite of the hurtful words he had just spoken she would always have a soft spot for the man. But she knew, too, what a lousy judge of men she'd always been. Her husband! God! A quietly cultivated, top-of-the-head English don, incurably in the grip of the Oxford Disease – that tragic malady which deludes its victims into believing they can never be wrong in any matter of knowledge or opinion. What a disaster that had all been! Then a series of feckless, selfish, vain admirers . . . then Theo. Poor Theo! But at least he was – had been – an interesting and vital and daring sort of man.

Sheila walked slowly over to the window and watched Cedric as he wheeled his bicycle across Beaumont Street towards St Giles'. He never drove his car if he was having any drink with his lunch. Not like some people she'd known. Not like Theo, for instance . . . He'd been over the limit, they'd said, when he'd crashed his BMW, and there could have been no sympathy whatsoever for him from the relatives of the woman killed in the other car. *Or* from his wife, of course – his bloody wife! And yet there was the suggestion that he'd been just a little unlucky, perhaps? Certainly many people had mumbled all that stuff about 'there but for the grace of God . . .' And there *was* a lot of luck in life: some people would go to jail for badger-baiting; but if they'd baited just the foxes they'd like as not be having sherry the next day with the Master of the Foxhounds. Yes, Theo *may* have been a fraction unlucky about that accident.

Even unluckier now.

And Cedric? Was he right – about what he'd just said? Already that morning she had drunk more than the weekly average for women she'd noticed displayed on a chart in the Summertown Health Centre waiting-room. But when she was drinking, she was (or so she told herself) perfectly conscious of all her thoughts and actions. It was only when she was reasonably sober, when, say, she woke up in the morning, head throbbing, tongue parched, that she suspected in retrospect that she hadn't been quite so rationally conscious of those selfsame thoughts and actions . . .

God! What a mess her life was in!

She looked miserably back across the coffee-lounge, where several of the group were mumbling none too happily. Six o'clock. Morse had changed their departure-time to six o'clock, unless something dramatic occurred in the meantime.

She walked through into the Lancaster Room again, where Phil Aldrich was still scribbling away on the hotel's notepaper; and for the moment (as Sheila stood in the doorway) looking up with his wonted patience and nodding mildly as Janet propounded her latest views on the injustice of the tour's latest delay. But even as Sheila stood there, his mood had changed. None too quietly, he asked the woman if she would mind leaving him alone, just for a while, since he had something more important to do for the minute than listen to her gripes and belly-aching.

Who would have believed it?

Sheila had heard most of the exchange; and, with the volume of Janet's voice, so probably had several of the others too. It had been a devastating rebuke from the quiet little fellow from California; and as Sheila watched the hurt face of the formidable little woman from the same State (wasn't it the same Church, too?), she almost felt a tinge of sympathy for Mrs Janet Roscoe.

Almost.

Lewis, too, had been watching as Aldrich wrote out his statement; and wondering how a man could write so fluently. Huh! When Aldrich handed it to him there were only three crossings out in the whole thing.

Chapter Thirty-four

Thou hast committed –
Fornication; but that was in another country,
And besides, the wench is dead
(*Christopher Marlowe*, The Jew of Malta)

I was stationed in Oxford in early 1944
for training as a 22-year-old GI for the
forthcoming landings in Normandy. One night
in Chipping Norton I met a married woman
and I fell deeply in love with her. Her
husband had been serving in the British
Merchant Navy on the Russian Convoy run
but after 1943 he was receiving psychiatric
treatment in Shropshire somewhere for his
nerves. They said nobody survived that
posting without getting his nerves shattered.
Well while he was in hospital his wife
had gotten herself pregnant and she had
a baby daughter 2nd Jan. 1945. From
what I half learnt the father must have

been a forgiving sort of man because he
treates the daughter (my daughter) as if
she were his own little girl. But there was
some trouble with her in her early teens
and perhaps she'd guessed something of the
truth. The fact is she ran away from her
home in late 1962 and her mother heard
a few months later that she was living as
a common street girl near King's Cross
Station. I only knew something of all this
because the girl's mother kept in touch
with me occasionally through innocent looking
postcards and just the one phone call put
through to ~~our telephone~~ me when her
husband died in 1986. She moved soon
after that to Thetford in your E. Anglia
and I was able to phone her there a
few times. But I could tell there was no real
wish on her part to renew any old tie
of love and friendship and if I am going
to be honest no real wish on my part
either. I valued my independence too much

to get into any deep down involvement and
particularly with a woman who goddamit
I probably wouldn't have recognized anyway!
But I felt so different about my daughter
and tried to learn where she'd gotten to.
She attended the funeral so I guess there
must have been some contact there. Well
then her mother died last Feb. with some
awful cancer and her daughter had been
beside her when she died and probably
learnt then about the secret which must
have burdened her poor mother's life for
so many years. I guess I ought to be
more honest about this because my
daughter wrote me after her mother's funeral
and said she'd guessed what had happened
anyway. I'd never had other children of
my own and somehow she seemed very
prescious just then, but I never expected
to see her. She'd not given any address
but the stamp had a WC1 postmark. So
when this tour was advertised and I saw

three days would be spent in London. I
just decided to go, that's all. It would be
good to see old England again and even if
I didn't find her I could tell myself I'd
just tried that little bit. So when we were
there in London I asked around at several
centers for rehabilitating women and I struck
lucky. At one place there were about a dozen
young women having a lunch together. I don't
recall the name of the place but there was
royal blue woodwork there and grey walls
and all the pipes were bright red. It was
a biggish house in a terrace, yellowish brick
and white window frames about five or ten
minutes walk from King's Cross. The only
other thing I remember is that there was litter
everywhere in that street there. The Warden
was a wonderful guy and he mentioned my
daughter's name to these girls and one of
them knew her! There were a lot of street
walkers and petty criminals, he called
them his pros and cons, but one of them had

seen my daughter Pippa a week earlier in
a cafeteria somewhere near. So I left
her £10 and asked her to please tell the
warden if she saw her again so that he
could call me with any news. Yesterday
was the last possible day ~~we could have~~
on the tour that was near enough London
to get up there ~~easily~~, only about an hour
away. Then I had a phone call yesterday
from my daughter herself! I'd given
the warden details of our itinerary,
and the call got put straight through to
my own room here just before we went
for lunch. So we arranged to meet in the
Brunel Bar in the Great Western Hotel
at Paddington at a quarter after two
and I just decided to go without telling
anyone in the group. I got to Paddington
just after 2 o'clock right on skedule and
I walked straight over to the hotel bar and
gotten me a big whiskey because gee was
I nervous. You see, I'd never seen my

own daughter before. I waited and waited
and waited — until about 3 o'clock and
then when the bar closed until about 4
o'clock in the lounge here. But she didn't
come though I was willing and praying for
any women round forty-five or so who
came in to be her. So I caught the
4.20 train back to Oxford which stopped
at Reading and then Didcot. I didn't
see Eddie get on the train at Didcot but
I now know he saw me. I only know
because he told me this morning, he'd
not meant to say anything but his
conscience was worrying him so he
told me what he'd told you. I just hope
the police can come nearer solving the
murder if we all tell the truth even
if there are a few skeletons in the
cuboard. I only ask for my secret to
stay a secret. But just one more thing.
I asked ~~Janet~~ Mrs Janet Roscoe
to sign that she saw me yesterday

afternoon at one of the sessions. Please don't blame her because I just told her I'd gotten a bad headache. She is a much nicer lady than the others may think and I admire her such a lot.

Philip Aldrich

Chapter Thirty-five

Just a song at twilight
When the lights are low
And the flick'ring shadows
Softly come and go . . .
(From the English Song Book)

For all the swiftness of his thought, Morse was quite a slow reader. And as Lewis (who had already read through the statement) watched his chief going through the same pages, he felt more than a little encouraged. It was like finding a Senior Wrangler from Cambridge unable to add seventy-seven and seventeen together without demanding pencil and paper.

'Well?' asked Morse at long last. 'What did you make of that?'

'One odd thing, sir. It's an alibi for Aldrich all right, but not really one for Stratton, is it?'

'It isn't?'

'Surely not. Aldrich didn't actually *see* Stratton – on the train, did he?'

'You mean Stratton might *not* have been on the train? Ye-es . . . But if so, how did he know *Aldrich* was on the train?'

Lewis shook his head: 'I'm thinking about it, sir.'

'But you're right, Lewis,' added Morse slowly, as he sat back and stared at the ceiling for a few seconds. 'And I'll tell you something else: he writes well!'

'Clever man, sir!'

'More literate than his daughter, I should think. Only those couple or so spelling mistakes, wasn't it?'

'Only the two I spotted,' replied Lewis, his features as impassive as those of a professional poker-player, as

Morse, with a half-grin of acknowledgement, started shuffling inconsequentially through the completed questionnaires.

'Bit sad,' ventured Lewis, 'about Mr Aldrich's daughter.'

'Mm?'

'Wonder why she didn't turn up at Paddington.'

'Probably met a well-oiled sheik outside The Dorchester.'

'She'd *agreed* to meet him, though.'

'So he says.'

'Don't you believe him?' Lewis's eyes looked up in puzzlement. 'He can't have made up all that stuff about the army . . . or the train—'

'Not those bits, no.'

'But you don't believe the bits in the middle?'

'As you just said, he's a clever man. I think he went up to London, yes, but I'm not at all sure what he *did* there. All a bit vague, don't you think? Just as I'm not quite sure what *Kemp* was doing, after he left his publishers. But if they *met* each other, Lewis . . . ? Interesting, don't you think?'

Lewis shook his head. It was almost invariably the same: halfway through any case Morse would be off on some improbable and complicated line of thought which would be just as readily abandoned as soon as a few more facts emerged. And, blessedly, it was *facts* that Morse now seemed to be concentrating on as, forgetting Aldrich for the moment, he browsed once again through the questionnaires.

'See here, Lewis!' He passed over three of the sheets and pointed to the answers to question (e):

P. Aldrich   10–27–90

E. Stratton   27th Oct 1990

H. Brown   October 27

'Not conclusive though, is it, sir?'

But Morse appeared to have boarded a completely different train of thought: 'I was just wondering about their dates of birth . . .'

'Soon find out. I got Ashenden to collect in all their passports this morning.'

'You did?'

Lewis felt gratified to note the surprise and appreciation
in Morse's eyes and voice, and very soon he was back with
the passports.

'All here, are they?'

'Except Ashenden's. You're not, er, forgetting Ashenden,
are you, sir?'

'Oh no! I'm not forgetting Ashenden,' replied Morse
quietly, as taking out his Parker pen he wrote three d.o.b.s
on a table napkin:

Aldrich:	8.4.1922
Stratton:	29.9.1922
Brown:	3.8.1918

'Two of 'em sixty-eight now, and one seventy-two . . .'

'You wouldn't *think* Brown was the oldest, though, would
you, sir? He trots around like a two-year-old.'

'A two-year-old *what*?'

Lewis sighed, but said nothing.

'He stayed in his room when his wife went off for a
jaunt round Oxford, remember? And I still think one of the
oddest things in this case is why Stratton didn't see his wife
safely up to her room. It's not natural, Lewis. It's not how
things *happen*.'

'What are you suggesting?' asked Lewis, vaguely.

'Brown said he stayed in his room when his wife and
Stratton decided to look round Oxford. Said he was tired.
Huh! As you said, he's as sprightly as a two-year-old.'

'A two-year-old *what*, sir?'

But Morse appeared to have missed the question.

In the Annexe, as if on cue, a tune could be heard
quite clearly. First a few exploratory notes, presumably on
the Steinway Grand that Morse had earlier admired in the

Lancaster Room; then the whole melody as the pianist hired for the afternoon tea-room session fingered his way through the nostalgic chords of 'Love's Old Sweet Song'.

The two men listened in silence, before Morse resumed:

'You know, I'm beginning to wonder exactly who was having an affair with who.'

Lewis's eyebrows shot up yet again.

'All right! "Whom", if you prefer it. Stratton and Shirley Brown go out together and everybody says "tut-tut". Agreed? And we all focus our attention on the potential scandal – completely ignoring a far more suggestive state of affairs. Brown and Laura Stratton are there right next to each other in Rooms 308 and 310. It's shenanigans between the sheets, Lewis! It's a *crime passionnel*! Stratton comes back in and catches Brown in the missionary position – and all this Wolvercote Tongue business is just a secondary blind.'

But Lewis would have nothing to do with such futile speculation: 'She was tired, sir. She'd be far more interested in a bath than . . .'

'. . . than in a bonk?'

'Well, people that age—'

'What? I've heard that sex can be very good for the over sixty-fives.'

'Only ten years for you to go, then.'

Morse grinned, though with little conviction. 'I'm sure of it, though. It's Love's Old Sweet Song – that *must* come into things somewhere. A woman dies. An art-work goes missing. An art-expert gets murdered. You following me, Lewis? There's a link – there's got to be a *link*. But for the present I can't—' He broke off, and looked at the three dates again. 'You realise, don't you, that those three would have been – what? – twenty-two, twenty-two, and twenty-six in 1944?' His eyes gleamed with what might have been taken for some inner illumination. 'What about all of them being stationed in or near Oxford?'

'What difference would that make, sir?'

Morse seemed not to know.

Picking up Aldrich's statement, Lewis rose to his feet. 'Shall I go and get Howard Brown?'

But again Morse's mind seemed to be tuned to another wave-length. 'Why did you say he' – indicating the statement – 'he was a clever man?'

'Well, for a start, there's only the three crossings out, aren't there? And he just – well, he just sort of sat down and wrote it straight off.'

'Ye-es,' said Morse, but to himself, for Lewis had already left the Annexe to summon Brown.

He looked around at the two other tables occupied in the Bar-Annexe. At the first, a middle-aged woman with an enormous bosom was digging a fork into a plate of salad with the precision of an accountant jabbing at his calculator, before transferring the accumulated forkful up to her rapidly masticating jaws; and Morse knew that if he had married *her*, it would all have been over within the week. But there was another woman, at the second table: a woman only half the age of her executively suited escort; a woman who was having a fairly difficult time by the look of things, earnestly rehearsing a whole chapter of body language with her ringless hands. Perhaps, thought Morse, the illicit little office affair was drawing to its close. Then her sad eyes met Morse's in a sort of distant, anonymous camaraderie: she smiled across, almost fully. And Morse did the same, feeling for a few small moments an intense and splendid happiness.

Chapter Thirty-six

Their meetings made December June
(Tennyson)

Faced with the evidence of the tell-tale 7, Howard Brown capitulated immediately. Yes, Morse was right in one respect: Aldrich, Stratton, and himself had been stationed in or around Oxford in 1944, and he (Brown) had in fact known Stratton vaguely in those far-off days. They'd been delighted therefore to renew acquaintanceship at the beginning of the tour; and thereafter had spent many an hour together, talking about old comrades they'd known – those who'd come through, and those who hadn't . . . and reminiscing about some of the 'local talent' the GIs had been only too happy to discover, in Oxford itself and in some of the surrounding towns and villages. Brown had fallen miserably in love (so he said) with a girl named Betty Fowler, whom he'd met one Friday evening at a hop held in the Oxford Town Hall, and already on their second meeting they had vowed a mutual, eternal love.

Then, when the war ended in the summer of 1945, after being demobbed from Germany, he'd gone straight back to the US, with no possible hope of any real communication between them except for one or two impermanent and unreliable addresses. So, slowly, the memories of their idyllic times together had faded. He'd met up with a marvellous girl in Münster, anyway; then a fully consenting Hausfrau from Hamburg . . . and so it had gone on. He'd gradually come to terms with the fairly obvious fact (as most of his comrades already had) that wartime associations were almost inevitably doomed to dissolution.

Back home in California, he'd met Shirley; and married her. OK, there mightn't perhaps be all that much left over now from the early joys of their marriage; yet, in an odd sort of way, the longer they'd abjured the divorce-courts, the stronger had grown the ties that bound them together: home, children, friends, memories, insurance policies; and above all, perhaps, the sheer length – the ever-increasing length – of the time they'd spent together as man and wife. Forty-three whole years of it now.

Before marrying Shirley, he'd written an honourable and honest letter to Betty Fowler, but he'd received no reply. Whatever the actual reasons for this, in his own mind he'd singled out the fact that she must have got married. She was an extraordinarily attractive girl, with a pale complexion, a freckled face, and ginger hair: a girl for whom most of the other GIs would willingly have given a monthly pay-packet. Or an annual one.

Then, only six months since, he had received a letter ('Private and Strictly Confidential'). Although sent to his 1947 address in Los Angeles, it had finally, almost flukily, caught up with him – and thereby opened a floodgate of memories upon which the years had added their sentimental compound-interest. She had (Betty confessed) received his letter all that while ago; still had it, in fact. But by that time she had married a car-worker from Cowley, was four months' pregnant, and was eventually to become the mother of four lovely children – three girls and one boy. Her husband had retired in 1988 and then, so sadly, died only seven months later. She was all right, herself. No worries – certainly no financial worries. And eight (eight!) grandchildren, though she had not herself been tempted to enter the local 'Glamorous Grandmother' contest. So, the only reason for her writing was to say that if he ever *did* get the chance to come over to the UK again, well, she'd like – well, it would be nice . . .

From America, how earnestly he'd longed to reach her on the telephone! But she had given him neither an address nor a telephone number; and the complexities of finding either had posed rather too much of a problem on a transatlantic line. Yet here he was now – so near to her! And with his wife gone out for long enough with one of her admirers . . . So, he'd watched her go from the hotel, and then contacted Directory Enquiries from the phone-booth in the foyer. Miraculously, within a couple of minutes, he'd found himself speaking to a woman he'd kissed goodbye in the early May of 1944 – over forty-six years ago! Could she meet him? Would she *like* to meet him? The answer was yes, yes, yes. And so they *had* met (it had been *so* easy, as it happened, for him to sneak away the previous afternoon) nervously and excitedly outside the main entrance to the University Parks at 2.30 p.m.

'And *she* turned up, did she?' asked Morse.

'Yes.' Brown appeared a fraction puzzled by the question. 'Oh, yes! I'd walked up St Giles' about two o'clock, and then down Keble Road to the Parks. And, well, there she was – waiting for me.'

'Then you went to Parson's Pleasure and sat in one of the cubicles.'

'But you won't get me wrong, will you, Inspector? I want to set the record straight. We just had a quiet little kiss and cuddle together and – well, that was that, really.'

'My only wish,' said Morse, looking now with somewhat irrational distaste at the remarkably well-preserved Lothario from Los Angeles, 'is to set, as you say, the record straight. So thank you for your honesty!'

Brown stood up and prepared to leave. He looked, little doubt of it, considerably relieved, but clearly there was something on his mind, for he stood hesitantly beside the table, his eyes scouting around for some object upon which to focus.

'There *is* one thing, Inspector.'

'And that is?'

'When I was walking up to Keble Road yesterday I saw someone standing at the bus-stop outside St Giles' Church, waiting to get up to Summertown. Well, I suppose it was Summertown.'

'And who was that, sir?'

'It was Mr Ashenden.'

★ ★ ★

'I just don't believe all this,' said Morse after Brown had gone.

'You mean you wonder who *Ashenden* saw, sir?'

'Exactly.'

'He sounded as if he was telling the truth.'

'They all do! But *somebody* isn't telling the truth, Lewis. Somebody stole the Wolvercote Tongue, and somebody murdered Kemp! If only I could find the connection!'

'Perhaps there isn't a connection,' said Lewis.

But he might just as well have been talking to himself.

Chapter Thirty-seven

Sic, ne perdiderit, non cessat perdere lusor
(To recoup his losses, the gambler keeps on
backing the losers)

(*Ovid*, Ars Amatoria)

Ashenden, buttonholed as he was once again in the coffee-lounge by the diminutive dynamo from Sacramento, appeared only too glad to be given the opportunity of escaping, albeit to an interview with Chief Inspector Morse.

'Do you always get one like that?' sympathised Lewis.

'Well, she'd probably take the prize,' conceded Ashenden with a weary grin. 'But Janet's not such a bad old stick sometimes – not when you get to know her.'

'Makes you wonder how anyone ever married her, though.'

Ashenden nodded as he walked through into the Bar-Annexe: 'Poor chap!'

With this next hand (Ashenden), Morse took no finesses at all. Just played off his aces and sat back. Question: Why had Ashenden lied about his visit to Magdalen? Answer: It wasn't a lie really. He *had* gone up to Magdalen College, asked at the Porters' Lodge, discovered the grounds were closed; then just carried on walking over the bridge, around the Plain, and back again down the High. Silly to lie, really. But it was only to avoid any tedious and wholly incon-sequential explanation. Question: What about the previous afternoon, at about 2 p.m.? (Morse admitted his willingness to listen to a little more 'tedious and wholly inconsequential explanation'.)

'No secret, Inspector. In fact I'd told a couple of the group – Mr and Mrs Kronquist, I think it was – that I was going up to Summertown.'

'Why bother? Why explain? You're a free agent, aren't you, sir?'

Ashenden pondered the question awhile. 'I did realise, yesterday, that you perhaps weren't completely satisfied with the account of my whereabouts when, er—'

'The Wolvercote Tongue was stolen,' supplied Morse.

'Yes. That's why it seemed no bad idea for somebody to know where I was yesterday afternoon.'

'And where was that?'

Ashenden, looking decidedly uncomfortable, drew a deep breath: 'I spent the afternoon in the betting-shop in Summertown.'

Lewis looked up: 'Not a crime, that, is it?'

Morse seemed to appreciate the interjection: 'Surely Sergeant Lewis is right, sir? Certainly it's not a criminal offence to line a bookie's pockets.'

Ashenden suddenly seemed more relaxed: 'I had a tip. I met this fellow from Newmarket when we were at The University Arms in Cambridge. He said be sure to back this horse – over the sticks at Fontwell Park.'

'Go on.'

'Well, that's it, really. I picked another horse, in the race before – I'd got to the bookie's at about half-past two, I suppose. I put three pounds to win on a horse in the two-fifty, and then five pounds to win on the "dead cert" this fellow had told me about in the three-fifteen or three-twenty – something like that.'

'How much did you win?'

Ashenden shook his head sadly: 'I don't think you can be a racing man, Inspector.'

'Would they have records at the bookie's to show you'd been there, sir?'

It was Lewis who had asked the question, and Ashenden turned in his chair to face him: 'Are you suggesting I *wasn't* there?'

'No, sir. Certainly not. But it was the key sort of *time*,

wasn't it? Three o'clock time? Just the time when Dr Kemp was getting back to Oxford.'

'Yes,' replied Ashenden slowly. 'I take the point.'

'Would anyone recognise you,' continued Lewis, 'if you went there again?'

'I don't know. There were quite a few there during the afternoon – eight, ten – more, perhaps, for some of the time, some of the races. But whether anyone would recognise me . . .'

'They'd have your betting-slips, surely?' suggested Morse.

'Oh yes – they'd keep those – if the horses had won.'

'Bit of bad luck you didn't pick a winner, then. You could have collected your winnings and proved your alibi both at the same time.'

'Life's full of disappointments, Inspector, as I'm sure—' Suddenly he stopped; and his eyes lit up as he withdrew a black-leather wallet from the breast-pocket of his sports jacket. 'With a bit of luck . . . Yes! Thank goodness! I thought I might have torn them up.'

'They tell me betting-shops are littered with torn-up betting-slips,' said Morse, as he looked down at the two pink slips that Ashenden had handed to him.

'You might just as well tear those up as well, Inspector, I'm afraid.'

'Oh, no, sir. We mustn't destroy any evidence, must we, Lewis?'

Ashenden shrugged, and seemed for the moment somewhat less at ease. 'Anything else?'

'I think not,' said Morse. 'But it's a mug's game, betting, you know. A dirty game, too.'

'Perhaps you should go into a betting-shop yourself one day. It's quite a civilised business, these days—'

But Morse interrupted the man, and his eyes were ice. 'Look, lad! Once you've lost as much money as me on the horses – *then* you come and give me a sermon on gambling, all right?' He flicked his right hand in dismissal. 'And tell your coach-driver he can leave at *five* o'clock. That should please everybody. It's only thirty-seven or thirty-eight miles to Stratford – and Lewis here once managed it in half an hour.'

Chapter Thirty-eight

The west yet glimmers with some streaks of day:
Now spurs the lated traveller apace
To gain the timely inn
                    (*Shakespeare*, Macbeth)

On the coach, as it headed north up the Woodstock Road, and thence out on to the A34, the members of the touring party were mostly silent, their thoughts monopolised perhaps by the strange and tragic events they had left behind them in Oxford. What tales they would be able to tell once they got back home again! John Ashenden, seated alone in the front nearside seat, debated with himself about reaching for the microphone and saying a few words about Somerville College, the Radcliffe Infirmary, the Tower of the Winds, the large, late nineteenth-century redbrick residences, St Edward's School . . . But he decided against it: the mood was not upon him – nor upon anyone else in the coach, as far as he could gather.

Opposite him, in the seat immediately behind the driver, sat a sour-faced Mrs Roscoe, her nicely shaped little nose stuck deep into the text of *A Midsummer Night's Dream*. Immediately behind him sat Howard and Shirley Brown, silent and sombre, each thinking thoughts that were quite impossible for any observer to ascertain – even for the two of them themselves fully to comprehend. And behind the Browns, the enigmatic Kronquists, now the only other married couple registered on the tour, reluctant, it seemed, to engage in even the most perfunctory of conversations: she now reading *Lark Rise to Candleford*; he, the *Good Beer Guide* (just published) for 1991. At the back, as if distanced to the utmost from the woman who *ab initio* had publicly sought to claim him as escort, friend, and guide, sat Phil Aldrich, slowly reading the evening's edition of *The Oxford Mail*. Nor had the sudden coolness between himself and Mrs J. Roscoe escaped most of the other tourists; indeed, this development was proving one of the few topics of conversation as the coach accelerated along the dual carriageway towards Woodstock.

Only two of the party that had arrived at The Randolph, some fifty hours earlier, were no longer in their original seats – the seats immediately behind Mrs Roscoe. One of these missing persons was still lying (lying still, rather!) in the police mortuary in St Aldate's; the other person, with Morse's full permission, had that afternoon departed by train for London, not stopping on this occasion (as he had claimed to have stopped earlier) at Didcot Parkway, but travelling straight through – past Reading, Maidenhead, Slough – to Paddington, whence he had taken a taxi to the Tour Company HQ in Belgravia in order to discuss the last wishes and the last rites of his erstwhile legal spouse, Mrs Laura Mary Stratton.

As the coach pulled powerfully up the hill away from Woodstock, Ashenden once again looked slightly anxiously at his watch. He had rung through to the Swan Hotel in Stratford to set a revised time of arrival at 6.15 p.m.; but by the look of things it was going to be, in Wellington's words, 'a damn close-run thing'. Yet he made no attempt to harass the driver into any illegitimate speed. They'd arrive a little late? So what! Twenty-six plates of 'Mousse Arbroath Smokies' were already laid out, they'd said – with just the single carrot juice for just the single Vegan girl.

Was Inspector Morse (Ashenden pondered) quite the man most people seemed to think he was? A man with a mind that might have left even the mythical Mycroft just floundering a fraction? Ashenden doubted it, his doubt redoubling as the coach drew further and further away from Oxford along the A34.

Everything would be all right.

Chapter Thirty-nine

I feel like I done when Slippery Sun
Romped 'ome a winner at 30 to 1
> (*A. P. Herbert*, 'Derby Day')

From the street-window of the coffee-lounge, Morse and Lewis had watched them go.

'Think we shall be seeing any of them again, sir?'

'No,' said Morse flatly.

'Does that mean you've got some idea—?'

'Ideas, plural, Lewis! We've seldom had so many clues, have we? But I can't help feeling we've missed all the really vital ones—' Morse broke off and resumed the drift of his earlier thought. 'It's this wretched *love* business – and I still think that Kemp was killed because he had one too many fancy woman.'

'I know I keep on about Mrs Kemp, sir, but don't you think we ought—'

Morse ignored the interruption. '*Why* was he naked? I thought for a start it was because moving the dead body might have been a very messy business. Max said there'd have been buckets of blood, and if someone's going to get it all over a suit, or a dress . . . It's a possibility, Lewis. Or he may have been stripped to delay any identification, I suppose. The longer delayed it is—'

'—the more difficult it gets for us to disprove an alibi.'

Morse nodded. 'But I don't think it was either of those reasons.'

'You think he was making love to a lady?'

'Well, a *woman*, Lewis. And since we know that woman wasn't likely to have been his wife because she'd . . . well, because of the car crash, we've got to decide who it could have been. Just think a minute! We get the husband, or whoever the jealous party was, bounding into the boudoir and catching 'em copulating. Who was *she*, though? I can't for the life of me see how it could have been Sheila Williams he was with . . . No, we've got to look down the race-card for some attractive, available, acquiescent filly – and the likeliest filly is surely—'

Suddenly Morse stopped, his mind once more six furlongs ahead of the field. He had bought a copy of *The Times* before he had come to The Randolph that morning, but hitherto had not even glanced at the headlines. Now he looked again at the two betting-slips that lay on the table in front of him; then turned to the back of the Business section for the Sport, his eye running down the results of the previous day's racing at Fontwell Park. Ashenden's stake in the 2.50 race, £3 win on Golden Surprise, had contributed further, it appeared, to the luxurious life-style of the bookmaking fraternity. But as Lewis now saw them, Morse's eyes seemed to grow significantly in circumference as they fell upon the result of the 3.15:

1   THETFORD QUEEN (J. Francis) 30–1

'Bloody 'ell!' whispered Morse.

'Sir?'

'Ashenden backed a horse yesterday – a horse he said someone in Cambridge had tipped – he put a fiver on it – and it won! Thetford Queen. There! – it's on the betting-slip.'

'Whew! That means he's got a hundred and fifty pounds coming to him.'

'No. He didn't pay any tax on it, so he'd only get one hundred and forty back – including his stake.'

'I didn't realise you knew quite so much about the gee-gees, sir?'

But again Morse ignored the comment: 'He says he was there, Lewis – in the betting-shop. He's put his money on the hot tip, and the thing wins, and . . . he doesn't pick up his winnings!'

Lewis considered what Morse was saying, and shook his head in puzzlement. Surely Ashenden *would* have gone up to the Pay-Out desk immediately, if he'd been there – especially since that was the only time he was going to be in the betting-shop. And if for some strange reason he'd been misinformed, been told that the horse had lost, then it was difficult to see why he'd kept the slips so carefully in his wallet. Why not tear them up like everyone else and contribute to the litter found on every bookie's floor?

Morse interrupted Lewis's thoughts: 'Shall I tell you exactly what our leader was doing in the betting-shop? Establishing his alibi! If you've backed a couple of horses, and if you'll be gone the next day, you stay there like everybody else and listen to the commentaries. But if you pick a couple of complete no-hopers, rank outsiders, well, there's no need to stay, is there? Look at the odds on Golden Surprise! 50–1! So Ashenden spent eight quid of his money *in order to buy himself an alibi.*'

'Bit of bad luck the horse won, if you see what I mean, sir.'

'Where did he *go*, though?'

'Well he can't be that "jealous husband" you're looking for.'

'No, but he went somewhere he didn't want anyone to know about. I just wonder whether it might have been some-where like—'

The Manager walked swiftly through: 'Can you come to the phone, Inspector? Very urgent, they say.'

It was Max.

'Morse? Get over here smartish! Bloody Hell! Christ!'

'Tell me, Max,' said Morse softly.

'Mrs Kemp, that's what! Tried to cross the nighted ferry; might've made it but for a district-nurse calling unexpectedly.'

'She's not dead?'

'Not yet.'

'Likely to be?'

'Oh, I couldn't say.'

'*For God's sake, Max!*'
'Not even for His.'

Morse had never seen Mrs Marion Kemp, but from the marriage photograph that hung in the living room he realised that she must once have been quite a vivacious woman: dark, curly hair; slim, firm figure; and curiously impudent, puckish eyes. She had already been removed to the Intensive Care Unit at the JR2, but in the bedroom there seemed quite sufficient evidence that she had planned a deliberate departure. A brown-glass bottle of sleeping pills stood capless and empty on the bedside table, and beside it, lying on the top of a Georgette Heyer novel, was a short, soberly legible (though unsigned) note:

If found still alive, please let me die. If found dead, please contact Dr M. Davies at the Summertown Health Centre — the only man who ever tried to understand my suffering.

Chapter Forty

He
That kills himself to avoid misery, fears it,
And, at the best, shows but a bastard valour
(*Philip Massinger*, The Maid of Honour)

Morse and Max stood for a few moments silently just outside the front door of the Kemp residence. Nothing, as both men knew, could be quite as sombre and sickening as a suicide (or, as here, an attempted suicide), for it spoke not only of unbearable suffering but also of a certain misguided fortitude. Morse had looked quickly round the flat but had found nothing much to engage his interest.

'Let's try to keep her alive, if we can, Max,' he said quietly.

'Out of my hands, now.'

'Fancy a glass of Brakspear? Only just along the road here.'

'No time, dear boy! Presumably you consider the Henley branch of the Brakspear family to be greater benefactors than that St Albans fellow?'

'Wha—?' For a few seconds even Morse was lost a little; but then he grinned acknowledgement: 'You're a cultured sod.'

'You know, Morse,' panted Max as he eased his overweight frame into his car, 'I've always thought of myself more as a Renaissance man, actually.'

He was gone, and Morse looked around the area somewhat fecklessly. A maintenance man, with a garden fork and wheelbarrow, was tending the herbaceous border that stretched along the frontage of the flats and, in response to Morse's question, he said he was one of a small team that looked after the three blocks of flats that stood on the eastern side of Water Eaton Road. And yes, he'd been working there for several days. Had he seen anyone coming in, during the afternoon of the previous day? After three o'clock, say? But the man, looking to Morse far too young to have graduated with any glory from a landscape-gardening apprenticeship, shook his head dubiously.

'Difficult, innit? I mean, I was out the back most o' the time. There *were* some people comin' in, I remember, but they'd probably bin shoppin' and that, 'adn't they?'

'You saw this man?' Morse held up the photograph of Theodore Kemp which he had just removed from the living room. Clearly it had been taken several years earlier, but it showed, even then, the supercilious cast of a face which had looked into the camera with head held well back, and lips that seemed to smile with a curious arrogance above the Vandyke beard.

'Yea! I seen 'im before – but I dunno about yesterday. As I said, I was out the back most o' the time – doin' the bits by the river.'

The river . . .

Morse thanked the man, and walked along to the ramp at the side of the flats, and down to a concreted area where five garages directly in front of him shielded the immediate view. Then, turning to his right, he came to a stretch of well-trimmed lawn that sloped down to the river, the far bank of which was policed by a row of severely pollarded willow trees. Here the water was green-scummed and semi-stagnant. But a bridge ('Residents Only') led him across to the main channel of the Cherwell, where the water was still flowing fairly swiftly after the week's earlier rains, and where pieces of debris were intermittently knocking into the sides of the banks, and then turning and twisting, first one way then the other, like dodgem cars at the fun-fair. For several minutes Morse looked down at the turbid, turgid river; and his thoughts were as restless as the waters below him. Then, of a sudden, he nodded to himself firmly – and the look around his mouth was almost as arrogant as that of the late Theodore Kemp, who at some time, at some point, had recently been manoeuvred into these selfsame murky, swollen waters.

Lewis was waiting for him as he reached the road again.

'What now, sir?'

'What we need is a little liquid refreshment, and there's a little pub' – Morse got into the passenger seat – 'just along the road here.'

'Might as well walk, sir. It's only fifty yards.'

Morse said nothing, but sat where he was and picked up the *Railway Gazette* from the door-pocket and pretended to read it; then *did* read it – for a few seconds.

Lewis had backed the car a few feet down the ramp and was about to turn towards the Cherwell Arms when he heard his master's voice – a single hissed and incredulous blasphemy:

'Chrissst!'

'More clues, sir?'

'Look! Look at this!'

Lewis took the magazine and read through the brief article to which Morse was pointing:

GOLDEN OLDIES

> Members of the GWR Preservation Society will learn with particular interest that w.e.f. 21st October the world-famous Torbay Express will be making a nostalgic return visit to a few stretches of its old track, and will first be housed for three weeks in Railway Shed 4 at Plymouth.

His eyes looked across to Morse's: 'And he said he'd seen the Torbay Express at Didcot, didn't he? It's in his statement, surely.'

Morse stared in front of him, his eyes a-glitter: 'He's a liar, Stratton is; he's a bloody liar!'

'Is – is that a 1990 magazine?' asked Lewis diffidently.

Morse turned to the colourful cover, then placed the magazine back casually into the door-pocket.

'Well, sir?'

'September 1988,' said Morse, very quietly indeed.

'What's it all mean?' asked Lewis, as he sat at the table, with a pint of Brakspear for Morse and a half of the same for himself. He had never understood why Morse almost always expected *him* to buy the beer. It was as though Morse believed that he, Lewis, was on some perpetual expense-account.

'You mean about Mrs Kemp?'

'I mean about everything. I just don't know what's happening.'

'You think *I* do?'

'I thought you might have an idea.'

'Perhaps I have.' He drained his pint with extraordinary rapidity. 'Is it your round or mine?'

Lewis walked over to the bar with the single glass – almost happily.

Whilst he was gone, Morse turned to the back of *The Times* and had filled in the whole of the bottom right-hand quarter of the crossword when Lewis returned two minutes later.

'Do you always do crosswords that way round, sir?'

'Uh? Oh, yes! I always try solving problems by starting at the end – never the beginning.'

'I shall have to try that sometimes.'

'I didn't know you did crosswords, Lewis?'

'Yes! Me and the missus, we usually try to do the *Daily Mirror* Quick Crossword of an evening.'

'Oh!' said Morse, though without much wonderment in his voice. 'Well, let me tell you something. If I'm doing a crossword, and I think I'm getting stuck—'

'Not that you *do*, sir.'

'No. Not that I do – not very often. But if by some freak mischance I *do* get a bit stuck, you know what I do?'

'Tell me!'

'I *stop* thinking about the problem. Then, when I come back to it? No problem at all!'

'Have *we* got a problem, sir?'

'Oh yes! That's why we need the break – the drinking break.' Morse took an almighty swig from his replenished pint, leaving only an inch of beer in the glass. 'Our problem is to find the connection between the theft of the jewel and the murder of Kemp. Once we find that . . . So the best thing to do is to think of something completely different. Tell me about something, Lewis – something that's got nothing to do with Mrs Kemp.'

'I was just thinking about those betting-slips, sir. They've got the time on them – the time the bet was placed.'

'I said something *different*, Lewis! Anything. Tell me anything! Tell me the name of your first girl-friend! *Anything!*'

'I can't, sir. Not for the minute. I just think I let Mrs Kemp down . . . in a way.'

'What the hell are you talking about? It's *me* who let her down! How many times did you tell me I ought to see her?'

'Why do you think she tried . . . ?'

'How the hell do I know!'

'Just asked, that's all.'

'All right. What do *you* think?'

'I suppose she just felt life wasn't worth living without him – without her husband.'

'You didn't feel that, though, when you met her, did you? From what you told me, you seemed to feel the opposite: life might have been worth living if he *wasn't* there.'

Yes, Lewis knew that Morse was right. He'd felt the anger and the bitterness of the woman – far more than any sense of anguish or loss. He knew, too, that his lack of sleep was beginning to catch up with him.

'You talk about giving your mind a rest, sir, but I shall have to give my body a bit of a rest soon. I'm knackered – absolutely knackered!'

'Go home, then! What's stopping you? I can always get Dixon—'

'I don't want to go home, sir. We've got the decorators in and I keep getting nagged about getting new carpets and new curtains and—'

Morse jumped up from the table, his face radiant: 'You've done it, Lewis! You've done it again!'

Lewis too rose from his seat, a tired, bewildered expression across his honest features.

What had he just said?

Chapter Forty-one

Light thickens and the crow makes wing to
the rooky wood

(*Shakespeare*, Macbeth)

It was a quarter-past six when Sheila Williams saw the
police car draw up outside, and she answered the front
door immediately.

'Come in, Inspector!' The colourless liquid in the glass she
carried might just have been water, perhaps; but whatever it
was she seemed unwontedly sober.

'No. I – we've got a lot to do. Look. I'm very sorry to
have to tell you this – but Mrs Kemp tried to kill herself
this afternoon.'

Sheila's right hand jumped to her mouth with a convulsive
jerk: 'Oh, no!' she whispered.

'She took enough pills to kill a healthy elephant, Sheila,
but fortunately a nurse found her – in time, we think. If
only just.'

'Where—?'

'She's in the JR2. She's having the best care she could
get anywhere.'

Sheila took a deep breath. 'Oh dear!' she managed to
say in a broken voice as the tears began to trickle. Then,
somewhat to Morse's embarrassment, she suddenly buried
her head on his shoulder and clung tightly to him.

'Did she love him?' asked Morse gently.

'She *possessed* him!'

'But did she *love* him?'

Sheila Williams straightened herself and pulled away from
him, searching her pockets for a handkerchief. Her voice was

almost fierce as she answered: 'No! *I* was the only one who really loved him.'

'Do you know anyone else who loved him? Was there someone else? A *third* woman in his life?'

Sheila shook her head in deep anguish.

'You quite sure about it, Sheila? It's so very important that you're honest with me,' urged Morse.

'He said not. He swore it!'

'And you believed him?'

She nodded, and wiped her eyes. And Morse nodded, too, and looked very sad.

'All right. Thank you.' He turned to go, but she called him back, the tears springing once more.

'Inspector – please!'

Morse turned, and laid his right hand lightly on her shoulder. 'No need to tell me, really. I *know* there was another woman in his life.'

Her 'yes' was barely audible.

'And I think you knew who it was.'

She nodded again.

'It was only recently though, wasn't it, Sheila? Only recently that he'd started seeing Mrs Downes?'

Lewis, standing at the front gate, had managed to catch most of the exchanges; had watched Mrs Williams as she'd finally turned away from Morse in tearful distress. And now, as they got back into the car, both men sat in silence as they watched the light switched on in the front bedroom – and then the curtains being drawn across.

'Curtains!' said Morse, his voice sounding tired yet triumphant. 'As you said, Lewis – curtains.'

The Downes's house was in darkness, and the sound of the front-door bell seemed somehow to re-echo along empty passageways, around empty rooms. Morse looked at his watch: just after half-past six – and Downes would be meeting his wife at seven o'clock.

A wooden gate at the side of the house led to a neatly

tended garden at the back, the lawn sloping down to the river, with a path of paving stones laid along the middle, ending on the edge of the waters at what looked like a small landing-stage, perhaps once used to moor a small boat or punt, but apparently (as Lewis shone his torch across it) not in recent use.

'You think . . . ?' Lewis pointed down to the fast-flowing Cherwell.

'Launched from here? Yes, I do. Launched from here into eternity.'

'But *when*, sir? He wasn't back in Oxford—'

'All in good time, Lewis! For the moment, be a good boy-scout and shine your little torch over those back windows?'

As in the front, the windows here were fully curtained, all of them looking decidedly posh and new; and all of them with some approximation to those French pleats whose acquaintance Lewis had so recently made – and, if truth were told, Morse too.

'You see, Lewis,' began Morse, as the two strolled back to the front of the property, 'Kemp had grown tired of Sheila Williams and was starting out on a new conquest – the delectable Lucy Downes. Unfortunately for Kemp, however, Cedric Downes discovered the guilty pair *in flagrante delicto*, which as you will remember, Lewis, is the Latin for having your pants down. He's got to have a woman, has Kemp. His motto's *amo amas amat* it again. And he's at it again when Downes hits him with whatever's to hand; kills him; wonders where he's going to dump the corpse; can't dress him – far too difficult dressing a corpse—'

' 'Specially for a woman, sir.'

'What?'

'Don't you think it might have been a jealous *woman*? Not a jealous man?'

'No, no, Lewis! Not Sheila Williams.'

'She left the group, though – she went to the pub—'

'She hadn't got the *time*! Whoever killed Kemp had time:

time to cart him off to the river, and dump him there – *gently*, Lewis – without even a splash to startle the cygnets . . .'

'But it *couldn't* have been like that. The times are all wrong.'

'Speak on, Lewis! Like the murderer, we've got plenty of time.'

'We're waiting *here*, you mean?'

'Oh, yes! I'm very much looking forward to meeting Mr and Mrs Downes again.'

'And you think, in that suitcase of hers . . . ?'

But as the two detectives stood beside the car, the radio crackled into life.

'Lewis here!'

'Bad news, Sarge. Mrs Kemp died at the JR2 – fifty minutes ago. We've only just heard.'

Morse stood where he was, listening, and staring up at the sky as if viewing the unsuspected behaviour of some distant galaxy. His shoulders were sagging, and his face looked sad, and very weary.

'You look all in, sir.'

'Me? Don't talk so daft!' Morse looked quickly at his watch. 'He's meeting her in seven minutes! Put your foot down!'

'I thought you said we were waiting here?'

'Get *on* with it Lewis – and turn the bloody siren on!'

Chapter Forty-two

No one came
On the bare platform
(*Edward Thomas*, Adlestrop)

The police car drove into the Bus and Taxi area in front
of the railway station. Across on Platform 2, the train from
Paddington was just pulling in; and passengers were already
beginning to stream across the new pedestrian bridge as
Morse and Lewis first ascended, then descended the steps,
darting challenging looks around them as they dodged their
way through the bustling contra-flow.

The train still stood at the platform; and a group of Post
Office workers were lobbing a stack of bulging mail-bags into
the guard's van. And there – yes, there right in front of them! –
passing from one window to another, peering into each of the
carriages, his face drawn and anxious, was Cedric Downes.
Morse placed a restraining hand on Lewis's arm, and the two
of them stood watching the man while two or three heavily
luggaged travellers finally made their way along the platform.
Soon Downes had reached the last carriage, in front of the
diesel locomotive, staring quickly through the windows of the
compartment as the few doors still remaining open were
banged shut and a whistle blew, and with a slight chug and
then with a mighty heave the long, north-bound train began
slowly to move forward, gradually picking up a little speed,
before moving out and away along the curving stretch of line
that led to Banbury.

Downes looked down at his wristwatch, and at last turned
away, walking back along the bare platform towards the foot-
bridge – where he was confronted by the bulk of the broad-
shouldered Lewis.

'Good evening, sir. We *have* met before.'

Downes seemed slightly surprised – but hardly more than that: 'It's about Theo, I suppose? Theo Kemp?'

'Er – yes.' Lewis hardly managed to climb up to any plateau of assertiveness.

'Well, I've nothing more to tell you, I'm afraid. Nothing I can add to the statement I've already—'

'Meeting your wife, Mr Downes?' interrupted Morse.

'Pardon? Just a minute, Inspector! I . . . just a minute, please.' Downes fitted a hearing-aid taken from his pocket into his right ear, the aid promptly emitting a series of shrill whistles as he fiddled rather fecklessly with the controls.

'I was asking whether you were meeting—' bawled Morse – to no avail, as it appeared.

'If you'll just bear with me a few minutes, gentlemen, I'll just nip along to the car, if I may. I always keep a spare aid in the glove compartment.' The beseeching grin around the slightly lop-sided mouth gave his face an almost schoolboyish look.

Morse gestured vaguely: 'Of course. We'll walk along with you, sir.'

In front of the railway station, a second police car (summoned by a confident Morse as Lewis had driven him from North Oxford) was now waiting, and the Chief Inspector nodded a perfunctory greeting to the two detective-constables who sat side by side in the front seats as they watched, and awaited, developments; watched the three men walk over to the twenty-minute waiting-area set aside for those meeting passengers from British Rail journeys – an area where parking cost nothing at all; watched them as they passed through that area and walked into the main car-park, with the bold notice affording innocent trespassers the clearest warning:

> PARKING FOR BRITISH RAIL
> PASSENGERS ONLY.
> FOR OTHER USERS WITHOUT
> PARKING-TOKENS, £10 PER DAY

'Mind telling me, sir, why you didn't just wait in the twenty-minute car-park? Parking where you have done seems a rather unnecessary expense, doesn't it? Doesn't it . . . ?'

'Pardon, Inspector? If you give me just a second . . . a second or two . . . just . . .'

Downes took a bunch of car-keys from his pocket, opened the door of a British-Racing-Green MG Metro, got into the driver's seat, and leaned over left to open the glove compartment.

Both Morse and Lewis stood, rather warily, beside the car as Downes began to fiddle (once more) with a hearing-aid – one which looked to them suspiciously like the model that had earlier given rise to such piercing oscillation.

'There we are then!' said Downes, as he got out of the car and faced them, his face beaming with an almost childlike pleasure. 'Back in the land of the living! I think you were trying to say something, Inspector?'

'No. I wasn't *trying* to say anything, Mr Downes. I *was* saying something. I was saying how odd it seemed to me that you didn't park your car in the twenty-minute car-park.'

'Ah! Well, I did in a way. I seem to have collected an awful lot of those parking-tokens over the last few months. You see, I often have to go to London and sometimes I don't get back until pretty late. And late at night the barrier here where you slip in your parking-token is often open, and you can just drive straight through.'

'But why *waste* one of your precious tokens?' persisted Morse.

'Ah! I see what you're getting at. I'm a very law-abiding citizen, Inspector. I came here a bit early this evening, and I didn't want to risk any of those clamps or fines or anything. There's an Antiques Fair this week just along Park End Street, and I'd got my eye on a little set of drawers, yew-wood veneer. Lucy's birthday's coming up, November the seventh . . .'

'And then you called in the Royal Oxford, no doubt?'

'I did *not*! I no longer drink and drive. Never!'

'Some people do, sir,' said Morse. 'It's the most common cause of road accidents, you know.'

There was a silence between the three men who now stood slightly awkwardly alongside the MG Metro. Downes, as it appeared, had read the situation adequately, and was expecting to accompany the policemen – well, somewhere! – and he opened the driver's door of the Metro once more. But Morse, leaning slightly towards him, opened his right palm, like a North-African Berber begging for alms.

'We'd like you to come with us, sir. If you just hand over your car-keys to me, Sergeant Lewis here will see that your car is picked up later and returned to your home address.'

'Surely this isn't necessary, is it? I know where the police station is, for Christ's sake!' Suddenly, within the last few words, Downes had lost whatever composure he had hitherto sought to sustain.

'The keys, please!' insisted Morse quietly.

'Look! I just don't know what all this bloody nonsense is about. Will you please *tell* me.'

'Certainly! You can *hear* me all right now?'

Downes almost snarled his reluctant 'Yes'; and listened, mouth agape with incredulity, as Morse beckoned over to the two detective-constables from the second police car.

'Cedric Downes, I arrest you on suspicion of the murder of Dr Theodore Kemp. It is my duty to advise you that anything you now say may be noted by my sergeant here and possibly used in evidence in any future criminal prosecution.'

But as one of the detective-constables clicked a pair of handcuffs round his wrists, Cedric Downes was apparently in no state at all to mouth as much as a monosyllable, let alone give utterance to any incriminating statement. For many seconds he just stood where he was, as still as a man who has gazed into the eyes of the Medusa.

Chapter Forty-three

As usual he was offering explanations for what other
people had not even noticed as problems
(*Bryan Magee*, Aspects of Wagner)

After Downes had been driven away, Morse and Lewis walked
back to their own car, where Morse gave urgent instructions to
the forensic lab to send a couple of their whizz-kids over to the
railway station – immediately! – and to Kidlington HQ to see
that a breakdown van would be available in about an hour's
time to ferry away a certain Metro.

'You're absolutely sure about Downes, aren't you,' said
Lewis. But it was a statement, not a question.

'Oh, yes!'

'What now, sir?'

'We'll wait for forensics. Then we'll go and see how
Downes is making out – do him good to kick his heels in
a cell for half an hour. He was lucky, you know, Lewis.
Bloody lucky, one way or another.'

'Hadn't you better start at the beginning, sir? We've
got a few minutes' wait, like as not.'

So Morse told him.

The key thing in the case was the phone call made
by Kemp. And, yes, it *was* made by Kemp, although
some doubt could quite properly have been harboured on
the matter: Ashenden knew the man, and knew his voice;
and in spite of what was probably a poorish extension-line,
confirmation that the call *was* from Kemp had come from
the telephone-operator, someone else who knew him – knew
him very well, in fact. No, the call was not made by anyone
pretending to be Kemp. But Kemp had not made the call, as
he'd claimed, from Paddington! He'd made it from *Oxford*.

He was anxious about making absolutely sure that another
person was present in The Randolph at the lunch session with
the American tourists; and he learned quite unequivocally
that this person *was* there, although he didn't actually speak
to him. Furthermore, Kemp's absence that afternoon would
mean that this other person – yes, Downes – would be all the
more committed to *staying* with the tourists for the scheduled
'informal get-together'. This arrangement, cleverly yet quite
simply managed, would give him a couple of hours to get on
with what he desperately wanted to get on with: to climb into
bed with Downes's beautiful and doubtlessly over-sexed wife,
Lucy, and get his bottom on the top sheet before his time
ran out. The pair of them had probably not been having an
affair for long – only perhaps after Kemp's long infatuation
with the semi-permanently sozzled Sheila had begun to wear
off. But where can they meet? It has to be at Downes's
place: Kemp hasn't got a room in college, and it can't be
at Kemp's place because his wife is a house-bound invalid.
So, that morning presented a wonderful opportunity – and
just a little compensation perhaps for the huge disappointment
Kemp must undoubtedly have experienced over the theft of
the Wolvercote Tongue. The jewel was almost in his grasp;
almost about to be displayed and photographed and written
up in all the right journals: a jewel he himself had traced, and
one he'd worked so hard to get donated to the Ashmolean.
No wonder his interest in swopping pleasantries with ageing
Americans had sunk to zero; no wonder the prospect of the
lubricious Lucy Downes proved so irresistible. Now the
deception practised by Kemp was a very clever one. If he
was going to be late on parade – 3 p.m., he'd promised –
every pressure would be on the other two group leaders,
Sheila Williams and Cedric Downes, to keep the tourists
adequately amused by each of them shouldering an extra
responsibility. It would not, incidentally, have occurred to
Kemp that a consequence of such last-minute re-arrangements
was that several members of the group took the opportunity
this afforded to perform a strange assortment of extra-mural

activities – from viewing steam locomotives to tracing lost offspring. Red herrings, all.

But then things started to go wrong. Downes is not very deaf at all yet; but sometimes, with certain kinds of background noise, and when people are asking questions, well, there can be difficulty. A deaf person, as Lucy Downes told us, is not so much worried about not knowing the answer to any question put to him; he's worried, embarrassingly so, *about not hearing the question*. And at lunchtime – there are witnesses – Downes's hearing-aid began to play up and he discovered he wasn't carrying his spare aid with him. He decided to go home and pick it up, and in fact he was *seen* going up St Giles' on his bicycle towards North Oxford. It's hardly difficult to guess the sequence of events immediately after he'd quietly inserted his key in the Yale lock. He may have had a sixth sense about the presence of some stranger in the house; more likely he saw some physical evidence – a coat, a hat – belonging to a person he knew. He picked up a walking-stick – or something – from the hall-stand, and leapt up the stairs to find his wife and Kemp *in medio coitu*, both of them completely naked. In a fury of hatred and jealousy he thrashed his stick about Kemp's head while Kemp himself tried to extricate himself from the twisted sheets, to get out of the bed, and to defend himself – but he didn't make it. He staggered back and fell, and got his head crashed – a *second* time, as we know – against the corner-post of the double bed or the sharp edge of the fireplace. He had a thin skull – a medical fact – and there was a sudden, dreadful silence; and a great deal of blood. The despairing, faithless, gaping, horrified wife looked down at her lover, and knew that he was dead. Now, sometimes it is extremely difficult to kill a man. Sometimes it is quite extraordinarily easy, as it was then . . .

And Downes himself? The emotions of hatred and jealousy are immediately superseded by the more primitive instinct of survival, and he begins to realise that all may yet be well if he can keep his head. For he is suddenly, miraculously, aware that he has got a wonderful – no! – a *perfect* alibi; an alibi which has been given to him *by the very person he has just killed*. O lovely irony! Kemp had told Ashenden, and Ashenden had then told everyone else, that he (Kemp) would not be back from London until 3 p.m. And that meant that Downes could not *possibly* have killed Kemp before that time, and Downes was going to make absolutely certain – as he did – that he was never out of sight or out of touch with his group – except for the odd, brief visit to the loo – at any time that afternoon or early evening.

It is hardly difficult to guess what happened at the Downes's residence immediately after the death of Kemp. Downes himself could not stay for more than a few minutes. He instructed his panic-stricken, guilt-ridden wife to pack up Kemp's clothes in a suitcase, and to clean up the bloody mess that must have been left on the carpet, and probably on the sheets. The body was left – *had* to be left – in the bedroom. Downes himself would have to deal with that. But later. For the present he seeks to compose himself as he cycles back down to The Randolph.

That evening, at about seven o'clock, he returns to his house in Lonsdale Road, the very far end of Lonsdale Road, where the lawn slopes down directly to the bank of the River Cherwell. He manoeuvres Kemp's body down the stairs and carries it across the lawn, probably in a wheelbarrow. It was a dark night, and doubtless he covered the corpse with a ground-sheet or something. Then slowly, carefully, without even the suspicion of a splash perhaps, he slid Kemp into the swift-flowing waters of a river swollen by the recent heavy rains. Two hours later, the body has drifted far downstream, finally getting wedged at the top of the weir in Parson's Pleasure – the place where the careless Howard Brown had earlier left his yellow programme – and his continental seven . . .

It was at this point in Morse's recapitulation that the forensic brigade arrived; and soon afterwards a royal-blue BMW carrying no lesser a personage than Chief Superintendent Bell from the City Police.

'You know, Morse,' began Bell, 'you seem to breed about as many problems as a pregnant rabbit.'

'You could look at it the other way, I suppose,' replied the radiant Morse. 'Without me and Lewis half of these fellows in forensics would be out on the dole, sir.'

About an hour before these last events were taking place, the American tourists had registered into the two-star Swan Hotel in Stratford-upon-(definitely 'upon')Avon. As throughout the tour, Ashenden had observed the opportunist self-seekers at the front of the queue (as ever) for the room-keys; and in the rear (as ever) the quieter, seemingly contented souls who perhaps knew that being first or last to their rooms would make little difference to the quality of their living. And at the very back, the small, patient figure of Phil Aldrich, seeking (of this, Ashenden could have little doubt) to avoid the embarrassment of refusing to sign Janet Roscoe's latest petition.

The evening meal had been re-scheduled for 8.30 p.m.; and with time to spare, after throwing his own large hold-all on to the counterpane of his single bed, Ashenden joined a few of the other tourists in the Residents' Lounge, where he took some sheets of the hotel's own note-paper, and began to write a letter. When he had finished, he found a red, first-class stamp in his wallet, fixed it to the envelope, and walked out into Bridge Street to find a pillar-box. The letter was addressed to Chief Inspector Morse, St Aldate's Central Police Station, Oxford, and in the top left-hand corner was written the one word: URGENT.

Chapter Forty-four

'When my noble and learned brother gives his Judgment, they're to be let go free,' said Krook, winking at us again. 'And then,' he added, whispering and grinning, 'if that ever was to happen – which it won't – the birds that have never been caged would kill 'em.'

(*Dickens*, Bleak House)

Unwontedly, Lewis was philosophising as he and Morse sat in the canteen at St Aldate's: 'Amazing, really: you get all these statements and alibis and secret little meetings, and then really, in the end, it's just – well, it's just the same old story, isn't it? Chap goes home and finds the missus in bed with one of the neighbours.'

'Remember, though, this is only *half* the case. And we've got to get some evidence. No, that's wrong! We've *got* some evidence – or we shall have, very soon.'

'Perhaps we shouldn't wait too much longer, sir?'

'It'll be here. Patience, Lewis! Eat your cheese sandwich!'

'I couldn't help feeling just a bit sorry for him, though.'

'Sorry? Why do you say that?'

'Well, you know, it might have been a bit sort of – *accidental*, don't you reckon?'

'I do *not*,' replied Morse, with the fullest conviction.

Downes sat at the table in Interview Room Two on the ground floor, spell-bound and motionless, as if a witch had drawn a circle round him thrice. Seated opposite, Sergeant Dixon was finding the silence and the stillness increasingly embarrassing.

'Like a cuppa tea?'

'No! Er, yes! Yes please.'

'Milk and sugar?'

But Downes appeared not to hear the supplementary questions, and Dixon nodded to the constable who stood at the door, the latter now making for the canteen on a less than wholly specific mission.

At the Swan Hotel in Stratford, Mrs Roscoe had just completed her evening meal, a concoction of beans so splendidly bleak as to delight the most dedicated Vegan. She immediately wrote a brief congratulatory note, insisting that the waiter convey it forthwith to the chef de cuisine himself.

At this same time (it was now 9 p.m.) Eddie Stratton was sitting on the only chair in a small third-floor room of a hotel just north of Russell Square. The facilities here were minimal – a cracked wash-basin, one minuscule bar of soap, and one off-white towel. Yet the bed looked clean-sheeted and felt comfortable; and there was a lavatory just along the corridor (the lady had said), a bathroom one floor down, and a Residents' TV Lounge beside Reception. On the bedside table was a Gideon Bible, and beside it an entry form which, if and when completed and dispatched, would entitle the fortunate applicant to inclusion in a free draw for a ticket to one of the following summer's golfing championships. Stratton availed himself of neither opportunity.

Earlier he had visited the American Consulate, where an attractive and sympathetic fellow countrywoman from North Carolina had advised him on all the sad yet necessary procedures consequent upon the death of an American national in Britain, and acquainted him with the costs of the transatlantic conveyancing of corpses. And now, as he sat staring fixedly at the floral configuration on the faded green carpet, he felt a little sad as he thought of Laura, his wife for only the last couple of years. They had been as contented together as could have been expected, he supposed, from a union which had been largely one of convenience and accommodation; and he would always remember, with a sort of perverse affection, her rather loud voice, her over-daubed war-paint – and, of course, the painful state of those poor feet of hers . . . He nodded slowly to himself, then looked up and across at the lace-curtained window, like a bird perhaps suddenly spotting the open door of its cage. And an observer in that small room would have noticed the suspicion of a smile around his loose and slightly purplish lips.

It was just after 9 p.m. that a PC arrived from the railway station carrying a small brown envelope, which Morse accepted with delight, smiling radiantly at Lewis but saying nothing as he slit open the top and looked briefly inside. Then, with smile unfading, he handed the envelope to Lewis.

'Wish me luck! I'll let you know when to come in.'

Chapter Forty-five

Perchance my too much questioning offends
(*Dante*, Purgatorio)

At least Morse spared Cedric Downes the charade of a
cordial re-greeting; he even forbore to express the hope that
conditions were satisfactory and that the prisoner was being
well treated. In point of fact, the prisoner looked lost and
defeated. Earlier he had been officially advised that it was
his legal right to have his solicitor present; but surprisingly
Downes had taken no advantage of the offer. A cup of tea
(sweetened) stood untouched at his right elbow. He raised his
eyes, morosely, as Morse took Dixon's seat opposite him and
pulled another chair alongside for a very blonde young WPC,
who amongst other accomplishments was the only person in
St Aldate's HQ with a Pitman shorthand qualification for
130 w.p.m. Not that she was destined to get any practice at
such a mega-speed, since Downes, at least for the first half
of the interview, was to enunciate his words with the slow
deliberation of a stupefied zombie. Morse waited patiently.
That was always the best way, in the long run. And when
Downes finally spoke, it was to ask about his wife.

'Did someone meet the train, Inspector? The next train?'

'Please don't worry about her, sir. She'll be looked after.'

Downes shook his head in stupefaction. 'This is madness
– absolute madness! There's been some dreadful misunder-
standing somewhere – don't you understand that? I – I can't
think straight. I don't know what to say! I just pray I'm going
to wake up any second.'

'Tell me about Dr Kemp,' said Morse.

'Tell you what? Everyone knows about Kemp. He was
the biggest philanderer in Oxford.'

'You say "everyone"?'

'Yes! Including his wife. *She* knows.'

'*Knew*. She died this afternoon.'

'Oh God!' Downes closed his eyes and squeezed them tightly shut. Then he opened them, and looked across at Morse. 'I think I know what you're going to ask me now, Inspector.'

Morse tilted his head to the left: 'You do?'

'You're going to ask me whether Lucy – whether my wife was . . . is aware of it, too.'

Morse tilted his head to the right, but made no reply.

'Well, the answer's "yes". Once or twice he'd – well he'd tried to make some sort of advances to her. At receptions, parties – that sort of thing.'

'Your wife *told* you about this?'

'She was a bit flattered, I suppose.'

'Was she?'

'And amused. More amused than flattered, I think.'

'And you? You, Mr Downes? Were *you* amused?'

'I could have killed the bloody swine!' So suddenly, so dramatically, the manner had changed – the voice now a harsh snarl, the eyes ablaze with hatred.

'It's not all that easy actually to kill a man,' said Morse.

'It isn't?' Downes's eyes appeared perplexed.

'What exactly *did* you hit him with? When you went home for – for whatever it was?'

'I – pardon? – you don't—'

'Just in your own words, sir, if you will. Simply what happened, that's all. The WPC here will take down what you say and then she'll read it back to you, and you'll be able to change anything you may have got wrong. No problem!'

'Wha—?' Downes shook his head in anguished desperation. 'When am I going to wake up?'

'Let's just start from when you put your key – Yale lock, isn't it? – into the front door, and then when you went in . . .'

'Yes, and I got my other hearing-aid, and some notes—'

'Whereabouts do you keep the spare hearing-aid?'

'In the bedroom.'

Morse nodded encouragement. 'Twin beds, I suppose—'

'Double bed, actually – and I keep my spare aid in a drawer of the tallboy' – he looked directly into Morse's eyes again – 'next to the handkerchiefs and the cufflinks and the arm-bands. You do want me to be *precise* about what I tell you?'

'And your wife was in the double bed there – yes, we do want you to be precise, sir.'

'Wha—? What makes you think my wife was in bed? This was at *lunchtime*.'

'Where was she?'

'In the living room? I don't know! I forget. Why don't you ask *her*?' He suddenly sprang to his feet. 'Look! I've got to talk to her! Now! You've no right to hold me here. I know you've got your job to do – I understand that. Some people get held on suspicion – *I know!* But I must speak to Lucy!'

His voice had become almost a screech of anger and frustration. And Morse was glad of it. So often the loss of self-control was the welcome prelude to a confession – a confession that was usually, in turn, a vast relief to the pent-up pressures of a tortured mind. And already Downes seemed calmer again as he resumed his seat, and Morse resumed his questioning.

'You understood, didn't you, the real point of Dr Kemp's phone call? No one else did – but *you* knew.' In contrast to the crescendo of fury from Downes, Morse's voice was very quiet indeed, and beside him WPC Wright was not absolutely sure that she'd transcribed his words with total accuracy.

As for Downes, he was leaning across the table. 'Could you please speak up a bit, Inspector? I didn't hear what you said, I'm afraid.'

It is likely, however, that he heard the loud knock on the door which heralded the entry of a rather harassed-looking Lewis.

'Sorry to interrupt, sir, but—'

'Not *now*, man! Can't you see—?'

'It's very urgent, sir,' said Lewis, in a voice of hushed authority.

WPC Wright had heard what Sergeant Lewis said all right; and she glanced across at Downes. Had *he* heard? Something in his face suggested to her that he might well have done, perhaps.

But it was difficult to tell.

Chapter Forty-six

I do love to note and to observe
(*Jonson*, Volpone)

'I just don't believe it!' declared Morse.

It had been Lewis himself who a few minutes earlier had taken the call from the Met.

'Trying to cross over the road by King's Cross Station – about five-thirty – hit by a car. From Oxford she is. A Mrs Downes: Mrs Lucy Claire Downes according to her plastics. Lonsdale Road.'

'She – is she dead?' Lewis had asked.

'ICU at St Pancras Hospital. That's all we know.'

'Was she carrying a case?'

'No more details – not yet, Sarge. Seems she just stepped off the pavement to get in front of a row of people and . . .'

Morse sat down and rested his forehead on his right hand. 'Bloody 'ell!'

'Circle Line from King's Cross to Paddington, sir – about twenty minutes, say? She must have been going for the six o'clock train, and she was probably in a dickens of a rush when . . .' Lewis had taken the news badly.

'Yes? Dickens of a rush when she *what*?'

'When she stepped off the pavement—'

'An intelligent woman deliberately stepping out into the London traffic – in the rush hour? Do you really believe that? Or do you think she might have been pushed? Do you hear me, Lewis? *Pushed.*'

'How can you *say* that?'

For a few moments Morse sat where he was. Then he

rose to his feet, slowly – his eyes glowing savagely. 'He did it, Lewis. *He* did it!'

'But he was in *Oxford*!'

'No he wasn't! He wasn't waiting on the Oxford platform at all. *He'd just got off the train.* And then he saw *us.* So he turned round the second he did, and made it look as though he was waiting for the woman he'd just tried to kill – when they were walking along together . . . He loved her, you see – probably never loved anyone in the world except his Lucy. And when he saw her copulating with Kemp . . . He just couldn't get it out of his mind, not for one second. He thought he was never going to be able to get it out of his mind.' Morse shook his head. 'And I'm an idiot, Lewis. That key! The key they found under the floor-mat in the car, or wherever. I'd guessed that Downes wanted to go back to his car to hide *something*, so I played along with all that hearing-aid rubbish. And when they brought the key, I knew exactly what it was – a left-luggage locker-key. But tell me this, Lewis! How the hell did *he* get hold of that key if he hadn't met his wife?'

'That's what it is, sir? Left-luggage key? You're sure of it?'

Morse nodded. 'And I'll tell you which station, unless you want to tell *me*.'

'King's Cross.'

'Could be Paddington, I suppose.'

'The *bastard*!' muttered Lewis, with an unwonted show of emotion.

Morse smiled: 'You like her, don't you?'

'Lovely woman!'

'That's what Kemp thought.'

'Perhaps . . . ?' started Lewis.

'Oh, no! We shall waste no sympathy on Kemp. Look! I want you to get someone to drive you up to the hospital to see her. All right? You can get a bit of kip in the car. Then go to King's Cross and see if there's anything in locker sixty-seven. If there is, bring it back. And if you can get anything in the way of a statement – fine. If not, well, just try to see what she's got to say.'

'If she's . . . shall I say we've got *him* here?'

'Perhaps not . . . I dunno, though. Play it by ear!'

'OK, sir.' Lewis stood up and walked over to the door, where he halted. 'Have you ever thought it might have been *Mrs* Downes who killed Dr Kemp? What if when her husband came home he found Kemp already dead, and then he did all this stuff, you know, to cover up for *her*?'

'Oh, yes, Lewis. I've thought of every possibility in this case. Including Lucy Downes.'

'You don't think—?'

'I think you will be *completely* safe in London. I don't think you'll be in the slightest danger of being knifed as you practise your bedside-manner sitting by a semi-conscious young woman in an intensive care unit.'

Lewis grinned weakly, and felt in his pocket to make sure that the brown envelope containing a small red key, number 67, was still there.

Janet Roscoe had finished re-reading *A Midsummer Night's Dream*, and felt just a little less certain now about her long-held view (she had earlier been an actress) that Mr Shakespeare was sometimes way below his best when it came to the writing of comedy. And she had just turned on the TV, hoping for a late news-programme, when she heard the light knock on her bedroom door. It was Shirley Brown. She had been stung by *something*, and could Janet help? But of course she *knew* Janet could help! Invited in, Shirley watched the little woman delving into her capacious handbag (a gentle little joke with the rest of the group) from whose depths had already emerged, in addition to the usual accessories, a scout-knife, an apostle spoon, and a miniature iron. And something else now: two tubes of ointment. A little bit of each (Janet maintained) could do no possible harm, unsure as Shirley was whether the offending insect had been wasp, bee, gnat, flea, or mosquito.

For five minutes after the medication, the two women sat on the bed and talked. Had Janet noticed how quiet

Mr Ashenden had seemed all day? Not his usual self at all, one way or another. Janet had noticed that, yes: and he *was* the courier, wasn't he? Got *paid* for it. And Janet added something more. She thought she *knew* what might have been on his mind, because he'd been writing a letter in the Lounge. And when he'd put the envelope down to put a stamp on it – '*Face upwards*, Shurley!' – why, she couldn't *help* noticing who it was addressed to, now could she?

Suddenly, and perhaps for the first time, Shirley Brown felt a twinge of affection for the lonely little woman who seemed far more aware of what was going on than any of them.

'You seem to notice everything, Janet,' she said, in a not unkindly way.

'I notice most things,' replied Mrs Roscoe, with a quiet little smile of self-congratulation.

Chapter Forty-seven

Some circumstantial evidence is very strong – as when
you find a trout in the milk
(*Henry Thoreau*, unpublished manuscript)

'Are you going to save us an awful lot of time and
trouble, sir, or are you determined to burden the taxpayer
further?'

Downes licked his dry lips. 'I don't know what this is all
about – except that I'm going mad.'

'Oh, no! You're very sane—' began Morse. But Downes,
at least for the moment, had taken the initiative.

'And if you're worried about the taxpayer, shouldn't you
perhaps be attending to the urgent little matter your sergeant
told you about?'

'You *heard* that?' asked Morse sharply.

'He speaks more clearly than you do.'

'Even when he whispers?' For a few seconds a bemused-
looking Morse appeared slightly more concerned with the
criticism of his diction than with the prosecution of his case,
and it was Downes who continued:

'You were commenting on the degree of my sanity,
Inspector.'

WPC Wright glanced at Morse, seated to her left. She
had never worked with him before, but the man's name was
something of a legend in the Oxfordshire Constabulary, and
she was experiencing a sense of some disappointment. Morse
was talking again now, though – getting into his swing again,
it seemed, and she took down his words in her swift and deftly
stroked outlines.

'Yes. *Very* sane. Sane enough to cover up a murder! Sane
enough to arrange for your wife to cart off the incriminating

evidence to King's Cross Station and stick it in a left-luggage locker—'

'I can't be *hearing* you right—'

'No! Not again, sir – please! It's getting threadbare, you know, that particular excuse. You used it when Kemp rang up – *rang up from your own house*. You used it again when you'd just got off the train from Paddington tonight, when you pretended you were waiting for Mrs Downes—'

In her shorthand book, WPC Wright had ample time to write the word that Downes now shrieked; write it in in long-hand, and in capitals. In fact she would have had plenty of time to shade in the circles in the last two letters.

She wrote 'STOP!'

And Morse stopped, as instructed – for about thirty seconds. No rush. Then he repeated his accusation.

'You got your wife to take Kemp's clothes to London—'

'Got my wife – got *Lucy*? What? What do you *mean*?'

'It's all right, sir.' Morse's tone now (thought WPC Wright) was rather more impressive. Quiet, cultured, confident – gentle almost, and understanding. 'We've got the key your wife gave you after she'd deposited the clothes and the blood-stained sheets—'

'I've been here all day – here in Oxford!' The voice had veered from exasperation to incredulity. 'I've got a marvellous alibi – did you know that? I had a tutorial this afternoon from—'

But Morse had taken over completely, and he held up his right hand with a confident, magisterial authority. 'I promise you, sir, that we shall interview everyone you saw this afternoon. You have nothing – nothing! – to fear if you're telling me the truth. But listen to me, Mr Downes! Just for a little while *listen* to me! When my sergeant came in to see me – when you yourself heard him – he'd just learned that on my instructions the locker had been opened in London. And that inside the locker was a case, the case your wife took with her to London today; a case which she told me – told me and Sergeant Lewis – contained some curtains. Curtains! We both *saw* her take it, in a taxi. And shall I tell you again what it *really* contained?'

Downes thumped the table with both fists with such ferocity that WPC Wright transferred her shorthand-book to her black-stockinged knee, and failed completely to register the next three words that Downes had thundered.

'No! No! No!'

But Morse appeared wholly unperturbed. 'Please tell me, Mr Downes, how the key came to be in your possession? Under the mat in the driver's seat, was it? Or in the glove compartment? Can you explain that? Are you going to tell me that it was someone who came back on the train from London who gave you the key?'

'Wha—?'

'Couldn't have been your wife, could it?'

'What's Lucy got to do with—?'

'The key!' roared Morse. 'What about the *key*?'

'Key? You mean . . . ?' Downes's cheeks were very white, and slowly he started to get up from his chair.

'Sit down!' thundered Morse with immense authority; and simply, silently Downes did as he was bidden.

'Do you remember the number of the key, sir?'

'Of course.'

'Please tell me,' said Morse quietly.

'Number sixty-seven.'

'That's correct. That's correct, Mr Downes.' Morse briefly placed his right hand on WPC Wright's arm, and gave her a scarce-perceptible nod of encouragement. It would be vital, as he knew, for the next few exchanges to be transcribed with unimpeachable certitude. But as Downes spoke, with a helpless little shrug of his shoulders, the newly sharpened pencil of WPC Wright remained poised above the page.

'That's the key to my locker at the North Oxford Golf Club, Inspector.'

Suddenly, Interview Room Two was still and silent as the grave.

Chapter Forty-eight

Darkness is more productive of sublime ideas
than light
(*Edmund Burke*, On the Sublime and Beautiful)

The traffic along Western Avenue had been quiet, and it
was only an hour and a quarter after leaving Oxford that
Lewis was speaking to the Night Sister on the third floor
of the hospital, a neat, competent-looking brunette who
appeared rather more concerned about the unprecedented
police interest in matters than in the medical condition of her
most recent road-casualty, now lying behind a curtained bed
in Harley Ward. A casualty not all *that* badly injured, anyway:
broken left humerus, broken left clavicle, some nasty bruising
and laceration round the left shoulder – but no broken legs or
ribs, and fairly certainly no head injuries, either. Yes, said
Sister, Mrs Downes had been remarkably lucky, really; and,
yes, Sergeant Lewis could see her for a short while. He would
find her under sedation – a bit dopey and drowsy, and still in
a state of some disorientation and shock. Quite lucid, though.
'*And*,' added Sister, 'you'd better have something ready to
tell her if she asks you when her husband's coming. We've
put her off as best we can.'

Lewis stood by the bed and looked down at her. Her eyes
were open, and guardedly she smiled an instant recognition.
She spoke softly, lisping slightly, and Lewis immediately
noticed (what he had not been told) that two teeth in the
upper left of her jaw had been broken off.

'We met this morning, didn't we?'

'Yes, Mrs Downes.'

'Cedric knows I'm all right, doesn't he?'

'Everything's in hand. Don't worry about anything like
that.'

'He'll be here soon, though?'

'I've told you,' said Lewis gently, 'we're looking after everything. No need for you to worry at all.'

'But I want to *see* him!'

'It's just that the hospital don't want you to have any visitors – not just for the time being. The doctors, you know, they've got to patch you up a bit.'

'I want to thee Thedric,' she moaned quietly, her lips quivering and her eyes now brimming with tears as the good Lewis laid a hand on the pristine-white plaster encasing her upper arm.

'Soon. In good time. As I say—'

'Why can *you* see me if he can't?'

'It's just routine – you know – accidents. We have to make reports on—'

'But I've seen the police already.'

'And you told them—?'

'I told them it was my fault – it wasn't the driver's fault.' Her eyes looked pleadingly up at Lewis.

'Would you just repeat what you said. Please, Mrs Downes.'

'There was nothing *to* say. It was my fault, what else do you want me to say?'

'Just *how*, you know . . .'

'I was walking along there. I was in a hurry to catch the tube – it was the rush hour – I didn't want to miss the train – Cedric . . . you see, Cedric was waiting—'

'At Oxford, you mean? He was waiting at Oxford?'

'Of course. I was just trying to get past some people in front of me and I stepped off the pavement and the driver – he didn't have a chance. It was *my* fault, don't you believe me? He braked and . . . It was the *case* really. If it hadn't been for the case, I think perhaps . . .'

'The car hit the case, you mean? Hit the case first?'

Lucy nodded. 'It sort of, well – cushioned things, and I hit a litter-bin on the kerb and . . .' She lifted her right hand and pointed vaguely across to the left-hand side of her body.

'So you still had the case with you, then? When the car hit you?'

For the first time the hitherto lucid Lucy looked a little bemused, as if she was unable to follow Lewis's last question. 'I don't quite follow . . . I'm sorry.'

'I just wanted to know if you were carrying the case, that's all.'

'Of course I was.'

'Do you – do you know where it is now, Mrs Downes?'

'Isn't it still under the bed, Sergeant?'

Morse took the call just after 11 p.m.

'You'll never guess what's happened, sir!'

'Don't put your bank balance on it, Lewis!'

'She's going to be all right, they think, sir. The Met got it wrong about the ICU.'

Morse said nothing.

'You are – well, pleased about *that*, aren't you?'

'I take no delight in death, Lewis, and if one thing worries me above all else it is accidents – the random concourse of atoms in the void, as Epicurus used to say.'

'You feeling tired, sir?'

'Yes.'

'You *knew* it was an accident all the time?'

'No. Not all the time.'

'You're losing me – as usual.'

'What is this news of yours, Lewis, that I shall never guess?'

'The case, sir! The case we both saw Mrs Downes take up to London.'

'We both saw her put in the *taxi*, if we are to be accurate.'

'But she did bring it to London! And you won't guess what was in it.'

'Curtains, Lewis? Any good? Curtains with French pleats? By the way, remind me one day to explain this business of French pleats to you. Mrs Lewis would be glad if you took a bit more interest in household furnishings and interior decoration.'

'What do you want me to do about this left-luggage key, sir?'

'What are you talking about? What makes you think that's a left-luggage key?'

After Lewis had rung off, Morse sat at his desk and smoked three Dunhill International cigarettes one after the other. He'd been shaken, certainly, when Cedric Downes had invited him to go along to the North Oxford Golf Club and knock up the caretaker if necessary. And Lewis's phone call had surely hammered the last coffin-nail into the Cedric–Lucy theory. Yet Morse's mind was never more fertile than when faced with some apparently insuperable obstacle, and even now he found it difficult to abandon his earlier, sweet hypothesis about the murder of Theodore Kemp. He gazed out through the curtainless window on to the well-lit, virtually deserted parking-area: only his own red Jaguar and two white police cars. He could – should! – get off now and go to bed. He would be home in ten minutes. Less, perhaps, at this hour . . . Yes, it was extremely useful to have a car, whatever people said about traffic and pollution and expense . . . yes . . .

Morse was conscious that his mind was drifting off into an interesting avenue of thought, but also that he was drifting off to sleep, as well. It was the cars that had started some new idea . . . For the minute, though, it was gone. Yet there were other new ideas that jostled together in his brain for some more prominent recognition. First, the conviction that there was – must be! – a link, perhaps a blindingly obvious link, between the theft of the Wolvercote Jewel and the murder of Theodore Kemp. Second, the growing belief that *two* people must have been involved in things, quite certainly in the murder. Third, the worrying suspicion that amongst the evidence already accumulated, the statements taken, the people interviewed, the personal relationships observed, the *obiter dicta*, the geography of North Oxford – that amongst all these things *somewhere* there was a fact that he had seen or heard but never fully recognised or understood. Fourth, the strange reluctance he felt about abandoning Downes as Suspect Number One. And as Morse opened his passenger door, he stood for a while looking up at the Pole Star, and asking himself the question he had been asking for the past two hours: was there *any* way in which Downes could still have been the murderer after all?

Many of Morse's ideas were either so strange or so wildly improbable that most of them were always doomed to early disappointment. Yet, as it happened, he was registering well above par that evening, for three of the four ideas he had formulated were finally to prove wholly correct.

Lewis had fallen fast asleep on the back seat of the police car and remained so for the whole of the journey back to Oxford. In his younger days, he had been a middle-weight Army boxing champion, and now he dreamed that he was in the ring again, with a right-cross from a swarthy, swift-footed opponent smashing into the left-hand side of his jaw. He had tried to feel inside his mouth to see if any teeth were broken or missing, but the great bulk of his boxing-glove precluded any such investigation.

When the car finally pulled up in St Aldate's, the young driver opened the rear door and shook Sergeant Lewis awake, failing to notice that the first action of his passenger was to run the forefinger of his left hand slowly along his upper teeth.

Part Three

Chapter Forty-nine

Where water, warm or cool, is
Good for gout – at Aquae Sulis
(Graffito in the Pump Room, Bath, *c*.1760)

'Bairth? This is *Bairth*?'

Seated on the nearside front seat of the luxury coach, John Ashenden glanced across at the diminutive septuagenarian from California. 'Yes, Mrs Roscoe, this is Bath.'

With less than conspicuous enthusiasm, he leaned forward for his microphone, turned it on, and began. Not quite so confidently as in Stratford; or in Oxford, of course, where he had memorised whole sentences from the Jan Morris guide.

'Bath, ladies and gentlemen, is the site of a Roman spa, *Aquae Sulis*, probably built in the first and second centuries AD. A good deal of the extensive baths has been excavated and the city presents the tourist of today with perhaps the most splendidly restored of all Roman remains in Europe.'

On either side of the central aisle, heads nodded at the buildings and streets around them as a now livelier Ashenden continued, himself (like the site, it appeared) splendidly restored from whatever malaise had affected him over the previous two days, a malaise which had been noted and commented upon by several others of the group besides Mrs Shirley Brown – the latter sitting comfortably now in her usual seat, the effects of the sting having cleared up fairly quickly under the twin application of Mrs Roscoe's unguents.

'Looks a swell place, Shirl,' ventured Howard Brown.

'Yeah. Just wish Laura was with us – and Eddie. It all seems so sad.'

'Too right! Bus seems sorta empty somehow.'

As scheduled, the tourists had lunched at Cirencester, after leaving Stratford earlier that Sunday morning. The weather was still holding, if only just: another golden day in late autumn. And perhaps in the minds of many, the memories of their tragic stay in Oxford were slowly softening at the edges.

One of the slightly younger widows, Mrs Nancy Wiseman, a librarian from Oklahoma City, was seated at the back of the coach beside Phil Aldrich. She had observed with a quiet pleasure how the strident Roscoe woman had markedly cooled towards her former partner after his refusal (and that of most of the others) to sign her petulant letter of complaint concerning Sheila Williams. Although Phil had been slightly reserved in his manner towards her (Nancy), she knew that that was his way and she was enjoying the company of that wiry, small-boned, gently spoken citizen from Sacramento who almost invariably found himself at the back of every queue that ever formed itself. Yes, the tour was definitely looking up a little, and only the previous evening she had written a card to her daughter to say that in spite of a death and a theft and a murder she was 'beginning to make one or two very nice friends on the trip'.

In truth, however, Phil himself was finding Nancy Wiseman a little too effusive for his liking and – perversely, as it seemed – would have preferred sitting next to Janet Roscoe, up there at the front of the coach, as he listened to (and indeed almost wholly managed to hear) the end of Ashenden's introduction to Bath:

'In the eighteenth century the city was transformed into a resort for English high society – being particularly associated, of course, with the name of Beau Nash, the great dandy and gamester who lived here during the 1740s and 50s. Among its many literary connections, Bath can number such great figures as Henry Fielding, Fanny Burney, Jane Austen, William Wordsworth, Walter Scott, Charles Dickens – and most famous of all, perhaps, Geoffrey Chaucer and *The Wife of Bath's Tale*.'

It was a good note on which to end.

Opposite him, he noticed that Janet Roscoe had delved once more into the deep handbag, this time producing a very slim volume, whose title it was impossible for him not to see, and which he could have guessed in any case: CHAUCER, *Tale of the Wyf of Bathe.*

He smiled across at her, and as she opened her book at the Prologue, she smiled quite sweetly back at him.

It seemed a good omen for the stay in Bath.

Only seemed.

Chapter Fifty

During late visits to Stinsford in old age he would
often visit the unmarked grave of Louisa Harding
(*Florence Emily Hardy*, The Early Life of Thomas Hardy)

According to the hospital bulletin on the Monday afternoon,
the condition of Lucy Downes was now officially listed
as 'comfortable', one notch above the 'satisfactory' of the
Sunday, and two above the earlier 'stable'. Three visits from
her husband had helped, perhaps (the first in the small hours
of the Sunday morning, two hours after his release from
custody), but some slight complications had arisen with
continued internal bleeding, and she had become deeply and
embarrassingly conscious of how she must appear to everyone
whenever she smiled. So she forbore to do so altogether, even
to Cedric, and as she lay in her bed that day, her arm now
beginning to give her some considerable pain, she would willingly (she knew) have cracked two of her ribs rather than
chipped a couple of her teeth.

Vanity, all is vanity, saith the preacher. And 'satisfactory'
was arguably too favourable a judgement on her circumstances.
But that was the word Morse repeated to the first question
Lewis put to him about Lucy's progress at 8.30 a.m. on the
Tuesday. It may have been that Morse had smiled a little at
the question. But it may not.

Activity in the two days following Cedric Downes's release
had hardly afforded a model of investigative collaboration,
with Morse sleeping through until the late afternoon of the
Sunday, then idling away most of the Monday in his office,
moodily perusing the documents in the case; and with Lewis
doing the converse, making what he felt had been a fairly
significant contribution to the case on the Sunday afternoon,
and then spending the whole of the Monday abed, where he

had lain dead to the wideawake world, and where, even when Mrs Lewis had gently rocked his shoulder at 6.30 p.m. and quietly breathed the prospect of egg and chips into his ear, he had turned his head over into the pillow and blissfully resumed his slumbers. But now he felt fully refreshed.

By the look of him, however, his chief had not perhaps shared a similarly successful period of recuperation, for he sounded tetchy as he picked up the brief note Lewis had left him.

'You say Stratton *was* quite definitely out at Didcot when Kemp was being killed?'

'No doubt about it, sir. I went over there yesterday—'

'You were in bed yesterday.'

'Sunday, I mean. They remembered him.'

'Who's "they"?'

'One of 'em took a photo of him on the footplate of "The Cornishman". He'd already got it developed and was going to post it to America. Stratton gave him a fiver. He's going to get a copy and send it here.'

'And it *was* Stratton?'

'It was Stratton.'

'Oh!'

'Where does all this leave us, sir? I just don't know where we are.'

'And you think *I* do?' mumbled the ill-shaven Morse. 'Here! Read this – came this morning.'

Lewis took the envelope handed him, postmarked Stratford-upon-Avon, and withdrew the two hand-written sheets.

> Swan Hotel,
> Stratford,
> Saturday, 3rd Nov
>
> Dear Inspector,
> My conscience has troubled me since I left Oxford. When you asked about the phone call I

tried to remember everything and I don't know
what else I could have told you. I want to repeat
that the line was faint but it was definately
Dr Kemp on the phone and that what I wrote was
as near as anyone could get to what he said.
But I lied about the afternoon and I was worried
when you wanted to keep the betting slips
because you probably know that one of the horses
won and I would have won quite a lot of money
if I'd stayed in the betting shop. I wanted
people to think I'd gone to Summertown and I
could prove it if necessary. So I went to
Ladbrokes and picked two rank outsiders and
put some money on them and left. The only
reason I did this was because I didn't want
anyone to know where I really went which was
to a flat in Park Town where I am ashamed to
say I watched some sex videos with three
other people. I think one of them would be
willing to back up my story and if its necessary
I will give you a name if you can promise it
can all be done with no charges brought. I am
worried as well about the way you asked me
where I went after we'd arrived in Oxford
because I didn't tell you the truth then either,
I went to Holywell cemetery and went to the grave
of a friend of mine. He wrote to me before he died

and I didn't write back and I just wanted to
make up for it in some way if I could. His name
was James Bowden.
I am sorry to have caused trouble.

John Ashenden

P.S. I forgot to say that I left a small memento
at his grave.

P.P.S. I shall be glad if you can pick up
my winnings and give the money to Oxfam.

'Well?'

'I suppose you want me to tell you how many spelling
mistakes he's made.'

'That would be something.'

'Looks all right to me. There's an apostrophe missing,
though.'

Morse's face brightened. 'Well done! Excellent! There *is*
the one spelling mistake, but you're *definitely* improving
. . . That's a clue, by the way . . . No? Never mind!'

'At least we're getting some of the loose ends tied up.'

'You mean we cross Ashenden off the suspect-list?'

'Don't know, sir. But we can cross Stratton off, I reckon.
He was in Didcot most of the afternoon. That's for sure.'

'So he couldn't have killed Kemp?'

'I don't see how.'

'Nor do I,' said Morse.

'Back to square one!'

'You know where we went wrong, don't you? It was that

phone call that sent me up the cul-de-sac. You see, we can't get away from the fact that if Kemp *was* in London, he could easily have caught an earlier train. That still puzzles me! He rang at twelve-thirty-five and there was a train at twelve-forty-five. Ten minutes to walk across from the phone to the platform!'

'You know, we haven't really checked that, have we? I mean the train could have been cancelled . . . or something.'

Morse said, 'I've checked. It's almost the only profitable thing I did yesterday.' He lit a cigarette and sat staring gloomily out of the window.

Lewis found himself looking at the back page of *The Oxford Times* which lay on the desk. Morse had not started the crossword yet ('Ichabod' this week), but just to the right of it Lewis noticed a brief item on a fatal accident at the Marston Ferry Road traffic lights: a young student who had been taking a crash course in EFL. *Crash* course! Huh!

'Don't tell me you've done one across, Lewis?'

'No. Just reading about this accident at the Marston Ferry lights. Bad junction, you know, that is. I think there ought to be a "filter right" as you go into the Banbury Road.'

'Fair point!'

Lewis read on aloud. ' "Georgette le . . . something . . . daughter of M. Georges le . . . something of Bordeaux . . ." ' But now his eyes had spotted the date. ' 'Sfunny! This accident was a week last Saturday, sir, at half-past five. That's exactly one week earlier than Mrs Downes.'

'Life's full of coincidences, I keep telling you that.'

'It's just that when you get two things happening like that, people say there's going to be three, don't they? That's what the wife always says.'

'Look, if a third accident'll please you, volunteer for the ambulance crew this morning. It's a fiver to a cracked piss-pot that some irresponsible sod—' Suddenly Morse stopped, the old tingle of high excitement thrilling strangely across his shoulders.

'Christ! What a fool you've been!' he murmured softly to himself.

'Sir?'

Morse rattled out his words: 'What's the name of Kemp's publisher? The one you rang to make sure he'd been there.'

' "Babington's". The fellow there said it was named after Macaulay' (Lewis smiled with distant memories) 'Thomas Babington Macaulay, sir – you know, the one who wrote the *Lays of Ancient Rome*. That's the one poem I—'

'Get on to the American Consulate! Quick, for Christ's sake! Find out where Stratton is – they'll know, I should think. *We've got to stop him leaving the country.*'

Morse's blue eyes gleamed triumphantly. 'I think I know, Lewis! I think I *know*.'

But Eddie Stratton had left the country the previous evening on a Pan Am jumbo bound for New York – together with his late wife Laura, the latter lying cold and stiff in a coffin in a special compartment just above the undercarriage.

Chapter Fifty-one

At day's end you came,
and like the evening sun,
left an afterglow
(*Basil Swift*, Collected Haiku)

Lewis was enjoying that Tuesday, the day on which Morse had suddenly spurted into a frenetic flurry of activity. Six extra personnel: Sergeant Dixon, three detective PCs, and two WPCs for the telephones. The administrative arrangement and supervision required for such teamwork was exactly the sort of skill in which Lewis excelled, and the hours passed quickly with the progressive gleaning of intelligence, the gradual build up of hard fact to bolster tentative theory – and always that almost insolent gratification that shone in Morse's eyes, for the latter appeared to have known (or so it seemed to Lewis) most of the details before the calls and corroboration had been made.

It was just after a quick, non-alcoholic lunch that Morse had sought to explain to Lewis the nature of his earlier error.

'I once did a crossword in which all of the clues were susceptible of two quite different solutions. A sort of *double-entendre* crossword, it was. Get on the wrong wavelength with one across, and everything fits except one single interlocking letter. Brilliant puzzle! – set by Ximenes in *The Observer*. That's what *I* did – got off on the wrong foot. And I did it again in this case, with Downes. You know what one across was? That bloody phone call! I'd assumed it was important, Lewis, and I was *right*. But right for the wrong reasons. When I first learned that the line was bad, I thought it possible – likely, even – that the caller *wasn't Kemp at all*. Then, because he said he'd missed the train – although there was still ten minutes to go – I thought he wasn't at Paddington at all: I thought Kemp was probably in Oxford. And it all fitted, didn't it? Except for that one single letter . . .

'But all the time, that poor line we kept hearing about *was* of crucial significance, but for a totally different reason! It was Kemp all right who made the call. But he wasn't at *Paddington*: he was still at his publisher's in London – Babington Press, Fine Arts Publications, South Kensington – and doubtless he referred to it, like anyone would, as Babington's. Oh, yes! That's where he was, and he did *exactly* what he said he'd do. He caught the next train and arrived in Oxford, dead on schedule.'

In the circumstances 'dead on schedule' hardly seemed to Lewis the happiest of phrases, but he knew that Morse was right about the call from Babington's. It had been he himself, Lewis, who had finally got on to the man there who was in the process of completing the proofs for the forthcoming seminal opus entitled *Pre-Conquest Craftsmanship in Southern Britain*, by Theodore S. Kemp, MA, DPhil; the man who had been closeted with Kemp that fateful morning, and who had confirmed that Kemp had not left the offices until about 12.30 p.m.

Sergeant Dixon (stripes newly stitched) was also enjoying himself, although initially he had serious doubts about whether he – or anyone else, for that matter – could successfully handle his assignment in the ridiculously short period of the three or four hours which Morse had asserted as 'ample'.

But he had done it.

He had not realised quite how many customers were attracted by the Car Hire firms of Oxford, especially American customers; and checking the lists had taken longer than he'd imagined. In this particular respect Morse (suggesting the likelihood of the Botley Road area) had got things quite wrong, for it was at the Hertz 'Rent-a-Car' offices at the top of the Woodstock Road where Dixon had finally spotted the name he was looking for with all the excitement of a young angler just hooking a heavyweight pike.

Tom Pritchard, the manager, went through the key points of the car-hire catechism to be faced by every client:

- Full name and home address?
- How many days' hire?
- Make of car preferred?
- Which dates?
- One driver only?
- Method of payment? (credit card preferred)
- Valid driving licence? (US licence OK)
- Telephone number of one referee?

After that, the manager went through the procedure adopted: a telephone call to the reference number cited; verification of credit card; verification of driving licence; verification of home address (the last three usually completed within ten minutes or so on the International Information Computer); preparation, presentation, and signing of the contract (including appropriate insurance clauses); then, paperwork now completed, the car brought round to the outer forecourt, with an assistant to give the client a quick run-over of the controls, and to hand over the keys. *Bon voyage*, cheerio, and Bob's your uncle.

By good fortune it had been the manager himself who had effected this particular transaction, and who remembered the occasion reasonably clearly. Well, it was only five days ago, wasn't it? The reference call to the hotel, The Randolph – that's what he'd remembered clearest of all, really: he'd looked up the telephone number and then been put through, on the extension given to him by his client, to the Deputy Manageress, who had promptly and effusively vouched for the *bona fides* of Rent-a-Car's prospective customer. Naturally, the manager had more details to offer: the car hired had been a red Cavalier, Registration H 106 XMT; it had been hired at 1.45 p.m. and returned at some time after the offices had closed at 6.30 p.m., with the keys pushed through the special letter-box, as requested. Mileage on the speedometer had been clocked as only 30.7. Probably, thought the manager, the car hadn't left Oxford at all?

Yet for all his own pleasure at tracing this evidence, Dixon could see little in his report which might have accounted for the look of extraordinary triumph he had seen on Morse's face when he reported in at 2.45 p.m.

Sergeant (with a 'g') Lewis's own, self-imposed task would, he suspected, be a fairly tricky undertaking. But even here the gods appeared to be smiling broadly on Morse's enterprise. The distinguished personage known as the Coroner's Serjeant (with a 'j') had been willing to sacrifice what he could of his time if the interests of Justice (capital 'J') were really being served. Yet it had still taken the pair of them more than two hours to assemble and photocopy the material that Morse had so confidently predicted would be found.

And was found.

But by far the most difficult and tiresome task had been that of the telephone girls, who had made scores and scores of transatlantic calls that Tuesday morning, afternoon, and early evening: calls made to one address that led to calls to another address; calls to one friend that led to another friend or colleague; from one police department to another; one State to other States; calls for one set of records that referred to another set of records that led . . . *ad* apparently *infinitum*.

'Couldn't it have waited?' Chief Superintendent Strange had asked, calling in briefly in mid-afternoon. 'Waited till tomorrow?'

But Morse was a man who could never abide the incomplete; could never abide the not-knowing-immediately. One clue unfinished in a *Listener* puzzle, and he would strain the capacity of every last brain-cell to bursting point until he had solved it. And equally so, as now, in a murder case. Tomorrow

was too far distanced for his mind to wait for the last piece
of evidence – a mind so ceaselessly tossing, as it had been
ever since Lewis – wonderful Lewis! – had mentioned that
seemingly irrelevant item in *The Oxford Times*.

Those names!

And it was Morse himself who had initiated the arrest
of Mr Edward Stratton as he stepped off his plane in New
York; Morse himself who had spoken with the aforementioned
Stratton for forty-six minutes, seven seconds – as measured by
the recently installed meter in the recently constituted Telephone Room at St Aldate's. But not even the penny-pinching
Strange could have complained overmuch about the price that
had been paid for the extraordinary information Morse had
gleaned.

It was Morse himself, too, who at 8.30 p.m. had called a halt
to everything. He had not returned any fulsome gratitude to
his staff for all the work they had put in during the day; but
he always found it difficult to express his deeper feelings. However, he *had* returned all but three of the tourists' passports to
the safe-keeping of the Manager at The Randolph – the latter
just a fraction irked that it now appeared to be his own responsibility to return these passports to whatever location the
departed tourists happened to find themselves in.

At 9 p.m. Morse, hitherto that day most remarkably
under-beered, made his way up through Cornmarket to the
Chapters Bar of The Randolph. There were many times in
Morse's life when he needed a drink in order to think. On
occasion though (such as now), he needed a drink because he
needed a *drink*. What's more, having left the Jaguar down in
the police car-park, he was *going* to drink.

And compulsively, happily, thirstily – he drank.

One and a half hours later, as he still sat on a high stool at
the bar, he looked down and saw the fingers of a beautifully
manicured hand against his left arm, and felt the ghost of a
touch of the softest breast against his shoulder.

'Can I buy you a drink, Inspector?' The voice was slightly

husky, slightly slurred, and more than slightly disturbing.

Morse had no need to look round. He said, 'Let me buy *you* one, Sheila.'

'No! I insist.' She took his arm, gently squeezing it against herself, then pressed her lips – so full, so dry! – against a cheek that had been hurriedly ill-shaven some fourteen hours earlier.

For the moment, Morse said nothing. The day that would soon be drawing to its close had been one of the most wonderful he had experienced: the theft, the murder, the link *between* the theft and the murder – yes, all now known. Well, almost known. And he'd solved it all himself. He'd needed help – yes! Help in crossing the 't's and barring the '7's and dotting the 'j's. Of course he had. Yet it had been his own vision, his own analysis, his own solution.

His.

'What are you doing here?' he asked.

'Annual Dance. Lit and Phil Society. Bloody booring!'

'You with a partner?'

'You don't come to these do's without a partner.'

'So?'

'So he kept trying to get a bit too intimate during the Veleta.'

'Veleta? God! That's what I used to dance . . .'

'We're none of us getting much younger.'

'And you didn't want – you didn't want that?'

'I wanted a drink. That's why I'm here.'

'And you told him . . .'

'. . . to bugger off.'

Morse looked at her now – perhaps properly for the first time. She wore a black dress reaching to just above her knees, suspended from her shoulders by straps no thicker than shoelaces; black stockings, encasing surprisingly slim legs, and very high-heeled red shoes that elevated her an inch or so above Morse as he stood up and offered her his stool. He smiled at her, with what seemed warmth and understanding in his eyes.

'You look happy,' she said.

But Morse knew, deep down, that he wasn't really happy at all. For the last hour his progressively alcoholised brain had reminded him of the consequences of justice (small 'j'): of bringing a criminal before the courts, ensuring that he was convicted for his sins (or was it his crimes?), and then getting him locked up for the rest of his life, perhaps, in a prison where he would never again go to the WC without someone observing such an embarrassingly private function, someone smelling him, someone humiliating him. (And, yes, it was a *him*.) Humiliating him in that little paddock of privacy just outside the back of the house where he would try so hard to keep all that remained of his dignity and self-esteem.

'I'm not happy,' said Morse.

'Why not?'

'G and T, is it?'

'How did you guess?'

'I'm a genius.'

'I'm quite good at some things myself.'

'Yes?'

'Do you want me to make you happy for tonight?' Her voice was suddenly more sober, more sharply etched – and yet more gentle, too.

Morse looked at her: looked at the piled-up hair above her wistful face; looked down at the full and observably bra-less bosom; looked down at the taut stretch of black stocking between the knee and the thigh of her crossed right leg. He was ready for her, and she seemed to sense it.

'I've got a wonderfully comfortable bed,' she whispered into his left ear.

'So have I!' said Morse, oddly defensive.

'But we wouldn't argue *too* much about that sort of thing, would we?' Sheila smiled and reached for her drink. 'Aren't you having another one?'

Morse shook his head: ' "It provokes the desire, but it takes away the performance." '

'Do you know, I've never met anyone before who's quoted that thing correctly.'

Perhaps she shouldn't have said it, for suddenly its implications stirred Morse to an irrational jealousy. But soon, as she linked her arm possessively through his, collected her coat from Cloaks, then steered him across towards the taxi-rank in St Giles', he knew that his lust for her had returned; and would remain.

'I ought to make it quite clear to you, ma'am,' he murmured in the taxi, 'that any knickers you may be wearing may well be taken down and used in evidence.'

For the first time in many days, Sheila Williams felt inordinately happy. And was to remain so – if truth is to be told – until the early dawn of the following day when Morse left her to walk slowly to his bachelor flat – only a short distance away up the Banbury Road – bareheaded in the beating rain which an hour since had obliquely streaked the windows of Sheila Williams's front bedroom.

Chapter Fifty-two

Rigid, the skeleton of habit alone upholds the human frame

(*Virginia Woolf*, Mrs Dalloway)

Morse and Lewis arrived at the Chesterton Hotel in Bath at 10.35 a.m. the following morning. Morse had insisted on travelling by what he called the 'scenic' route – via Cirencester – but, alas, the countryside was not appearing at its best: the golden days were gone, and the close-cropped fields where the sheep ever nibbled looked dank and uninviting under a sky-cover of grey cloud. Little conversation had passed between the two detectives until, an hour out of Oxford, Morse (looking, as Lewis saw him, still rather tired) had crossed those final 't's.

'All a bit unusual, though, isn't it, sir?'

'You think so?'

'I do. About as unusual as a . . .' But Lewis found himself unable to dredge up the appropriate simile.

' "Unusual as a fat postman",' supplied Morse.

'Really? Our postman looks as if he tips the scales at about twenty stone.'

Morse inhaled deeply upon yet another cigarette, half closed his eyes, shook his head, and relapsed into the silence that was customary for him on any journey.

Behind, in a marked police car, Sergeant Dixon sat beside his driver, a moderately excited PC Watson.

'Drives pretty quick, don't he?' ventured the latter.

' 'Bout the only thing he does do quick, I reckon,' said Dixon.

It seemed to Watson a cruel, unfair remark. And Dixon himself knew it was unfair, for a little while regretting having said it.

* * *

It had been forty-five minutes earlier when Dr Barbara Moule had parked her Fiesta at the Chesterton Hotel, finding John Ashenden waiting for her a little anxiously. The first part of her illustrated lecture was scheduled for 10–11 a.m., followed by a coffee break, and then further slides and questions from 11.30 to noon. Ashenden himself had carried the heavy projector to the Beau Nash Room at the rear of the hotel, where most of the tourists were now foregathering. The room was of a narrow, oblong shape, with the plastic chairs set out two on each side of the central gap in which, at the front, the projector was placed. Looking around, Ashenden noted yet again the readily observable fact that (doubtless like animals) tourists from very early on staked out their territories: find them sitting at one particular table for dinner and almost invariably, for breakfast next morning, you would find them sitting at the very same table; allocate them to particular seats in a coach on the first part of a journey, and as if by some proprietorial right the passengers would thereafter usually veer towards those selfsame seats. And the Beau Nash Room might just as well have been their luxury coach: twenty-three of them only for the minute, with Eddie Stratton now being held in custody by the New York Police, distanced by only a few yards, as it happened, from the mortal remains of his former wife; and with Sam and Vera Kronquist, one of the three married couples originally listed on the tour, still in their room on the second floor of the hotel – Sam watching a mid-morning cartoon on ITV, and Vera, fully dressed, lying back lazily against the pillows of their double bed, reading the previous February's issue of *Country Life*.

'You won't forget, Birdy' (Birdy?) 'that you're supposed to be having a headache, will you?'

His wife, not deigning to look up from the page, smiled to herself slightly. 'Nobody ain't coming in here, Sam – not if we leave that notice there on the door-narb.'

On the front row of the Beau Nash Room, only one of the chairs was occupied – Number 1, if the chairs had been numbered, from left to right, 1, 2, 3, 4 – the seat Janet Roscoe had invariably occupied on every single leg of the coach trip. Behind her the two seats were empty, a troublous reminder of where Eddie and Laura had sat side by side when the coach had first set off from Heathrow Airport . . . had first arrived at the eastern outskirts of Oxford.

At the back of the room, solitary now, and perfectly prepared to be wholly bored for the next hour (or was it two?) sat Mr Aldrich. His interest in Roman remains was minimal, and in any case his ears (incipient otosclerosis, his personal physician had diagnosed) seemed to be filling up with thicker and thicker wads of cotton-wool each day. He would have liked to exchange a few words with Cedric Downes at Oxford – surely a man suffering from the same kind of trouble? But the opportunity had not arisen, and Aldrich had taken no initiative in effecting any introduction.

Odd, really: Aldrich, with his increasing hearing problems, sitting right at the back of the class; and Mrs Roscoe, whose hearing was so extraordinarily acute, ever seated at the front . . .

So be it!

Three rows in front of Aldrich, on his left-hand side as he looked at the backs of their heads, sat Howard and Shirley Brown.

'Hope these slides are better than your sister's lot on Ottawa.'

'Hardly be wurse,' agreed Shirley, as Ashenden launched into a well-rehearsed eulogy of Dr Moule's incomparable pre-eminence in the field of Romano-British archaeology in Somerset – before walking to the entrance door at the rear, and turning off the lights.

At 10.50 a.m., Aldrich looked across at the two men who had entered quietly by the same door. Surprisingly, he was hearing Dr Moule quite loud and clear, for she had a firm and resonant voice. What's more, he thought, she was good; he *wanted* to hear what she was saying. And everybody thought she was good. Indeed, only three or four minutes into her talk, Shirley Brown had leaned across and whispered into Howard's ear: 'Better than Ottawa!'

Dr Moule had been momentarily conscious, albeit with her back turned, of some silent addition to the audience, though giving this no further thought. But after she had finished the first part of her lecture; after slightly nodding her head to the generous applause; after the lights had gone up again; after Ashenden had said (as every chairman since Creation had said) how much everyone had enjoyed the talk and how grateful everyone was that not only had the distinguished speaker fascinated each and every one of them but also had agreed to answer any questions which he was absolutely sure everyone in the room was aching to put to such a distinguished expert in the field . . . it was only then that Dr Moule was able to survey the two intruders. Sitting together on the back row: the one nearer the exit a burly-looking fellow, with a rather heavy, though kindly mien; and beside him a slimmer, clearly more authoritative man, with thinning hair and pale complexion. It was this second man who now asked the first, the last, question. And it was to this man that almost everyone now turned as the rather quiet, rather cultured, rather interesting, wholly English voice began to speak:

'I was a Classic in my youth, madam, and although I have always been deeply interested in the works of the Roman poets and the Roman historians I have never been able to summon up much enthusiasm for Roman architecture. In fact the contemplation of a Roman brick seems to leave me cold – quite cold. So I would dearly like to know why it is that you find yourself so enthusiastic . . .'

The question was balm and benison to Barbara's ears. But then the questioner had risen to his feet.

'. . . yes, it would be extremely interesting for all of us to learn your answer. But not – not for the moment, please!'

The man now walked down the central aisle and halted beside the projector, where he turned and spoke. Was it to her? Was it to her audience?

'I'm sorry to interrupt. But the people here know who I am – who we are. And I shall have to ask you, I'm afraid, to leave the next half hour to Lewis and to me.'

Dr Barbara Moule almost smiled. She'd picked up the literary allusion immediately, and enjoyed those few seconds during which the man's intensely blue eyes had held her own.

It was Ashenden who went upstairs to knock on the door of Room 46.

'But didn't Sam here explain? I have a headache.'

'I know. But it's the police, Mrs Kronquist.'

'It is?'

'And they want everybody to be there.'

'Oh my Gard!'

Chapter Fifty-three

And summed up so well that it came to far more
Than the Witnesses ever had said
          (*Lewis Carroll*, The Barrister's Dream)

The beautiful if bemused Dr Moule, invited to stay if she
so wished, took a seat in the front row. The man spoke, she
thought, more like a don than a detective.

'Let me outline the case, or rather the two cases, to you all.
First, a jewel was stolen from Mrs Laura Stratton's room in
The Randolph. At the same time – whether just before or just
after the theft – Mrs Stratton died. What is medically certain
is that she died of coronary thrombosis: there is no question of
any foul play, except of course if the heart attack was brought
on by the shock of finding someone in her room stealing the
jewel she had come all the way from America to hand over to
the Ashmolean Museum, or more specifically to Dr Theodore
Kemp on behalf of the Museum. I tried to find out – I may be
forgiven – who would benefit from the theft of the jewel, and
I learned from Mr Brown here' (heads swivelling) 'that Mrs
Stratton was always slightly mysterious – ambivalent, even –
about her own financial affairs. So I naturally had to bear in
mind the possibility that the jewel had not been stolen at all
by any outside party, but "caused to disappear", let us say,
by the Strattons themselves. It had been the property of Mrs
Stratton's first husband, and it was he who had expressed the
wish, as stated in his will, that it be returned to England to
find a permanent place in the Ashmolean Museum with its
counterpart, the Wolvercote Buckle. As a piece of treasure
of considerable historical importance, the Wolvercote Tongue
was of course beyond price. In itself, however, as an artefact
set with precious stones, it was, let us say, "priceable", and

it was insured by Mrs Stratton for half a million dollars. I am not yet wholly sure about the specific terms of the policy taken out, but it appears that in the eventuality of the jewel being stolen, either before or after her death, the insurance money is payable to her husband – and is not to be syphoned off into some trust fund or other. At any rate, that is what Eddie Stratton believed – believes, rather – for I learned most of these facts yesterday from Stratton himself, who is now back in America.' Morse paused a moment and looked slowly around his audience. 'I don't need, perhaps, to underline to you the temptation that faced Mr Stratton, himself a virtually penniless man, and a man who knew – for such seems to be the case – that his wife had run through almost all of the considerable money she had inherited from her first husband.'

Several faces looked pained and incredulous, but Janet Roscoe was the only person who did not restrain her disquietude:

'But that could nart *be*, Inspector! Eddie was out walk-ing—'

Morse held up his right hand, and spoke to her not un-gently:

'Please hear me out, Mrs Roscoe . . . It was easy to pin-point the period of time within which the theft must have occurred, and not too difficult – was it? – to find out where the great majority of you had been during the crucial forty-five minutes. Not *all* of you felt willing to be completely honest with me, but I don't wish to labour that point now. As I saw things – still see things – the thief had to be one of you here, one of the touring party, including your courier' (heads swivelling again) 'or one of the staff at The Randolph. But the latter possibility could be, and was, fairly quickly discounted. So you will be able to see where things are heading, ladies and gentlemen . . .

'The immediate effects of the theft were considerably lessened both by the death of Laura Stratton and on the very next day by the murder of Dr Kemp, the man to whom the

Tongue was due to be handed over that day at an official little ceremony at the Ashmolean. Now one of the jobs of the police force, and especially the CID, is to try to establish a *pattern* in crime, if this is possible, and in this instance both Sergeant Lewis and myself found it difficult not to believe there was some *link* between the two events. They may of course have been quite coincidental; but already there *was* a link, was there not? Dr Kemp himself! – the man who had one day been deprived of a jewel which he himself had traced to an American collector, a jewel for which he had been negotiating, a jewel that had been found in the waters below the bridge at Wolvercote in 1873, a jewel which once united with its mate would doubtless be the subject of some considerable historical interest, and bring some short-term celebrity, possibly some long-term preferment, to himself – to Kemp. Indeed a photograph of the re-united Buckle and Tongue was going to be used on the cover of his forthcoming book. And then, on the very next day, Kemp is murdered. Interesting, is it not? Did, I asked myself, did the *same* person commit both the theft and the murder? It seemed to me more and more likely. So perhaps I needed just the one criminal, not two; but I needed a reason as well. So my thinking went a little further in that direction – the correct direction. If the criminal was the same in each case, was not the *motive* likely to have been the same? In both crimes, the person who had suffered by far the most had been the same man, Kemp. In the first, he had been robbed of something on which he had set his heart; in the second he was robbed of his life. Why? – that is what I asked myself. Or rather that is *not*, in the first instance, what I asked myself, because I was driven to the view – incorrectly – that there could be no link between the two crimes.

'So let us come to Kemp himself. It is a commonplace in murder investigations that more may often be learned about the murderer from the *victim* than from any other source. Now what did we know of the victim, Dr Kemp? He was a Keeper of Antiquities at the Ashmolean, a man somewhat flamboyant in dress and manner, not only a ladies' man but one of the most dedicated womanisers in the University; a man who patently, almost on first sight, appeared self-centred and self-seeking. Yet life had not gone all his way: far from it. The University had recognised Kemp for what he was: his promotion was slow; a full fellowship was withheld; no family; a very modest two-bedroomed flat in North Oxford; and, above all, a great personal tragedy. Two years ago he was involved in a dreadful crash on the western Ring Road in which his wife, who was sitting beside him in the passenger seat, received such serious injuries to the lower half of the body that for the rest of her life – a life which ended tragically last week – she was confined to a wheel-chair. But that was only the half of it. The driver of the other car was killed instantaneously – a Mrs Mayo from California who was in England doing some research project on the novels of Anthony Trollope. The settlements of the dead woman's Accidental Death Benefit, and of the policy covering the "passenger-liability" responsibility of the surviving driver – a driver by the way almost completely unscathed – were finally settled. But the legal tangle surrounding "culpability" was never really unravelled: no eye-witnesses, contradictory evidence on possible mechanical faults, discrepancies about the time recorded for the breathalyser test – these factors resulted in Kemp getting away comparatively lightly, being banned from driving for three years only, with what must have seemed to many the derisory fine of only four hundred pounds. What had really confused everyone was the fact that Kemp always carried a hip-flask of brandy in the car's glove compartment, and that he had given his wife – trapped by the legs beside him – several sips from this flask before the ambulance arrived; and had even drunk from it himself! Everyone who subsequently learned of this action condemned it as utterly stupid and irresponsible, but perhaps such criticism may be tempered by the fact that the man was in a deep state of shock. At least that was what he said in his own defence.

'But let me revert to the crimes committed last week.

The crucial happening, whichever way we look at things, was the telephone call made by Kemp. I formed several theories about that call – all wrong, and I will say nothing about them. Kemp had reported to the group that he would be arriving in Oxford at 3 p.m. – and the simple truth is that he *did* arrive in Oxford at 3 p.m. And somebody knew about that telephone call, *and met Kemp at the railway station*, doubtless informing the taxi-driver who had been hired that he was no longer required.'

Janet Roscoe half opened her mouth as if she were contemplating breaking the ensuing silence. But it was Morse who did so, as he continued:

'A taxi, you see, would have been easily traceable, so a different plan was adopted. Someone went to a car-rental firm in North Oxford in the early afternoon and hired a Vauxhall Cavalier. There was only one real difficulty: after vehicle-licence, credit-worthiness, and so on, were formally checked, the firm required some reference to establish the *bona fides* of the client. But this difficulty was quickly and neatly overcome: the man who hired the car – a *man*, yes! – gave the telephone number of The Randolph, and as the firm's representative was dialling the number he casually mentioned that the Deputy Manageress of The Randolph could be immediately contacted on a certain extension. The call was put through, confirmation obtained, and the car handed over. You will appreciate of course that an *accomplice* was essential at this juncture, but not just someone prepared to perform a casual favour. No! Rather someone who was prepared to be an accomplice to *murder*. Now, I believe it to be true that before this tour – with one exception – none of you had known each other. That exception was Mr Stratton and Mr Brown, who had met in the Armed Forces. But at the time the car was being hired, Mr Stratton was on his way to Didcot Railway Centre – of that fact there can be no doubt whatsoever. And Mr Howard Brown' (Morse hesitated) 'has given a full and fairly satisfactory account of his own whereabouts that afternoon, an account which has since been substantially corroborated.' Lewis's eyebrows shot up involuntarily, but he trusted that no one had noticed.

'There were one or two other absentees that afternoon, weren't there? Mr Ashenden for one.' The courier was staring hard at the patch of carpet between his feet. 'But he was up in Summertown for the whole of that afternoon with friends – as we've now checked.' (Lewis managed to keep his eyebrows still.) 'And then, of course, there's Mr Aldrich.' Heads were swivelling completely round this time – to the back row where sat Phil Aldrich, nodding his head in gentle agreement, a wry smile on his long, lugubrious face. 'But Mr Aldrich can't possibly have been our guilty party either, can he? He went up to London that day, and in fact was travelling on the same train as Stratton when the two of them arrived back in Oxford. Mr Aldrich himself claims, and I am fully prepared to believe him, that he did not see Mr Stratton on the train. *But Mr Stratton saw Mr Aldrich*; and so in an odd sort of way, even if we had no proof of Stratton being in Didcot, the pair of them quite unwittingly perhaps had given each other an utterly unshakeable alibi. And in addition we now *know* that Stratton was in Didcot most of that afternoon. You see, ladies and gentlemen, whatever happens in life, no person can ever be in two places at the same time, for the laws of the Universe forbid it. And the person perfecting his plans in Oxford, the person who had taken possession of the red Cavalier, that person had plenty to do, and precious little time in which to do it – to do it *in Oxford*. There is, perhaps, a brief additional point to be made. It occurred to me that if Stratton and Brown had known each other, so might their wives, perhaps. But one of these wives was already dead; and it was a *man*,' said Morse slowly, 'and not a woman, who hired the car that afternoon.

'Are we running out of suspects, then? Almost, I agree. Your tour started with only three married couples, did it not? And already we have eliminated two of these: the Strattons and the Browns.' In the tense silence which followed this remark, all eyes now turned upon the couple who had been fetched from their bedroom; the couple who had decided that any further diet of delightful architecture would have amounted to a sort of cultural force-feeding. But the pivoting glances which now fell full upon Sam and Vera Kronquist almost immediately reverted to Chief Inspector Morse as the latter rounded off his background summary.

'But Mr Kronquist, as several of you already know, was assisting Mrs Sheila Williams during most of the afternoon in question with the temperamental kaleidoscope allocated to her for her illustrated talk on "Alice". Now Mr Kronquist may be a very clever man, but *he* is not permitted, either, to suspend the physical laws of the Universe. And you do see, don't you, that Mrs Williams, too, must now be crossed off our list of suspects? And finally we shall cross the name of Cedric Downes off that same list, and for exactly the same reason. If anyone from the group here met Kemp at 3 p.m., it wasn't Downes, because nine or ten of you here will willingly testify to the incontrovertible fact that he was talking to you from that time onwards. Did I say running out of likely suspects? And yet, ladies and gentlemen, someone *did* meet Kemp at the railway station that afternoon.

'One of *you* did!'

Chapter Fifty-four

Either what woman having ten pieces of silver, if she
lose one piece, doth not light a candle, and sweep the
house, and seek diligently till she find it?

(*St Luke*, ch. 15, v. 8)

Throughout the morning on which Morse was addressing
his audience in Bath, and stripping away the deceptions
and the half-truths which hitherto had veiled the naked
truth of the case, there was much activity at the Trout
Inn, a fine riverside hostelry set between the weir and the
Godstow Lock in the village of Wolvercote, only a couple
of miles out on the western side of North Oxford. During
the summer months hordes of visitors regularly congregate
there to eat and drink at their leisure on the paved terrace
between the mellow sandstone walls of the inn itself and the
river's edge, where many sit on the low stone parapet and
look below them through the clear, greenish water at the
mottled dark-brown and silvery backs of the carp that rise
to the surface to snap up the crisps and the crusts thrown
down to them.

But that Wednesday morning, the few customers who
had called for an early drink were much more interested in
other underwater creatures: four of them, with sleek black
skins and disproportionately large webbed feet, circling up
and down, and round and round, and sweeping the depths
diligently below the weir, streams of bubbles intermittently
rising to the surface from the cylinders strapped to their
backs. Each of the four was an experienced police frogman,
and each of them knew exactly what he was looking for –
knew indeed the exact dimensions of the object and the
positioning of the three great ruby eyes once set into it.

Thus far they had found nothing, and above the bed of the river their searchings were stirring up a cloudy precipitate of mud as the white waters gushed across the weir. Yet hopes were reasonably high. The frogmen had been briefed – and with such a degree of certitude! – as to the exact point on the hump-backed bridge whence the Tongue had been thrown. So they were able to plot their operation with some precision as first they swam slowly abreast across the river, then turning and recrossing the current, ever feeling, ever searching, as they worked their way slowly downstream into the more placid reaches of the water.

But nothing.

After its discovery in 1873, the Tongue had found its way into the hands of a treasure-hunter, who had kept quiet about it and sold it to a London dealer, who in turn had sold it to an American collector, who had lent it to an exhibition in Philadelphia in 1922 – which latter appearance had provided the clues, sixty-five years later, for a detective-story-like investigation on the part of Theodore Kemp of the Ashmolean Museum – a man who now lay dead in the mortuary at the Radcliffe Infirmary. But the man who had agreed to tell Chief Inspector Morse precisely where he had stood, and with what impetus thrown the Tongue back into the river at Wolvercote – this man was seated, very much alive, in the vastly confusing complex of Kennedy Airport. Beside him sat a man of such immense proportions that Eddie Stratton wondered how he could ever fit into the seat that had been booked for him on the flight to Heathrow, scheduled to leave in forty minutes' time. He wondered, too, whether the man would be willing to unlock the handcuff that chafed away at his right wrist. For he, Stratton, was contemplating no high-jinks or high-jacks in mid-Atlantic flight.

Chapter Fifty-five

In great affairs we ought to apply ourselves less to
creating chances than to profiting from those that offer
(*La Rochefoucauld*, Maxims)

It was way past coffee-break time in the Chesterton Hotel,
but no one seemed to notice.

'Kemp was met at the railway station,' continued Morse.
'He was there told something – I'm guessing – which
persuaded him to accompany the driver to his own flat
in Water Eaton Road. Perhaps he was told that his wife
was suddenly taken very ill; was dead, even. Perhaps some
less dramatic disclosure sufficed. There, at Kemp's home –
again I'm guessing – a quarrel took place in which Kemp
was struck over the head and sent stumbling in his own
living room, where his right temple crashed against the
kerb of the fire-place – and where he died. I'm amazed
how difficult it is occasionally for a murderer to despatch his
victim: in the Thames Valley we once had a case where no
fewer than twenty-three vicious stab-wounds were insufficient
to complete the sorry business. But at the same time it is
occasionally so terribly easy to rob a fellow human being of
his life: a slight nudge, let us say, from a car-bumper, and a
cyclist is knocked down and hits his head against the road –
and in a second or two a life has gone. In this case, Kemp
had a thin skull, and his murder was no problem. But the
body? Oh yes, the body was a problem all right!

'Now, if the murder took place at about three forty-five
p.m., as I believe it did, why do we find Kemp's wife,
Marion, doing nothing about it? For we can be absolutely
sure she was there, the whole time. Maybe the reason for this
was that she was vindictively happy *not* to do anything, and

it is the opinion of my sergeant here that she probably hated her husband almost as intensely as the murderer himself did. But Marion Kemp could not, in my view, have killed her husband, and quite certainly she could hardly have moved the body a single centimetre from where it lay. On the other hand, Kemp was a slimly built, light-boned man, and it *would* have been possible for most people here, let us say – anyone reasonably mobile, reasonably fit – to have moved that body at least some small distance. *Even for a woman*, if she were sturdily or athletically built.'

The innuendo in this remark proved too much for the petite figure in the front row, who during the last few words was showing signs of unmistakable distress.

'Inspector! Chief Inspector, rather! For you even to *suggest* that I, for one, could have shifted a bardy, why, that is utterly absurd! And if you think that I am going to sit here—'

Morse smiled wanly at the lady as she sat in the front row, a lady turning the scales at not much more, surely, than around five stone.

'I should never accuse *you* of that, Mrs Roscoe. Please believe me!'

Mollified, it seemed, Janet sat back primly and slimly in her seat, as John Ashenden, seated immediately opposite (beside Dr Moule), looked across at her with a troublous, darkling gaze. And Morse continued:

'In the concreted yard at the back of the flats at Water Eaton Road stood a light-weight, rubber-wheeled, aluminium wheelbarrow which one of the maintenance men had been using earlier that day. It was into this barrow, under cover of the night, at about seven p.m., that the body was put, covered with plastic sacks, themselves in turn covered with a fair sprinkling of autumn leaves, before being wheeled across the low wooden bridge there, across a well-worn path through the field, and across to the swiftly flowing current of the River Cherwell, where unceremoniously the body was tipped into the water. And as I say' (Morse looked slowly around his audience) 'it was one of your own group who performed this grisly task – a *man* – a man who would have felt little squeamishness about first stripping the dead man of his clothes – for there had been much blood, much messy, sticky blood which almost inevitably would have transferred itself to the clothes of the man disposing of the body; a man who for the last ten years of his working life had been inured to such gruesome matters, as a moderately competent "mortician" in America.'

There was a sudden communal intake of breath from the audience, and clearly no need for Morse to spell things out further. But he did:

'Yes! *Mr Eddie Stratton.*'

'*No*, sir!'

The voice from the back of the room caused every head to crane round, although the mild tones of Phil Aldrich were known so well by now to everyone.

'You have my testimony, sir, and you have Eddie's too that we—'

'Mr Aldrich! I do accept your point, and I shall explain. Let us return to Stratton briefly. He had become a small-time mortician, specialising in the beautification – please allow the word! – of corpses that had died an ugly or disfiguring death. And a bachelor. Until two and a bit years ago, that is, when he met and married the widow of a middle-bracket philanthropist. The marriage was mostly an accommodation of interests; a convenience. Eddie did the shopping, tended the garden, mended the taps and the fuses, and serviced the family car. Laura – Laura Stratton as she now was – was reasonably content with the new arrangements: she was less anxious about burglars, she was chauffeured to her twice-weekly consultations with the latest chiropodist, she forgot most of her worries about the upkeep of the household, and she still found herself able to indulge the twin passions of her life, smoking cigarettes and playing contract bridge – simultaneously, wherever possible.

'But there had been disappointed expectations, on both sides, when the estate of the late philanthropist had finally,

well almost finally, been settled, with the lawyers still growing
fat on the pickings. *Objets d'art* there were aplenty, but most
of them were held in trust for some collection or gallery. And
so the prospects of a happily-monied marriage of convenience
were ever diminishing, until an idea occurred to the pair of
them – certainly to Laura Stratton. The Wolvercote Tongue
was insured for half a million dollars, and one of the safest
ways of transferring it over to England had got to be on the
person of the traveller: few people would entrust such an item
to letter-post or parcel-post or courier-service; and even if they
did, the insurance-risk premium would be prohibitive. So the
Strattons took it themselves – *and then made sure it was stolen.*
That was their plan. The reason the plan went so sadly askew
was the not-wholly-unexpected but extremely untimely death
of Laura Stratton herself, though whether this was occasioned
by her own complicity, excitement, remorse – whatever! – we
shall never really know. The plan – a simple one – was for the
Tongue to be stolen immediately after Laura had installed
herself in her room at The Randolph. She would be sure to
make such a song and dance about her aching feet that she
would get right to the head of the queue for the room-key –
well, apart from Mrs Roscoe, naturally!'

For the first time during Morse's analysis, his audience
was seen reluctantly to smile as it acknowledged the primacy
of the perpetually belly-aching little lady from California.

'Once she had the key, and whilst her husband signed the
formalities, she was to go up to her room, put the handbag
containing the Tongue – and money, pearls, and so on – on
a ledge as near as possible to a door which was going to be left
deliberately ajar. Meanwhile Eddie Stratton was to enthuse
about a quick stroll around the centre of Oxford before it got
too dark, and an invitation to accompany him was accepted by
Mrs Brown, a woman with whom he'd become friendly on the
tour, and who probably felt a little flattered to be asked. All he
had to do then was to make it known that he had promised
to leave Laura alone so that she could have a rest in peace,
to make an excuse about paying a brief visit to the Gents, to

go up to his room – probably via the guest-lift – to stick his hand inside the room and grab the handbag, to take out the jewel before dumping the handbag, and then . . .'

Morse stopped, but only briefly. 'Not a *terribly* convincing hypothesis, are you thinking? I tend to agree with you. Everyone would be trying to use the lift at that point – probably queuing for it. And it would be impossible to use the main staircase, because as you'll recall it is immediately next to Reception there. And where does he ditch the emptied handbag? For it was never found. However quickly he may have acted, the actual taking of the handbag must have taken more *time* than seems to have been available – since Eddie Stratton and Shirley Brown were seen walking out of The Randolph almost immediately, if the evidence of at least two of you here is to be believed, the evidence of Mr Brown and Mrs Roscoe. So! So I suggest that something a little more sophisticated may have taken place. Let me tell you what I think. The plan, whatever it was, must have been discussed well in advance of the tour's arrival in Oxford, but a few last-minute recapitulations and reassurances would have been almost inevitable. Perhaps you've noticed that it's often difficult, on a bus or a train, to assess how loudly you are talking? Yes? Too loudly? And where were the Strattons sitting?' Morse pointed dramatically (as he hoped) to the two empty seats just behind Janet Roscoe. 'If they *did* discuss things on the coach, who were the likeliest people to eavesdrop? I'm told, for example, that you, Mrs Roscoe, have quite exceptionally acute hearing for a woman of—'

This time the little lady stood up, if thereby adding only some seven or eight inches in stature to her seated posture. 'Such innuendo, Chief Inspector, is wholly without foundation, and I wish you to know that one of my friends back home is the fiercest libel lawyer—'

But, again, and with the same patient smile, Morse bade the excitable lady to hold her peace, and bide her time.

'You were not the only one in earshot, Mrs Roscoe. In the seats immediately across the gangway from the Strattons sat

Mr and Mrs Brown . . . and in front of them, in the courier's
seat . . .' Eyes, including Morse's, now turned as if by some
magnetic attraction towards John Ashenden, who sat, his eyes
unblinking, in the front row of the seats.

'You see,' resumed Morse, 'Stratton never went up at all
to his room in The Randolph – not at that point. But someone
did, someone *here* did – someone who had overheard enough
of the original plan; someone who had sensed a wonderfully
providential opportunity for himself, or for herself, and who
had capitalised upon that opportunity. How? By volunteering
to steal the Wolvercote Tongue, in order that the Strattons
could immediately claim – claim without any suspicion
attaching to them – the tempting prize of the insurance
money!

'Let me put the situation to you simply. The person
who had eavesdropped on the proposed intrigue *performed
Stratton's job for him*; stole the jewel; slid thereafter into
the background; and disposed at leisure of the superfluous
pearls and the petty cash. And *that*, ladies and gentlemen, is
no wild hypothesis on my part; it is the truth. Stratton was
presented with an offer he could hardly refuse. At the time,
though, he was not aware – could never have been aware – of
the extraordinary service he would have to render as the *quid
pro quo* of the agreement. But he was to learn about it soon
enough. In fact, he was to learn of it the very next day, and
he duly performed his cwn half of the bargain with a strangely
honourable integrity. As it happens' – Morse consulted his
watch ostentatiously – 'he is very shortly due to take off from
Kennedy Airport to fly back to Heathrow, and he has already
made a substantial confession about his part in the strange
circumstances surrounding the Wolvercote Tongue and Dr
Theodore Kemp. But – please believe me! – it was not *he*
who actually stole the one . . . or murdered the other. Yet
I am looking forward to meeting Mr Stratton again, because
thus far he has refused point-blank to tell me who the
murderer was . . .'

* * *

At the Trout Inn, the frogmen were now seated before a blazing log-fire in the bar. The landlady, an attractive, buxom woman in her mid-forties, had brought them each a hugely piled plate of chilli-con-carne, with a pint of appropriately chilly lager to wash it all down. None of the four had met Morse yet, and didn't know how strongly he would have disapproved of their beverage. But they knew they were working for him, and each of them was hoping that if the jewel were found it would be *he* who would have found it. Some acknowledgement, some gratitude from the man – that was an end devoutly to be wished.

But still nothing. Nothing, that is, except a child's tricycle, an antique dart-board, and what looked like part of a fixture from a household vacuum-cleaner.

Frequently, when Eddie Stratton had flown in the past, his heart had missed a beat or two whenever he heard the 'ding-dong' tones on the aircraft intercom. Indeed, he had sometimes felt that the use of such a system, except in times of dire emergency, should be prohibited by international law. No one Eddie had ever met wished to be acquainted with the pilot and his potential problems. So why not keep an eye on the steering, and forgo any announcement to interested passengers that there was now, say, a splendid view of the Atlantic Ocean down below? *No* announcements, *no* news – that's what passengers wanted. But now, ten minutes before take-off, Stratton felt most curiously relaxed about the possibility of an aerial disaster. Would such an eventuality be a welcome release? No, not really. He would speak to Morse again, yes. But Morse would never learn – at least not from *him* – the name of the person who had murdered Theodore Kemp.

Chapter Fifty-six

And as the smart ship grew
In stature, grace, and hue,
In shadowy silent distance grew the Iceberg too
(*Thomas Hardy*, 'The Convergence of the Twain')

Sergeant Lewis had been gratified by the brief mention of himself in despatches, and he was in any case revising (upwards) his earlier judgement on Morse's rhetorical skills. All right, he (Lewis) now knew the whole picture, but it was good to have the details rehearsed again in front of a different audience. He had never been near the top of the class in any of the subjects he had been taught at school, yet he'd often thought he wouldn't have been all that far below the high-fliers if only some of the teachers had been willing to go over a point a second time; or even a third time. For once Lewis *did* get hold of a thing firmly – suggestion, idea, hypothesis, theory – he could frequently see its significance, its implications, almost as well as anyone; even Morse. It was just that the initial stages were always a bit of a problem; whereas for Morse – well, *he* seemed to jump to a few answers here and there before he'd even read the question-paper. That was one of the big things he admired most about the man, that ability to leap ahead of the field almost from the starting-stalls – albeit occasionally finding himself on completely the wrong race-course. But it wasn't the *biggest* thing. The biggest thing was that Morse appeared to believe that Lewis was not only usually up with him in the race, galloping happily abreast, but that Lewis could sometimes spot something in the stretches ahead that Morse himself had missed, as the pair of them raced on towards the winning-post. It was ridiculous, of course. But Lewis ever found himself trusting that such a false impression might long be perpetuated.

The man's diction is slightly pedantic, thought Dr Moule, but he actually speaks in *sentences* – unusual even for a preacher, let alone a policeman. And – heaven be praised! – he doesn't stand there with his hands jingling the coins in his pockets. He reminded her of her Latin master, on whom she'd had an extra-special crush, and she wondered whether she wouldn't have had the same for this man. He looked overweight around the midriff, though nowhere else, and she thought perhaps that he drank too much. He looked weary, as if he had been up most of the night conducting his investigations. He looked the sort of man she would like to be going with, and she wondered whether he'd ever been unfaithful to his wife . . . But surely no wife would allow her husband abroad in such an off-white apology for a laundered shirt? Dr Moule smiled quietly, and trusted she was looking her attractive best; and tried to stop herself hoping he had holes in his socks.

As the TWA Tristar turned slowly at the head of the runway, Lieutenant Al Morrow tried to pull out a final inch or two from the safety-belt that clamped his enormous girth to the seat. At the same time he unfastened the handcuffs which united him to his fellow-passenger. Morrow had a good deal of experience of the criminal classes, but this particular villain was hardly one of the potentially-dangerous-on-no-account-to-be-accosted variety. OK. He'd accompany him to the loo. But for the rest, the fellow would be fine, imprisoned in his window-seat between the fuselage on the one side and the mighty mountain of flesh that was Morrow on the other. The lieutenant opened his reading matter, *The Finer Arts of Fly-Fishing*, and, as the great jet raced and roared its engines, glanced quickly once again at the man who sat beside him: the features immobile, yet in no way relaxed; the eyes staring, yet perhaps not seeing at all; the forehead

unfurrowed, yet tense, it seemed, as though his mind was
dwelling on unhappy memories.

'You want sump'n to read, pal?'

Stratton shook his head.

It was as the lieutenant had suspected . . .

. . . It had been extraordinary how the two things had
synchronised so perfectly at Oxford: a bit like the iceberg
growing as the SS *Titanic* drew ever closer.

It was Laura's fault, of course! The woman could never
keep her voice down – a voice that was usually double the
decibels needed in normal conversation; and in whispered,
conspiratorial communication, just about as loud as normal
speech. And particularly on any form of public transport
the dotty but endearing old biddy could never seem to gauge
the further limits of her penetrating tones. Constantly, had
she been fitted with a volume-control attachment somewhere
about her person, Stratton would have turned it down.
Frequently, as it was, he had inquired of his fairly recently
acquired bride whether she was anxious for *the whole world*
to know her business! Well, perhaps that was a bit of an
exaggeration. Yet someone *had* overheard their plan; or heard
enough of their plan to make a firm four out of two and two.
And the glory of the thing had been that this someone had
been just as anxious – more anxious! – to spirit away the
Wolvercote Tongue as Laura was. As *he* was.

It had been the night at the University Arms in Cambridge
that Plan B had been agreed. Such a *simple* plan, that 'plan'
seemed far too grand an appellation: audibly (not a difficult
task!) Laura would complain about her feet on the journey
to Oxford; quite naturally (for her regular seat was on the
row second to the front) she would be first in the queue at
Reception in The Randolph – even Mrs Roscoe probably
conceding her customary prerogative; she would leave her
handbag immediately inside the allocated, unlocked bedroom;
she would take a bath; she would leave the thief the childishly
simple assignment of putting a hand inside the door. His own

rôle? Principally to keep as far away from his room as possible. The police (no way in which they could not be involved) would be primarily interested in who was going to profit from any insurance, and he, Stratton himself, would have to vie with Caesar's wife in immunity from any suspicion. As it happened, he'd already prepared the ground for that by making something of a fuss of Shirley Brown; not at all difficult, because he *wanted* to make a fuss of Shirley Brown; and that lady had been flattered to follow his suggestion for a twilit stroll round Radcliffe Square – a stroll on which they'd seen their courier, Ashenden, and in turn been seen by the all-seeing Roscoe, a woman whom no one could abide, yet one whom everyone believed. Clever little touch, that! The problem that had worried Stratton about the earlier (now discarded) Plan A was where on earth he was going to dispose of the handbag. But need he have worried? Would it really have mattered if the bag had been found fairly soon in the nearest litter-bin? No, it wouldn't! The only thing that had to be disposed of was the jewel itself – not only because the insurance money must not be put in jeopardy, but also because someone else desired *Kemp* to be deprived of it. Desired it desperately.

Then Laura had to put her foot in it! Put her goddamned, aching, corny, foot right in it.

She'd gone and died.

Not that he (Stratton) had been involved in any way in that first death. No! But as far as the second death was concerned? Ah! That was a different matter. And whatever happened he would never tell the whole truth about that to anyone – not voluntarily – not even to that smart-alec copper, Chief Inspector Morse himself.

Yet he respected the man; couldn't help it, remembering the initial broadside on the transatlantic telephone, when Morse had immediately breached the outer fortifications.

'No, Inspector. There's nothing I can tell you about Kemp's death. Nothing.'

'I was more interested in the jewel, sir.'

'Ah! "The jewel that was ours", as Laura used to think of it.'

'Come off it!'

'Pardon, Inspector?'

'I said "Bullshit!" '

Chapter Fifty-seven

What's in a name? that which we call a rose
By any other name would smell as sweet
(*Shakespeare*, Romeo and Juliet)

Although it had been a rather chilly morning, several of the people seated in the Beau Nash Room wished that the central heating could be turned down a few degrees. Howard Brown wiped his high forehead with a large handkerchief, and John Ashenden brushed the sleeve of his sports jacket across his upper lip where he felt the sweat-prickles forming. Morse himself drew a forefinger half a circuit round the neck of his slightly over-tight collar, and continued:

'I know who stole the Wolvercote Tongue. I know where it is, and I am quite sure that it will soon be recovered. I also know which one of you – which one of you here – killed Dr Kemp.' The hush was now so intense that Lewis found himself wondering whether his involuntary swallow had been audible, as for thirty seconds or so Morse stood silent and still, only his eyes moving left and right, and left and right again across the central aisle. No one in the audience moved either. No one dared even to cough.

'I'd hoped that the guilty person would have come forward by now. I say that because you may have read of several cases in England recently where the police have been criticised – in some cases rightly so – for depending for a prosecution on the uncorroborated confessions of accused persons, confessions which, certainly in one or two cases, might have been extorted in less than safe and satisfactory circumstances. How much better it would have been, then, if Kemp's murderer came forward – *comes* forward – in the presence of his friends and fellow tourists . . .' Morse again

looked around the room; but if there were any one person
upon whom those blue eyes focused, it was not apparent to
the others seated there.

'No?'

'No?' queried Morse again.

'So be it! There is little more to tell you. The biggest
single clue in this case I passed over almost without reading it,
until my sergeant jogged my memory. It was contained in a
police report of the road accident in which Kemp crippled his
wife – and also killed the driver of the other car, a Mrs P. J.
Mayo, a thirty-five-year-old woman from California: Mrs
Philippa J. Mayo, whose husband had earlier been killed in a
gunnery accident on the USS *South Dakota*. That would have
been bad enough for Philippa Mayo's parents-in-law, would it
not? But at least the man had been serving his country; at least
he'd died for some *cause* – whether that cause was justified
or not. What of Philippa's own parents, though, when *she*
is killed? Their daughter. Their only daughter. Their only
child. A child killed needlessly, pointlessly, tragically, and
wholly *reprehensibly* – by a man who must have appeared to
those parents, from the reports they received, as a drunken,
selfish, wicked swine who deserved to be as dead as their
daughter . . . Above all, I suspect, the parents were appalled
by what seemed to them the quite extraordinary leniency of
the magistrates at the criminal hearing, and they came over to
England, father and mother, to lay the ghost that had haunted
them night and day for the past two years. But why only then,
you may ask? I learn that the wife had been suffering from
cervical cancer for the previous three years; had just endured
her second massive session of chemotherapy; had decided that
she could never face a third; had only at the outside six more
months to live. So the pair came over to view the killer of
their daughter, and if they deemed him worthy of death,
they vowed that he would die. They met him the once only,
on the night before he died: a cocky philanderer, as they saw
him; a cruel, conceited specimen; and now a man who, like
Philippa Mayo's mother, had so very little time to live. The

link between the two crimes, and the motivation for them, was
clear to me at last, and the link and the motivation merged into
a single whole: the implacable hatred of a man and his wife for
the person who had killed their daughter.

'For Theodore Kemp.

'I keep mentioning "man *and* wife" because I finally persuaded myself that no one single person on his own could have
carried through the murder of Kemp. It could have been
any two people, though, and we had to try to find out as
much about all of you as we could. When you signed in at
The Randolph, you all filled in a form which asked over-
seas visitors to complete full details of nationality, passport
number, place passport issued, permanent home address, and
so on. But, as you know, I also had to ask Mr Ashenden
to collect your passports, and from these, my sergeant here'
(the blood rose slowly in Lewis's cheeks) 'checked all the
details you had given and found that two of you lived in
the same block of retirement flats. But these two were not
registered as man and wife; rather they had decided to play
the waiting game, to take advantage of anything that might
crop up, to "optimise the opportunity", as I believe you say
in America. And that opportunity materialised – in the person
of Eddie Stratton.

'Stratton had been out at Didcot on the afternoon Kemp
died, and what is more he could prove his presence there
conclusively – with photographic evidence. And I – we –
were led to believe that his quite innocent statements about
his train journey back to Oxford were equally true. *But they
weren't.* Cleverly, unwittingly, as it seemed, he gave a wholly
unimpeachable alibi to a man he saw in the carriage ahead of
him – a man to whom he owed a very great deal. But he did
not see that man, ladies and gentlemen! Because that man
was *not* on the Didcot–Oxford train that afternoon. He was
in Oxford . . . murdering Dr Kemp.'

The last few words sank into the noiselessness of the
stifling room. And then Morse suddenly smiled a little, and
spoke quietly:

'Can you hear me all right at the back, Mr Aldrich?'

'Pardon, sir?'

'Don't you think it would be far better if you . . .' Morse held out the palm of his right hand and seemed to usher some invisible spirit towards the front row of the seats.

Aldrich, looking much perplexed, rose from his seat and walked forward hesitantly down the central aisle; and, turning towards him, Janet Roscoe smiled expectantly and pointed her hand to the empty seat beside her. But Aldrich ignored the gesture, and slipped instead into one of the empty seats immediately behind her.

'As I say,' resumed Morse, 'the person Stratton claimed to have seen was never on the train at all. That person told me he'd been to London to see his daughter; but he'd only ever had the one daughter . . . and she was *dead*.'

Morse's audience was hanging on his every word, yet few seemed able to grasp the extraordinary implications of what he was saying.

'Names, you know' (Morse's tone was suddenly lighter) 'are very important things. Some people don't like their own names . . . but others are extremely anxious to perpetuate them – both Christian names and surnames. Let's say, for example, that Mr and Mrs Brown here – Howard and Shirley, isn't it – wanted to christen their house, they might think of sticking half of their two names together. What about "W-a-r-d" from his name and "l-e-y" from hers? Make a reasonable house-name, wouldn't it? "Wardley"?'

'Gee, that's exactly—' began Shirley; but Howard laid a hand on her arm, and the embarrassed lady held her peace.

'Not much good trying to perpetuate a surname, though – not if your daughter gets married. She *can* keep her maiden name, of course. Can't she? *Can't* she . . . ? But it's easier with Christian names, especially sometimes. A father whose name is "George", say, can call his daughter "Georgie", "Georgina", "Georgette".' (Lewis glanced up at Morse.) 'And the woman who was killed in the road accident was called Mrs Philippa J. Mayo, remember? Her father couldn't give her his own name exactly, but he could give her the female equivalent of "Philip". And Philippa Mayo was the daughter of the only man here who has that name.

'*Wasn't she, Mr Aldrich?*' asked Morse in a terrifying whisper.

Chapter Fifty-eight

> . . . that fair field
> Of Enna, where Proserpin gathring flowrs
> Her self a fairer Flowre by gloomie Dis
> Was gathered, which cost Ceres all that pain
> To seek her through the world . . .
> (*John Milton*, Paradise Lost, Book IV)

'You're *serious* about all this, sir?' Phil Aldrich cocked his head to one side and his sad features seemed incredulous, and pained.

'Oh, yes,' said Morse, with a quiet simplicity – perhaps also with some pain. 'You've no daughter in London – or anywhere else now, I'm afraid. You've lost your alibi, too – the very clever alibi provided by Eddie Stratton as the first of his services for you . . . before he performed his *second* service, later that same day, by disposing of Kemp's body in the River Cherwell.'

Momentarily, it seemed, Aldrich was on the point of protesting, but Morse shook his head wearily:

'No point – no point at all in your saying anything to the contrary, Mr Aldrich. We've been in touch with the police department in Sacramento, with your neighbours, with the local institution there, including the High School your daughter attended. We've got your passport, and we've checked your home address, and it's perfectly correct. You carried through all your details accurately on to the t.h.f. Guest Registration Card at The Randolph, and doubtless here too, in Bath. But *your wife*? She was a little "economical with the truth", wasn't she? Your wife – *your accomplice*, Mr Aldrich – she made just a few little changes here and there to her details, didn't she? It was all right for it to be seen that you both lived in the same district, the same street, even – *but not in the same apartment*. Yet you do, don't you, live in the same apartment as your wife? You've been married together, happily married together, for almost forty-two years, if my information is correct. And apart from your daughter, there has only ever been one woman in life you have loved with passion and tenderness – the woman you married. She was a gifted actress, I learned. She was well known on the West Coast of America in many productions in the fifties and sixties – mostly in musicals in the earlier years, and then in a series of Arthur Miller plays. And being an actress, a successful actress, it was sensible for her to keep her stage name – which was in fact her maiden name. But she gave her Christian name to her daughter, just as you did. Philippa J. Aldrich – Philippa *Janet* Aldrich – that was her name.' Morse nodded sadly to himself, and to the two people who sat so near to one another now.

Then a most poignant and exceedingly moving thing occurred. Only a few minutes since, Phil Aldrich had rejected (as it seemed) the blandishments of a diminutive, loud-mouthed, insufferable termagant. But now he accepted her invitation. He rose, and moved forward, just the one row, to sit beside the woman in the front, and to take her small hand gently into his – the tears now spilling down his cheeks. And as he did so, the woman turned towards him with eyes that were pale and desolate, yet eyes which still lit up with the glow of deep and happy love as she looked unashamedly, unrepentantly, into her husband's face; the eyes of a mother who had grieved so long and so desperately for her only daughter, a mother whose grief could never be comforted, and who had journeyed to England to avenge what she saw as an insufferable wrong – the loss of the jewel that was hers.

Chapter Fifty-nine

Je ne regrette rien
(French song)

After the arrests, after the statements from the two Aldriches and from a repentant Stratton, after a second search of the Kemps' residence, the case – at least from Morse's point of view – was finished.

The major statement (the statement to which Morse awarded the literary prize) was made by Mrs Janet Roscoe, who properly insisted on vetting the transcription of her lengthy evidence typed out by WPC Wright. Except at one point, this agreed with the parallel statement made by Mr Phil Aldrich, with each, in turn, substantially corroborated by Mr Edward Stratton's testimony about his own collusion with the Aldriches. The one colossal discrepancy arose from the two wholly contradictory accounts of Kemp's death. Neither Mr or Mrs Aldrich was willing to give any detail whatsoever about what, as Morse imagined, must have been a savagely bitter altercation between Kemp and themselves before the fateful (though maybe not immediately fatal?) blow struck with the stick that originally had rested across Marion Kemp's knees as she sat in her wheel-chair, her eyes (in Janet's splendid phrase) 'glowing with a sort of glorious revenge'. So much was agreed. Kemp had stumbled blindly against a chair and then fallen heavily, the back of his head striking the corner of the fire-place with 'a noise reminiscent of a large egg trodden under foot – deliberately'. So much was agreed. Then there was all that blood. Such a surprising amount of it! And the carpet where most of it had dripped; and his clothes 'sticky and messy with the stuff'. So much was agreed. But which of the two it was who had lashed out ferociously at Kemp with that stick

('Please return to the Radcliffe Infirmary' branded upon it) – ah! that was proving so difficult to decide. It had been *Phil*, of course – Janet confessed: 'He must have gone quite berserk, Inspector!' But no! It had been *Janet* all the time, as Phil had so sadly admitted to Morse: a frenetic Janet who had been the happy instrument of eternal Justice. But when Morse had told Janet of the wild discrepancy, she'd merely smiled. And when Morse had told Phil of the same ridiculous discrepancy, he too had merely smiled – and lovingly.

There had been one or two minor surprises in the statements, but for the most part things had happened almost exactly as Morse had supposed. What finally, it appeared, had transmuted an intolerable grief into an implacable hatred, and a lust for some sort of retribution, was the fact that in all the reports the parents had received of the coroner's proceedings and the magistrate's hearing, *Philippa's name had never once occurred*. A curious catalyst, perhaps, and yet what a devastating one! But the name of Dr Theodore Kemp had been mentioned many, many times; and when they had read of the Historic Cities of England Tour, *they had seen that name again*. Their plans were made (for what they were) and they duly took their places on the tour – almost enjoying the distanced yet sometimes friendly rôles they had assumed. And it was on the coach that Janet had learned of the deceit that the Strattons were plotting . . . And after Janet had taken Laura Stratton's handbag, and put it immediately into her own, far more capacious one, she had gone to her own room, on the same floor, and happily discovered that the Wolvercote Tongue fitted almost perfectly into the small case she'd brought with her containing her portable iron . . .

Then it was the telephone call . . .

Janet had heard everything, *clearly*! And a plan was immediately formulated. Eddie Stratton was despatched somewhere – anywhere! – so long as he could establish a firm alibi *for himself*; and Phil sent off to a nearby car-hire firm, whilst she, Janet, remained seated by the extension-phone in her bedroom to deal with the necessary reference for the car firm. The confusion caused by Kemp's delay that day was a godsend; and Phil, after picking up Janet from Gloucester Green, had met Kemp at the railway station (his train two minutes early) informing him that his wife had been taken ill, that his duties were fully taken care of, and that he (Aldrich) was there to drive him directly up to his North Oxford home . . .

After the deed was done, Janet had found herself waiting anxiously for the return of Eddie Stratton; and as soon as she – and no one else! – had spotted him, she steered him away from The Randolph, handed him the Wolvercote Tongue and acquainted him with the *second* of his duties in the criminal conspiracy in which he was now a wholly committed accessory: the disposal of the body.

Marion Kemp (this from Stratton's evidence now) had admitted him at Water Eaton Road, where he had divested the corpse of its clothes – how else shift the body without staining his own? And . . . well, the rest was now known. It had not been an unduly gruesome task to a man for whom such post-mortem grotesqueries had been little more than a perfunctory performance. He had wrapped the carpet round the clothes of the murdered man, depositing the bundle behind the boiler in the airing-cupboard. And what of Marion Kemp? Throughout she had sat, Stratton claimed, in the hall-way. In silence.

'And greatly disturbed,' opined Morse.

'Oh no, Inspector!' Stratton had replied.

After leaving Water Eaton Road, Stratton had walked via First Turn and Goose Green to the Trout Inn at Wolvercote where he had thrown the Tongue into the river – and then caught a Nipper Bus back to St Giles', where he'd met Mrs Williams.

Sheila's evidence tallied with Stratton's account. She had invited Stratton back to her house in North Oxford, and he had accepted. Anxious as he was to drink himself silly, and with a co-operative partner to boot, Stratton had consumed considerable quantities of Glenfiddich – and had finally staggered into a summoned taxi at around midnight . . .

Such was the picture of the case that had finally emerged; such the picture that Morse painted on the Friday morning of that same week when Chief Superintendent Strange had come into his office, seating himself gruntingly into the nearest chair.

'None of your bullshit, Morse! Just the broad brush, my boy! I'm off to lunch with the C.C. in half an hour.'

'Give him my very best wishes, sir.'

'Get *on* with it!'

Strange sat back (and looked at his watch) when Morse had finished. 'She must have been an amazing woman.'

'She was, sir. I think Janet Roscoe is possibly the—'

'I'm not talking about *her*! I'm talking about the Kemp woman – Marion, wasn't it? Didn't the Aldrich pair take a huge gamble though? You know, assuming she would play along with 'em, and so on?'

'Oh, yes. But they were gambling all along – with the very highest stakes, sir.'

'And you just think, Morse! Staying in that house – with that bloody corpse – in her bedroom – in the hall – wherever – I don't know. *I* couldn't do it. Could *you*? It'd send me crackers.'

'She could never forgive him—'

'It'd still send me crackers.'

'She *did* commit suicide, sir,' said Morse slowly, beginning only now, perhaps, to see into the abyss of Marion's despair.

'So she did, Morse! So she did!'

Strange looked at his watch again and tilted his heavily jowled head: 'What put you on to 'em? The Aldriches?'

'I should have got there earlier, I suppose. Especially after that first statement Aldrich made, about his fictional trip to London. He wrote it straight out – only three crossings-out in three pages. And if only I'd looked at what he'd crossed out instead of what he'd left in! He was writing under pressure and, if my memory serves me, he crossed out things like "*we could have done something*" and "*our* telephone number". He was worried about giving himself away, because he was writing like a married man . . . He *was* a married man . . . And there was another clue, too. He even mentioned his daughter's name in that statement: "Pippa" – which as you know, sir, is a diminutive of "Philippa".'

Strange rose to his feet and pulled on his heavy winter coat. 'Some nice bits of thinking, Morse!'

'Thank you, sir!'

'I'm not talking about *you*! It's this Roscoe woman. Very able little lady! Did you know that a lot of 'em have been *little* – these big people: Alexander, Augustus, Attila, Nelson, Napoleon . . .'

'They tell me Bruckner was a very small man, sir.'

'Who?'

The two men smiled briefly at each other as Strange reached the door.

'Just a couple of points, Morse. How did Janet Roscoe get rid of that handbag?'

'She says she walked round the corner into Cornmarket, and went into Salisbury's, and stuck it in the middle of the leather handbags on sale there.'

'What about the murder weapon? You say you've not recovered that?'

'Not yet. You see, she walked along to the Radcliffe Infirmary, so she says, and saw a notice there about an Amnesty – for anything you'd had from the place which you should have returned: "Amnesty – No Questions Asked", it said. She just handed it in.'

'Why haven't you got it, then?'

'Sergeant Lewis went along, sir. But there were seventy-one walking sticks in the Physio department there.'

'Oh!'

'Do you want any forensic tests on them?'

'Waste of money.'

'That's what Sergeant Lewis said.'

'Good man, Lewis!'

'Excellent man!'

'Not so clever as this Roscoe woman, though.'

'Few cleverer.'

'She'd be useful in the Force.'

'No chance, sir. She had a thorough medical yesterday. They don't even give her a fortnight.'

'Any doctor who tells you when you're going to die is a bloody fool!'

'Not this one,' said Morse quietly – and sadly.

'Think you'll get that jewel back?'

'Hope so, sir. But *they* won't, will they?'

'Say that again?'

'The jewel that was theirs, sir. They won't ever get *her* back, will they?'

Was Morse imagining things? For a second or two he thought that Strange's eyes might well have glistened with a film of tears. But there was no way of telling this for certain, for Strange had suddenly looked down fixedly at the threadbare carpet beside the door, before departing for his lunch with the Chief Constable.

Chapter Sixty

Accipe fraterno multum manantia fletu,
   Atque in perpetuum, frater, ave atque vale
                                  (*Catullus*, Poem CI)

A week after his meeting with Strange, Morse took the
bus down from North Oxford to Cornmarket. He had
managed two complete days' furlough, had re-read *Bleak
House*, listened again (twice) to *Parsifal*, and (though he
would never have admitted it) begun to feel slightly bored.

Not today, though!

When he had said farewell to Sheila Williams the previous
week, he had suggested a second rendezvous. He was (he
assured her) a reasonably civilised sort of fellow, and it would
be pleasant for both of them to meet again fairly soon, and
perhaps have lunch together: the Greek Taverna, perhaps,
up in Summertown? So a time and a place were carefully
agreed: 12 a.m. (twelve *noon*) in the foyer (the *foyer*) of The
Randolph.

Where else?

As usual (for appointments), he was ten minutes early, and
stood for a while in the foyer talking to Roy, the bespectacled
Head Concierge, and congratulating this splendid man on his
recent award of the BEM. A quarter of an hour later, he
walked down the hotel steps and for several minutes stood
immobile on the pavement there, some of his thoughts centred
on the Ashmolean Museum opposite and on its former Keeper
of Anglo-Saxon and Mediaeval Antiquities; but most of his
thoughts, if truth be told, on Mrs Sheila Williams. At 12.20
p.m., when he found himself looking at his wristwatch about
three times per minute, he returned to the foyer, and stood
there rather fecklessly for a further few minutes. At 12.25

p.m., he asked the concierge if there'd been any messages.
No! At 12.30 p.m., he abandoned all hope and decided to
drown his disappointment in the Chapters Bar.

As he came to the door, he looked inside – and stopped.
There, seated at the bar, a large empty glass held high in her
left hand, her right arm resting on the shoulder of a youngish
(bearded!) man, sat Sheila Williams, her black-stockinged
legs crossed provocatively, her body disturbingly close to
her companion's.

'If you insist!' Morse heard her say, as she pushed her
glass across the bar. 'Gin – large one, please! – no ice – just
half a glass of tonic – slim-line.'

Morse held back, feeling a great surge of irrational
and impotent jealousy. About which he could do nothing.
Absolutely nothing. Like a stricken deer he walked back to
the foyer, where he wrote a brief note ('Unavoidable, urgent
police business'), and asked the concierge to take it through
to the bar in about five minutes or so, and hand it to a Mrs
Williams – a Mrs *Sheila* Williams.

Roy had nodded. He'd been there in the hotel for
forty-five years, now. That's why he'd been honoured
by the Queen. He understood most things. He thought he
understood this.

Morse walked quickly along the Broad, past the King's
Arms, the Holywell Music Room, the back of New College,
turned left at Longwall Street, and after two hundred yards or
so went through the wooden gate that led into Holywell Cemetery. He found the grave far more quickly than Ashenden had
done; and behind the squat cross the envelope that Ashenden
had left there, with the four lines written out neatly on a
white card therein. After replacing the envelope, Morse left
the cemetery and walked slowly back along Holywell Street
to the King's Arms, ordering there (as Ashenden had done
before him) a pint of Flowers Bitter. He found himself ever
thinking of Sheila, and at one point had been on the verge of
rushing up to The Randolph to see if she were still there in
the Chapters Bar.

But he hadn't.

And gradually thoughts of Mrs Williams were receding; and instead, he found his mind lingering on the sad quatrain he'd found beside the small stone cross in the Holywell cemetery:

Life divided us from each other,
Depriving friend of friend,
Accept this leave-taking – with my tears –
For it is all I have to bring.

At the Trout Inn, the frogmen had given it four days, then called off the search for the Wolvercote Tongue. Sensibly so, as Eddie Stratton (now facing charges of perjury and perverting the course of justice) could have told them from the beginning. It had been a sort of back-up insurance, really – prising out that single remaining ruby, and hiding it privily beneath the white-silk lining of Laura's coffin. In New York his plans had been thwarted, but the jewel would still be there, would it not? Whenever, wherever they finally buried her. Was *anyone* ever likely to suspect such duplicity, such ghoulish duplicity? Surely not. Surely not, reflected Stratton. Yet he found himself remembering the man who had been in charge of things.

Yes, just the one man, perhaps . . .